A WORTHY OPPONENT

WICKED VILLAINS #3

KATEE ROBERT

TRINKETS AND TALES

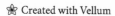

To Gina L. Maxwell.
Two Hooks are better than one!

ALSO BY KATEE ROBERT

Wicked Villains
Book 1: Desperate Measures
Book 2: Learn My Lesson
Book 3: A Worthy Opponent
Book 4: The Beast

The Island of Ys
Book 1: His Forbidden Desire
Book 2: Her Rival's Touch
Book 3: His Tormented Heart
Book 4: Her Vengeful Embrace

The Thalanian Dynasty Series (MMF)
Book 1: Theirs for the Night
Book 2: Forever Theirs
Book 3: Theirs Ever After
Book 4: Their Second Chance

The Kings Series
Book 1: The Last King
Book 2: The Fearless King

The Hidden Sins Series
Book 1: The Devil's Daughter
Book 2: The Hunting Grounds
Book 3: The Surviving Girls

This book contains an abusive ex-partner (emotional, physical). Most of it happens in the past, off page, but it may be triggering for some readers.

CHAPTER 1

TINK

"*T*wo more days, Tink."

I don't look up as I carefully set each drink on the table. Working at the Underworld feels a whole lot like swimming with sharks under the best of circumstances. Now, with a clock ticking down the seconds until I'm free, it's significantly more dangerous. I place the final drink down and glare at Gaeton Thibault. He's sprawled across half the booth, taking up more than his fair share, even considering how huge he is. He's cocky and irritating, and I usually enjoy sparring with him.

Not tonight. Not with him tossing the reminder of my deadline at my feet.

I glare. "Get your feet off the table. This isn't a barn."

He holds my gaze for a long moment. It's a struggle not to look away. Gaeton might have that easy charm that draws people to him, but he's dominant right down to his big bones. He doesn't fuck around, especially in this club. But I'm not the kind of submissive who will fall to their knees and play the silent partner to kinky bedroom games. I look down my nose at him. "Now, Gaeton."

1

"You're awfully bossy for a sub."

"You're awfully dense for someone who's a general to the Man in Black."

He chuckles and drops his feet back to the floor. "There. Are you happy now?"

Happy? As if that's even in the realm of possibility for me. *Happy* is for people who aren't walking around with my kind of sins tattooed on their soul. The weight of knowing what I left behind didn't used to bother me. The relief of being free was too strong. Or, if not actually *free*, then free of *him*. Working for one of the scariest people in Carver City has its perks, but free will isn't really one of them.

I realize I've been silent too long and snort. "You know better." I prop a hand on my hip. "Your clothing order will be in tomorrow."

He's watching me too closely. People see the muscles and his general hugeness and assume Gaeton is an idiot. It's something he's embraced because enemies always underestimate him. I've been watching people too long not to know better. He's smart as hell and has the kind of ambition that will either see him leading his own territory one day or burning the city to the ground around him.

Finally, he sits back and gives me a slow smile. "Why don't you deliver it yourself? A little one-on-one with my favorite submissive."

I don't bother to resist rolling my eyes. "I always deliver it myself, you ass."

"See you tomorrow, then." He sinks enough innuendo into the statement to make several people within hearing range glance over. But that's Gaeton; he likes a show, even at someone else's expense. Implying that we're meeting outside the Underworld—the neutral territory ruled by my employer, Hades—is a power play. An annoying one.

"Try to stay out of trouble in the meantime." I glance at

the other men at the table, but they're all minions. No one will cause any trouble tonight, and Gaeton is here without Beast, which means the furniture is probably safe. Those two really need to fuck and get it out of their system, but no one asks my opinion.

I head back toward the bar that dominates the center of the room. It's been built around a truly impressive marble sculpture that isn't *quite* an explicit orgy but is close enough to count. It's all very Hades, just like the rest of the Underworld. A sex club that specializes in kink and power, where all the main players in Carver City can come and spill their secrets into the willing ears of Hades's Dominants and submissives. For being some of the scariest people in existence, they're all too ready to do exactly that. It's mind-blowing.

I stop next to the bar and check the room. Most of the half-circle booths lining the walls are filled; people use the shadows for covert conversations and foreplay. In another hour or so, many of them will start filtering into the public playroom through the door at the back.

The bartender, Tisiphone, gives me a sympathetic look, which is just as much a warning as her pouring healthy splashes of whiskey into two tumblers. Tisiphone might be the nicest of Hades's three Furies, but she's no slouch. And she knows better than to handle me with kid gloves. She tucks a strand of long dark hair behind her ear. "Hades wants to see you. He says to bring him a drink."

Words I really, truly don't want to hear. I might have made a deal with Hades four years, eleven months, and twenty-eight days ago, but I've avoided him as much as possible since. All his deals come with teeth, and mine is no exception. Usually, he's content to let me work as long as I don't rock the boat, but with my contract end date coming up, apparently that's no longer the case.

3

Lucky me.

I down the whiskey and grimace. I prefer my drinks sweet enough to make my teeth ache, but desperate times and all that. I take the second glass and weave my way through the room to the door that leads to Hades's office. Or at least his public facing one. Very few people are allowed in his private office, and I've never been curious—or fatalistic— enough to investigate.

I knock on the door as I open it. The room is dimmer than I expected, and I hesitate just inside the door. Even knowing Hades doesn't harm the people under his care, I've long since learned the hard way that there are exceptions to every rule. I press my lips together to keep from calling out like some kind of heroine in a horror movie.

"Come in." He sounds as drily amused as ever. I hate that. I've always hated that. Being in the room with Hades makes me feel like I'm just short of understanding some kind of inside joke. He makes me feel like a silly child without even trying.

I straighten my spine and put some belligerence in my step as I move past the low couches to his massive desk. If I didn't know better, I'd suspect he shifted the lights in the room with the intention of creating shadows where he sits now. I carefully set down the whiskey glass. "You know, I *am* aware you have better shit in your private stash back here. You didn't need me to hand-deliver your drink."

His lips quirk, though I still can't see his eyes. I only get the impression of square black frames and a glint of silver in his hair. He steeples his fingers in front of his mouth. "Remind me when your contract is up."

I count to five slowly. It does nothing to stifle my emotional response to those words. Fear. Anger. The kind of elation that comes before a leap of faith and an unfortunate encounter with gravity. "Two days from now."

4

"Ah yes." He leans back, shielding his whole face in shadow. "My Meg tells me that you're requesting to stay on."

My mouth goes dry. I'd talked about it with Meg, yes. Meg, arguably the most powerful of the Furies, the trio of women at Hades's back. Tisiphone holds the bar and a number of secret assignments. Allecto runs security. Meg is queen to Hades's king.

She's also my direct boss. My friend, maybe, though the thought of labeling us as such about gives me hives. Friends are a lever just waiting to be pulled, a weakness to be exploited. "Yes, we'd talked about it."

"Allow me to add a clarifying viewpoint." He lets silence fill the room in slow ticks of the clock behind his head, until I have to clench my fists and press my lips together to keep from babbling like a fool just so we don't sit here for one more minute. Hades shakes his head slowly, breaking the spell. "Unless you can offer me something worth a deal, there will be no extension."

My breath rushes out, and I weave on my ridiculously high heels. "You're shitting me."

"I assure you, I am not."

Anger rises in a welcome wave. Foolish to let it gain hold here, but I feel particularly foolish in believing I might actually have a place here beyond my time as Hades's minion. "So that's it. Deal is done, you kick me out. I've been here *five years.*"

"Yes, you have. You've served me well and become a welcome asset. None of that changes the reality of your situation." He leans forward and the gentleness in his eyes is so much worse than the anger I expected. "You can't hide forever, Tink."

Easy enough for *him* to say. He's one step down from a god in the Underworld and his little square of neutral territory in Carver City. No one fucks with Hades, and that protection extends to all his people. He doesn't have to worry about the sins of his past coming for him, howling his name on the wind.

I lift my chin. "The second I leave, he'll try for me."

If anything, Hades's dark eyes go gentler yet. "You're not the same woman who showed up here that first night."

Really? Because I feel like that woman. With the threat of forcible freedom from this cage bearing down on me, it feels like being propelled back in time. Years, months, days, hours. They all peel back the strength I worked so hard to build up around me. I start to shake. I'm not strong. I can fake it with the best of them, but when push comes to shove, I'm nothing more than the girl who was too weak to save herself. "Please."

As soon as the word slips free, I want to snatch it back. I don't beg. Not to any of the Dominants I've shared scenes with over the years. Sure as fuck not to Hades.

I shake my head. "Forget I said that."

He nods slowly. "There's someone here to see you."

The change of subject leaves my head spinning. For one eternal moment, I'm sure it's *him*. The one I sacrificed everything to escape. But no, as cruel as Hades can be, he'd never throw me to the wolves so explicitly. I take a careful breath, and then another. When I answer, all the quaver is gone from my voice. "Who?"

Hades motions to the door behind me. "Room Two."

He's in one of the overnight rooms?

I cross my arms under my breasts. "I scene, Hades. I don't fuck like that. Not in the overnight rooms." I can't pretend I don't have sex on the job. I do. But it's only when *I* choose to offer it up in negotiations. Going to the private overnight rooms meant for patrons instead of the playrooms with built-in safety measures? Absolutely not.

"No one in my employ 'fucks like that.'" He pushes slowly to his feet. I don't believe in magic, but the way Hades unfurls his presence is as close to it as the real world is capable of. He's not a large man, but when he wants to be, he's overwhelming as hell. "He requests discretion for the conversation. This was the simplest way to honor that request. As always, Allecto and her people will monitor through video and microphone. I don't expect it to be an issue, but you'll hardly be alone."

Not yet, at least.

Not for two more days.

I give a shaky nod. I should probably apologize for assuming the worst, but I won't. I'm too raw, too exposed. "I'll go now."

He doesn't respond as I turn on a heel and stride out of the office. In the hallway, I briefly consider changing, but my black panties and equally lacy black bra aren't out of the ordinary for working a shift as a submissive. The only little rebellion I'm indulged with is wearing heels instead of having to go barefoot like the others. At five foot, two inches, I'm what Meg fondly calls pixie-sized. A plus-sized pixie, rather. I snort.

Whoever this guy is, he's obviously connected with the Underworld or Hades wouldn't allow this kind of meeting. Which means there's no need to change or worry about appearances. I don't allow myself to wonder why it's *me* meeting him instead of Meg or even Hercules. They're Hades's inner circle, the people who can make calls with the authority he extends to them. I'm only me.

I make my way up to the private bedrooms. They're usually reserved for people who choose to spend the night rather than people who want to fuck. In the Underworld, most of the sex happens out in the open, or at least in the individual rooms off the public playroom. They can be altered to fit a whole range of themes, all in the name of lust.

There's no point in knocking. Whoever is on the other

side of the door knows I'm coming. I cloak myself in anger, allowing it to soak into my very pores. A suitable shield if ever there was one. By the time I open the door, I'm fucking untouchable.

Until the man on the other side of the room turns to face me.

Hook.

CHAPTER 2

TINK

*A*ny other day, I would already be out of the room, throwing up a middle finger for good measure. For five years, I've gone out of my way to ensure I'm never alone with Jameson Hook. Apparently I no longer have that option. Even though I've seen him time and time again since I made my deal with Hades, I've never let myself *look*. It's only surprise that has my curiosity slipping its leash now. Shock at his presence in this room overriding what little good sense I have.

The man standing before me is a far sight from the skinny guy who used to look like a rough touch would shatter his bones. He looks good. His medium brown skin practically glows from health, and he's let his black hair grow out over the years. It's not tied back for once, falling to his shoulders in waves that gleam. He's filled out over the years, growing into his body in a way I intrinsically recognize.

I've done the same thing, after all, albeit in a different way. I love my curves, love the fact that *I* get to choose my beautiful. If anyone has a problem with that, they can fuck right off. Hook has gone in a different direction. His body looks like a sculptor spent a decade lovingly carving out the definition of his muscles. I can't see them now, not with him fully dressed in street clothes, but a person doesn't spend much time in the Underworld without getting pretty comfortable with public nudity. Especially if they have an exhibitionist streak.

Hook sure as fuck does.

Not that I've noticed. I've spent too much time determined *not* to notice.

I plant my hands on my hips and glare. Anger is the only thing I have left, but fortunately for me, the depths of my rage remain unplumbed when it comes to the man watching me with that glint in his dark eyes. I have to do something, say something, because standing here staring at him sends waves after waves of feelings through me that I am not prepared to deal with. Not today. Not ever.

My soul hates Hook. My body hasn't gotten the memo. But then, my desires always did get me into trouble. The difference is that now I know enough to tell the difference between lust and something as ill-advised as falling in love with the wrong person.

I shove the thought away. The past may lie in this room, thick enough to choke on, but I won't be the one to bring it up. "You know, normal people can take a hint. If not a hint, then my explicitly telling you to fuck off more times than I can count in the last five years."

"You wound me." He presses both hands to his chest.

Against my better judgement, I follow the movement to where his white T-shirt hugs his defined pectoral muscles. I jerk my gaze back to his face. "Not as thoroughly as I'd like to."

His grin is quick, a flash of white teeth against his neatly trimmed beard. It's gone before I can fully register its impact, leaving him serious. "There's trouble, Tink. Big trouble."

"I don't care."

"Yes, you do. If not about me, then about *this*." He hesitates, a pause barely long enough to allow me to brace for what I know is coming. Sure enough, Hook pulls my deepest fears forth and puts them into words. "He's making moves to take the territory back."

I desperately don't want to talk about this, to admit I know exactly who he's talking about, but denial has never been my strong suit. If there's one thing Hook and I share, and one thing only, it's the boogeyman stuffed into our respective closets. The man who's left scars on both our body and souls.

It's still no excuse for Hook's sins.

It's no excuse for mine, either.

I look away. I have to. "I don't see what that has to do with me."

"Really?" His dry tone cuts me directly to the bone. "You don't think it's the strangest coincidence that your contract with Hades is coming to a close and *now* is the time he's stirring up a coup? You're smarter than that."

The urge to flop onto the bed between us and bury my head in the pillows almost takes me to my knees. I don't want this. I don't want the responsibility Hook seems determined to lay at my feet. I don't want to be dragged kicking and screaming into the past I fought so hard to leave behind.

Apparently I didn't fight hard enough. Or run far enough.

It's cowardly to turn away, but I don't care. "It's not my problem."

"I see," he says slowly. "Are you saying that black eye you had not too long ago had nothing to do with Peter?"

I spin to face him. I didn't mean to react, but no one was supposed to know about that. Either Meg had talked—unlikely—or Hook had been watching me more closely than I realized. "Stalker much?"

"Don't do that."

"You don't get to tell me what to do." No one does. Not anymore. Yes, Hades technically owns my contract, and I may not like him even the smallest bit, but no one in the Underworld expects me to bow and flinch and keep my head down like the nearly-broken creature I was when I threw myself on Hades's dubious mercy.

The people here let me find my feet. They gave me the space to figure out who I was and learn to make no apologies for it. The thought of what Hook is asking me …

Wait. What *is* he asking me?

I can't do this. Reacting emotionally won't accomplish anything. Easy enough to realize that. Much harder to stuff all my messy feelings deep down until I'm able to face him again. I've never mastered the icy thing the way some people have, but I still try. "You're here for a reason."

His dark gaze flicks over my face before he nods slowly. "I'm here for a reason."

I wait. As difficult as it is to hold my questions, I force myself to do it. He came to me. He can be the one to break this stifling silence that stretches between us like taffy. Sticky and binding and horrible.

Finally, Hook curses. "There's no easy way to say this."

"Then say it the hard way."

"I can give you what you need."

I blink. If I'd allowed myself to anticipate his next words, those wouldn't even have made the list. "What are you talking about?"

"Revenge. His head on a platter, literal or otherwise." He doesn't smile, doesn't do anything to lessen the offer. "If you want him chained in a basement for four years while I personally deliver every single injury that he dealt out to you, I can do that, too."

I can't think. Can't do anything but stare. "You're drunk.

That's the only explanation for you spitting this madness at me."

"No, I'm not. I'm simply offering you something that even Hades won't."

Surely he can't know I asked Hades for more than sanctuary five years ago. I begged and pleaded and wept at his feet, desperate for him to remove the threat of Peter permanently. I know better now. Hades doesn't act directly against any of the territory leaders. It's the only way he's able to keep his precious neutral ground. I can respect that now, but I still can't forgive him for denying me the very thing Hook is offering now. There's only one question that remains; the most important one. "Why?"

"Because it's what we both want." He doesn't move, doesn't even appear to breathe. "But I require your cooperation to make it happen."

Here it is, the trap I sensed but couldn't see. He offers me the one outcome I want more than anything in the world as bait and slips a shackle around my ankle at the same time. "No."

"You may not have a choice."

"Wrong. I *always* have a choice."

Hook shrugs. He's not as big as Gaeton, but his frame is roped with muscle. "He might hesitate to cross Hades, but you're about to lose Hades's protection. He'll come for you. You know he will."

He's right. I hate that he's right. Peter will come for me, if not because I'm a toy that was taken from him before he finished with it, then because *I* tried to take away his new toy. That, he'll never forgive, and he certainly won't forget.

It wasn't something I was thinking about when I heard about the new girl. All I could focus on was that I knew exactly what she was going through, exactly how scared she must be to realize her Prince Charming was far more terrifying than anything she left behind. In those dark years, I hadn't allowed myself to pray, but if I had, I would have prayed for someone to get me out. So I tried to do that, to save her, to be the person my younger self needed.

I should have known better. She's not me. Or, more accurately, she's not me *now*. She's me five, six, eight years ago, when I attacked everyone who came close, because to do anything else was to welcome *his* suspicion and jealousy. To invite more pain.

Still, I can't quite stop blaming myself for her presence in his life. If I hadn't left, Peter wouldn't have needed to fill my place. She'd still be free.

I shake my head as Hook's words penetrate. "You can't honestly think he's going to come after me."

He doesn't blink. "I know he will."

A shiver of fear works its way down my spine. I haven't felt true terror in so long, but I recognize it intimately. "You show up here and offer me his head on a platter … Why?"

"Putting Peter six feet under benefits both of us."

I flinch at his name. Foolish to let something as simple as a name, five little letters, take on this kind of importance, but I can't shake the feeling that speaking his name will summon the man himself. It's everything I can do not to look over my shoulder.

Jameson—Hook—might be here under the guise of offering me help, but I know better than to expect it to come without strings attached. No one in our world offers something for nothing. Power, submission, sex; tit for tat. The form of repayment doesn't matter, only that repayment is expected.

I try very hard to keep the belligerent tilt to my head, to not let him see how spooked I am by the topic of our conversation, by the threat hanging over my head. "You know, if you want to fuck me this bad, there are easier ways to go about it."

He booms out a laugh and, despite myself, the joyful sound chases away some of the chill in my bones. He's always been able to do that, to turn on the charm and exude joy like it's Christmas morning or some shit, rather than whatever bleak reality we currently occupy. It's one of the reasons I distrusted him so intensely before—why I distrust him now; no one can survive Peter's court with that kind of joy in their heart. It's impossible.

He lets his laugh trail off and grins at me. "I don't want to fuck you, Tink."

"Yes, you do."

"Yes, I do," he agrees easily. His grin never wavers. "Let me clarify; I don't *just* want to fuck you."

It's a fight to stay on my feet, to stand strong against the sheer force of him. I make myself hold his gaze despite every instinct demanding I fall to my knees. "Stop playing coy and spit it out. What the hell do you want, Hook?"

Now he moves, stalking slowly around the bed toward me. His shadow grows behind him with every step closer to the light at my back until it threatens to swallow my world whole. When he finally stops, he's so close, I could lift my hand and touch him if I want.

I really don't *want* to want to touch him.

"You." He reaches out and runs his fingers through my long blond hair, his many rings glinting between the strands. "On your knees. In my bed." He catches my left hand, and I watch dazedly as he lifts it and strokes my knuckles. "My ring on your finger." He gives a slow grin that has my stomach tying itself in knots. "I want everything, *Tatiana*. Absolutely fucking everything."

I don't know whether to laugh or knee him in the balls. For saying all this shit I definitely don't want to hear. For calling me by a name I buried five long years ago. For all of it. "You're joking."

"Life would be easier if that were true."

Yeah, it really would. But Hook's similar to Gaeton in the way he moves through our world. His charm and devil-may-care personality makes people underestimate him. It always has. There's no amusement in his dark eyes now. No, he's serious as death.

I draw myself up. I have to. Standing this close to him is like standing in the eye of a hurricane. Scary. Powerful. Filled with promise of pain to come. I shiver. "You talk a good game, but it doesn't mean anything. It never did."

"You think I'm trying to ... What? Seduce you?" He tugs on my hair. Not to hurt. Simply to let me know he could. It should scare me. I've lived through a relationship gone off the rails, the home I thought I'd claimed morphing through a funhouse mirror into a nightmare prison that took *everything* I had to escape.

I still haven't escaped. I simply gave myself a five-year hiatus.

Hook tugs on my hair again, his dark brows lowering. "Fine. Let's be explicit. I will give you everything I said and more, on the single condition that you marry me."

Shock has a laugh bursting from my lips. "*Marry* you? You really *are* drunk."

"You know better."

I hate that he's right. Hook might have the appearance of a hard-partying asshole, but despite always having a drink close by, he's never once been drunk enough to so much as change his speech patterns, let alone get sloppy. I could chalk that up to the Underworld's strict two-drink policy for those who want to participate in scenes, but plenty of the others show up to drink in the lounge from time to time. Not Hook.

He releases me and takes a slow step back, every move

telegraphing that he's choosing this, not me. "That's the bargain. Take it or leave it."

"I'm leaving it." Bad enough that Hades is essentially kicking me out. But to voluntarily go back to the role as the little woman to the man who runs a territory? Been there, done that, bought a T-shirt, burned it to ash. I will not go back. Hook isn't Peter, but that doesn't mean a single damn thing. I've seen what it takes to hold on to power. It kills off a part of the person who wields it. If there was anything good in Hook—and that's highly debatable—then four years running his territory are enough to have cut it out of him.

He watches me for a long moment and finally shrugs. "The offer remains on the table." A plain black card appears in his hand as if by magic. I make no move to take it, but he catches my hand and presses it to my palm. "My personal number. Call it anytime, day or night, and I'll come for you."

I can't tell if he means the words like a threat, but that must be what they are. I don't believe in knights on white horses. Maybe I did once, but the only people out there searching for damsels in distress are more dangerous than anything said damsel leaves behind. Hook is just like the rest of them, always playing a deeper game.

I start to drop the card, but he catches my hand in his larger one and presses the card hard against my skin. "We both know you can't afford to ignore a helping hand, Tatiana. No matter how distasteful you find me."

He's right. I hate that he's right.

I reluctantly curl my fingers around the card, and he releases me. I can't tell what I'm feeling. Everything is all jumbled in my chest, and the confusion makes it hard to wrap myself in my normal snark. "I'm not going to say yes."

"Yes, you are." He gives me a slow grin. "I'm feeling generous, so when you come crawling to beg for my help, I won't even make you do it publicly."

I can picture it all too easily. Hook sitting in that casually dominant way he does, sprawled in a chair with his big legs spread and arms outstretched. The hard floor biting my knees and palms with each movement. My body heating under the intensity of his gaze. And when I reach him ...

It's everything I can do to fight down a blush and keep my tone cool. "I've said it before, and I'll say it again. Hold your breath while you wait for that. At least if you pass out, the rest of us get a break from your startling wit."

His grin doesn't dim. If anything, it widens. "We're going to have so much fun together, Tatiana. Just you wait."

CHAPTER 3

*T*here are times when forty-eight hours can stretch for what feels like weeks. Glorious nights spent playing the bratty submissive to my favorite Dominants followed by days working with Meg in the office and handling the various other duties that fall under my nebulous position as an assistant manager.

Not this time.

It feels like I blink and I'm in Hades's office again, though this time we aren't alone. Meg and Hercules stand at either side of him, a perfect little triangle of polyamorous love. It might make me sick if I didn't like Meg and Hercules so much, mostly despite myself. Impossible not to resent the place they've carved out for themselves, for each other. I dislike Hades intensely, but no one can argue that he runs his territory like the others in Carver City. He doesn't. I benefited from living under his rule.

He watches me with those cold dark eyes. "Our deal is now complete. Your price has been paid in full."

My throat burns, but I muscle down the physical reaction just like I have countless times in the past. There are submissives who don't mind crying in public. Or crying in general. I'm not one of them. I'll give up control of so much during a scene, but not that. Outside of a scene? Forget about it. "I'd say thank you, but you're kicking me out. Hard not to take it personally. I'm sure you understand."

Hercules opens his mouth like he might jump in, but Hades anticipates him and holds up a hand. "As token of my appreciation for the time you've spent here, you'll always maintain a membership here in the Underworld."

A membership. Not a job.

People would kill to have a membership here. They have in the past. It's outstandingly expensive, and Hades curates who he allows in, picking only the most powerful, and those who fit the tastes of the most powerful. Having this invitation extended to me is a big deal.

I still want to throw something.

"What am I supposed to do?"

Meg is watching me with her heart in her eyes, all sympathy and understanding, but again Hades is the one who speaks. "You've saved a significant amount of money in the last five years. You've started your own clothing business. The fact that you're asking me this question proves I'm making the right decision."

His tone is almost paternal. That is, if by paternal, I mean patronizing as shit. I glare. "If I wanted life advice, I would have asked for it."

"Then let me lay it out explicitly. I've allowed you to find your feet in more than one way while you lived under my roof and my protection. Despite our bargain, I only took five percent of your clothing profits, when we both know I was entitled to a much larger slice. You have resources. You have money. The only thing you're lacking is courage." He stands slowly, glowering down at me. "It's time to the leave the nest, Tink. Because these two have tender feelings for you, I am content to hold your possessions until you find a residence—within a reasonable timeline."

He just knocked the wind out of my best argument for more time. I swallow past my suddenly dry throat. "How long are you giving me?"

"Three days. That should be more than enough time to nail down living arrangements." He makes a show of looking at his watch. "That timeline starts now. I wouldn't linger."

None of them make a move as I turn on my heel and march out of the room. I won't hold this against Meg and Hercules later, but right now the betrayal lies thick on my tongue. I've made Hades a shit ton of money over the last five years, and the second he has a chance to drop me, he doesn't hesitate. For all his talk of loyalty and the like, he's a fucking hypocrite.

I absolutely refuse to see his side of things. I'm not interested in being fair right now. Only angry.

I stop on the employee residential floor to grab some things and stop short when I find Allecto leaning against the wall by my door. She's Hades's head of security, and she's so beautiful I'd be jealous if I didn't enjoy her snarky attitude so much. She's got her long black braids up in a messy bun on top of her head and is wearing combat boots, jeans, and a black tank top that shows off her impressive arm muscles. She catches sight of me and straightens. "You have ten minutes to grab your shit, and then I'm escorting you to the exit."

"Ten minutes and an escort." I try and fail to keep the hurt out of my voice. "Hades really is pulling out the stops."

Allecto shrugs, her dark brown skin gleaming in the soft light of the hallway. "Time to fly, little bird."

"I hate all of you."

"No, you don't. You're just pissed. You'll get over it." She motions to my door. "Clock's ticking."

As much as I'd like to stand here and yell at her until I can exorcise some of the horrible emotions tumbling through me, it won't make a difference. Allecto isn't responsible for this decision any more than I am.

I hurry into the room and bypass the racks half-filled with clothing from my last styling appointment and the compulsively organized corner of the room that houses my desk, sewing machine, and a small fortune's worth of fabric and accessories. I might not trust Hades as far as I can throw him, but I don't believe for a second that he'll mess with my things. He wants me gone, not broken. The two things feel remarkably similar in this moment, but with distance, that will change.

I've already been intimately acquainted with being broken. This isn't what it looks like. Not by a long shot. I'm pissed and my feelings are hurt, but that's the worst of it.

I wade into my walk-in closet and dig through the garment bags to the spot in the corner where the pink suitcase sits. It's shiny and new and has never been used. It's also packed with enough clothes to see me through a week of whatever the hell life can throw at me, duplicates of all my cosmetics and hair shit, and six pairs of shoes. Oh, and of course, a taser and two cans of bear mace. A woman has to be prepared, after all.

I heft it out of the closet and do a quick circuit of the room. My phone charger goes into my purse, the stash of cash I kept in a little fireproof safe in the nightstand follows. It's not everything I have, but it's more than enough for a month or two of rent to get me started.

I stop short. Holy shit, I'm going to have to find furniture, do my own grocery shopping, do *everything*. The sheer number of things I need to take care of has me wavering. Would Hades really put me out if I hid in my room until further notice?

I know the answer even before my mind finishes the thought. He would and he will. No, there's no option but to leave gracefully. Jump and figure it out on the way down.

I muscle open the door and haul the suitcase behind me. Allecto is exactly where I left her and she raises her eyebrows at the luggage. "Subtle."

"It's called character, asshole."

"You better take a cab or something. Dragging that shiny thing behind you is like carrying a neon sign just asking to get mugged."

As satisfying as it would be to tell her where to shove her opinion, she's right. "I'll call from the lobby. Wouldn't want to give you any excuse to drag me kicking and screaming from the building."

"Aw, Tink, you ruin all my fun." She gives me a wide grin and, even with my world turned on its head, it has heat licking up my spine. Allecto plays just as mean as I do, and we've had a lot of fun together in the past.

Will we still do scenes if I'm no longer on the payroll?

I shake my head and push the thought away. I have larger things than my sex life to worry about right now. And I certainly will *not* be thinking about Hook's offer.

Marriage. Fucking. *Him*.

It's more than that, though. If I agree to his terms, if I let him fight this battle for me, if I agree to forever, it wouldn't be as simple as signing a paper, putting a ring on my finger, and then lying back while I think of England. Hook would never settle for that. No, he wants me, body and soul.

I've only just gained ownership of both. I'm not in a hurry to give either away, let alone to a person I *know* I can't trust. Hook is a goddamn villain, no matter how pretty he smiles.

"Tink."

I blink. Allecto sounds annoyed enough that this can't be the first time she's said my name. "What?"

"The car."

"Right. My bad." I fish my phone out of my oversized purse and pull up the app to call the car service. It's only when I'm typing in the pickup address that I pause.

I have no idea where I'm going.

Staying in Hades's territory in the center of Carver City would be ideal, but even without having looked into it in detail, I know real estate prices are astronomical. Neutral territory is worth its weight in gold, and people are only too happy to pay through the nose to live inside his boundaries. It allows for dealings with a variety of criminal types without having to worry about stepping on territorial toes or pledging long-standing alliances to a single ruler.

I might be able to afford the cost of rent, but it would deplete my resources really fast. If I devoted more time to my fashion gig instead of using it as a side hustle the way I had for the last couple years, I might be able to make up the difference, but that is a lot of *might*. I can't pay my newly acquired bills with "might."

"Don't let all the possibilities hamper your decision-making abilities."

I give Allecto a sharp look. "I don't need you crawling around inside my head." I don't need *anyone* doing it.

She rolls her eyes. "You don't want me to guess what you're thinking, then you better work on your poker face. It's usually better than this." Her expression softens the tiniest bit, which is almost worse. All these scary people that I thought I earned my place beside as a near-equal, and they all pity me. I can't stand it.

"I'm fine." I take a deep breath and lay out my options. I could go to Jasmine. She's not as bad as some of the others, and she likes me enough to give me the space to work. I think. But then, she's less than a year into running her territory, and that will give her less leniency. She'll have to keep me under her thumb to avoid the appearance of favoritism or something else that will weaken her position. Dealing with Jafar is also a mark in the negative column. No, I'll only go there as a last resort.

Gaeton might take me in, at least for a little while, but it's even worse over there. The Man in Black is old, and rumor has it he's the kind of sick a person doesn't come back from. His daughters are strong enough to hold the territory, but the unrest will be bad for business. Bad for me if I'm there. Not to mention the Man in Black's youngest daughter has a history with Gaeton, and his helping me wouldn't earn me any points with her. If Isabelle Belmonte decides to blacklist me, that will cut out a *huge* stream of revenue to my business. I can't risk going that route, either.

There's no help for it. I'm going to have to bite the financial bullet and find a place in Hades's territory. At least for now. I'll figure out the rest once I get enough time and distance to be able to take an honest look at my current situation.

I try very hard not to think about how much I love my suite in the Underworld as I start walking with a vague wave in Allecto's direction. There's no point in calling a cab. Hades's reach is only a handful of blocks in any direction. There are a set of apartments a few streets down that might work. I've met clients there in the past, and while the spaces are small, they're really nice.

As I stop at the corner to wait for the light, the small hairs at the back of my neck raise and my skin prickles. Someone is watching me. I look around slowly, but it's midday and there's too much foot traffic to be able to tell who it is. That, and I'm too short to see over the shoulders of the people in front of me. The light changes, and they surge into motion, taking me with them. I focus on putting one foot in front of the other and try to watch the faces around me. No one seems to be paying me the slightest bit of attention. It should be enough to relax me, but my instincts aren't getting the memo.

I reach the other side of the street, and the guy on my left stumbles, knocking me aside right as I try to step on the curb. My heel turns, and then I'm falling. "Fuck!"

Hands grab my upper arms and haul me to my feet. I immediately start to step back, to thank the dude, but he doesn't let me go. *What the hell?* I jerk back harder. "Thanks. I got it."

"Do you?"

I freeze. Even five years later, I know that voice. My gaze goes up, up, up, and there he is. The specter in more night-mares than I care to count. My boogeyman. Peter. He doesn't look like he's aged a day since I saw him last, his light brown hair still cut short on the sides and left longer on top. His blue eyes twinkle at me, filled with the kind of mean amuse-ment that always comes before my pain. "Hey, baby."

No words come. I open my mouth, but a strange wheezing sound emerges. Apparently he takes that as a sign, because he shifts his grip to my wrists and starts pulling me down the block. "Been a while."

"Let go!"

"You know better. I'm just taking what I'm owed. And you owe me a *lot*, Tatiana." Step by step, despite my best efforts, we start down the street in the opposite direction of where I'd wanted to go.

I can't go with him. I know what happens if we get some-where private. What I *owe* him. He didn't kill me before, but he sure as fuck is going to now. Or worse. I can't think about worse right now. I can't think about anything. I dig in my heels, but he's always been stronger than me. Even though my body is nowhere near the weak thing it was at sixteen, at eighteen, at twenty, he still doesn't even seem to notice that I'm fighting him.

"Hey!"

A voice behind us, so familiar it makes me sag in relief. My breath sobs out. I twist and catch sight of Hercules wading through people behind us. His gaze lands on me and then on Peter, finally settling on where Peter's hands grind the bones of my wrist together. Hercules's eyes narrow. He's a total cinnamon roll, but right now he looks like he might tear Peter apart with his bare hands. "Let her go."

Peter looks down at me and chuckles. "You won't always have friends with you, baby. See you soon." He releases my wrists and melts into the crowd right as Hercules skids to a stop next to me.

Hercules goes down on one knee, completely ignoring how dirty the street must be, and examines my wrists. "Are you okay?"

Okay? I am so far from okay, I don't know where to begin. I blink down at him. "What are you doing here?"

"Hades has his reasons for making this call, but it's wrong to just toss you out without a parachute." He gives me a sweet smile. "I was going to help you find a place and get you settled in."

If he were anyone else, I'd accuse him of ulterior motives, but Hercules is one of those pure souls that defy explanation. He's a legitimately good guy, and I still don't quite under-stand how he and Hades and Meg ended up in a relationship that works. I guess it's enough that it does.

My body finally understands the threat has passed, and I start shaking and can't seem to stop. That was close. Too close. Not a single one of these strangers on the street even looked up from their phones long enough to realize they were witnessing an abduction. If Hercules wasn't too pure for this world, Peter could have taken me wherever he wanted to.

He won't stop. I knew it for truth even as I denied it to Hook, but there's no room for that kind of denial now. He will not stop. He will keep coming for me. I wasn't strong enough to stand against him on my own before.

I'm not strong enough now.

Hercules stands and pulls me into a hug. Part of me wants to fight him, but he's big and strong and smells really good. For a moment, I can almost fool myself into thinking I'm safe.

I'm not, though. I'll never be again.

Which means I have only one course of action left to me.

CHAPTER 4

HOOK

"*S*he's here."

I stare at Nigel for a full three seconds before speaking. "You're going to have to elaborate, cousin. There are a lot of 'she's' in my territory."

Nigel crosses his arms over his chest. He's built bulkier than I am, courtesy of his giant of a father, but we share our mothers' coloring. I've been in this world long enough to know that family doesn't mean shit unless you want it to, but I trust Nigel with my life. There are reasons he's my second-in-command, and cryptic statements aren't one of them. He relents before I do and snorts. "Short, curvy blonde. Mean as a fucking snake. You know exactly what *she* I'm talking about, so stop dicking around."

Tatiana. Or, rather, Tink. That's the name she's been going under since she got out.

I look at the old clock above the door. "That took less time than I expected."

"Yeah, yeah, I'll pay up." He digs his wallet out and passes me a hundred-dollar bill. "You going to keep gloating or you going to go get your woman?"

My woman.

Not yet. Not in any true way. But the fact she's here means she's going to say yes. She doesn't have a choice if she wants to stay in Carver City, and the sooner she realizes it, the better. Even Hades's neutral territory won't protect her if Peter decides to chase her down—and he's already decided it.

I check my pace and head for the door. She came to me. That puts me in exactly the position I need to get what I want. If I play my hand too freely, she'll realize my offer isn't as simple as it appears. She's smart enough to connect the dots and understand I need her just as much as she needs me. That shit will not fly.

Nigel put her in his office, which is just as well. I trust my men not to touch what's mine, but loyalty has been wavering over the last few months. I'll need to make an example of someone soon to ensure they fear me more than they fear the memory of Peter. The thought sits like lead in my stomach, but I knew what I was signing up for when I drove him out. This is the price I pay for safety, mine and my people's. I'm willing to bear the burden of it.

I should have killed him. I beat him within an inch of his life, but when it came time to finish him, I hesitated. Murder is what monstrous people did—what Peter and my father did. If I killed him, I'd be no better than him, so I had the few men loyal to him drag his bloody body out of the building and washed my hands of him.

Joke's on me. Four years later and I am *exactly* as monstrous as Peter and my father. Better that I'd lost my soul a few months earlier and removed the biggest threat to this territory, because my so-called morals didn't last the first year. One does not run an entire territory without being challenged, without being forced to make examples of people. I'm no exception. I can talk circles around most people, but there are situations that I simply can't charm my way out of.

Because of my weakness, Peter lives and now he's knocking on my door, threatening everything I've sold my soul to protect. If I fail, everything I've done to keep my people safe will be for nothing.

I can't let that happen. No matter the cost.

I step into the office and shut the door behind me. I'm not surprised to find Tink sitting at the desk and rifling through the unlocked drawers. She glares, silently daring me to say something.

I don't have to say shit. *She* came to me. She knows the offer on the table. If she wasn't willing to accept, she wouldn't have crossed into my territory, let alone shown up at the house itself. I sprawl into the chair across from the desk and wait.

She doesn't make me wait long. "I hate you." Tink's voice holds no heat, just a weary resignation.

"You've made that abundantly clear over the years." I only tried to talk to her once after she escaped Peter's clutches, a few months after she made her deal with Hades. She refused to see me, and every time since then, she has treated me like an enemy. Someone to be cut down verbally every time we shared the same space. I don't blame her for that. I'm a walking, breathing memory of years I'm sure she'd rather forget. And, fuck, but I enjoy seeing her snarl and snap instead of cowering like she did in the bad old days.

She props her hands on her generous hips. She's wearing a cute pink dress with black polka dots that hugs her tits and torso and then flares down to stop just below her knees. It's old school and a strange combination of prim and sexy that makes me want to sink my teeth into her.

She snaps her fingers next to her face. "Stop staring at my tits."

"I like the dress."

Her green eyes narrow. "I didn't put it on for you." She turns to look out the window, and I mourn the fact that the dress hides her ass and thighs. The woman is *thick*, and I fucking love it. She's always been beautiful, but when I knew her before, it was a fragile kind of thing that seemed on the verge of shattering. Too skinny. Too afraid. Not taking care of herself, though it was no fault of her own.

I've watched her find herself over the years. Find her style. Find her confidence. Find her Don't Fuck With Me attitude. The fact she won't give me the time of day only makes me respect her more. The woman she's become doesn't fuck around.

I'm putting her in one hell of a position, but I'm not a good enough person to be sorry for it.

She moves around the desk and perches on the edge of it. It puts her a few inches higher than me while I'm sitting, and I let her have the power position. Tink finally curses. "It's in your best interest for Peter to disappear. Explain to me why I need to marry you in order to make it happen."

Something went down since I saw her last. I study her expression. Evidence of it is there in the tight line of her mouth and the tense way she holds herself. I missed it before because I was too busy ogling her. She's *scared*.

I go still. "He got to you."

"He made an appearance," she agreed.

Fuck. I hadn't expected him to move so fast. She's been out from under Hades's thumb fewer than twelve hours. I thought we'd have more time to figure shit out, but I should have known better. "Agree to my bargain, Tink. I'll take care of it."

"I still don't get what *you* get out of it."

"I get *you*." *I get safety for my people ... until the next supposed badass with a grudge comes calling.* I wait for her to look at me

32

and give her a slow grin. "I think we can both agree that you're worth it."

She shakes her head. "You can't honestly think I'm naive enough to believe that."

No, I really don't. She's always been too smart for everyone else's good. She won't believe me if I tell her the truth. Tink has already cast me as the villain, and I'm more than happy to play to type. Easier than trying to explain what being the leader of this territory has cost me, what it will *continue* to cost me. I'm selfish enough to want a reward for all the sacrifices I've made, and that reward looks a whole lot like the pretty blond glaring at me right now. I shrug. "Believe what you want. I laid out the terms. Agree or don't." I make a conscious effort to stay relaxed and keep my breathing even. As if everything isn't hanging in the balance while she considers me.

"Let me see if I have this straight. In return for his head on a platter, I have to marry you, fuck you, and submit to you." She ticks each item off a finger, leaving her middle one up. "Sounds like bullshit from where I'm sitting."

"You submit in the bedroom. I'm not looking for a fucking slave." That kind of submission, the sort that bleeds over into every part of life, is exhausting just thinking about. I have enough people to worry about without adding that to my list. Beyond that, I *like* Tink's attitude and her determination to be a little fucking brat.

"I don't want to have sex with you."

I burst out laughing. She looks so cranky, I can't help it. "Lie to yourself if you want to. Don't lie to me. You most definitely want to have sex with me. It pisses you off, but it's the truth."

She looks like she wants to chuck something at my head. "Am I going to have to repeat every single thing I say to get it through that suffocating ego of yours? I. Do. Not. Want. To. Have. Sex. With. You."

"Fine. Sex is off the table."

If anything, she looks more suspicious. "You agreed to that too easily."

I want Tink in my bed, yes, but I want her there willingly. Breaking this woman isn't on my agenda. It never was. I stretch my arms over my head and fight a grin at the way she tries so hard not to check me out. "Here are the updated terms. I will not negotiate further. You marry me. I kill Peter. When you decide you're tired of playing hard to get, you'll crawl to me and beg for my cock. I'm all too happy to give it to you any way you like. *Every* way you like."

Her pretty pink lips form a perfect O of shock. "You've lost your mind."

"Wrong. I'm simply not in the habit of lying to myself the way you are."

She wipes the surprise from her expression and is back to glaring at me again. "What's the point of forcing me to marry you if it's a total sham of a marriage?"

I lift my brows. "Not all marriages have sex, Tink. That's a very narrow worldview you have."

"That's not what I mean and you know it. Stop baiting me."

"Stop making it so easy."

She makes a sound like a pissed off teakettle. "If you force the matrimony issue, and then turn around and fuck your way through the territory, it's going to make me look like a fool."

She's already decided to marry me. I have to work to keep the smugness out of my tone. Tink's exactly where I want her, and as soon as she signs the papers and accepts the ring, she'll be fighting herself as well as me to stay out of my bed. I idly twist the ring on my left thumb. "I'll honor my vows unless you tell me not to."

"What's that supposed to mean?"

"So suspicious." I laugh again, mostly to enjoy the twitch by her right eye that comes in response. "You've worked in the Underworld for five years. Even if you avoided me, you were too good an employee for Hades not to notice what I like." I know for a fact Hades has files on every single player in Carver City, including their kinks and whatever dirty secrets they let slip. Tink worked under Meg, which means she'd have access to those files, would be encouraged to keep her eyes open every time she's on the playroom floor.

"You like to share." She practically spits the words at me, and a flush spreads across her chest and up her neck. Fury or desire? Only time will tell.

I push slowly to my feet, giving her plenty of time to back up. She won't, but it's important to draw this line in the sand. "You will sleep in my bed. You'll be my wife in truth. I won't push the sex, but everything else holds."

"How long?"

I drag my fingers slowly through her long hair, enjoying how silky it feels. She's done something to the color to make the blond pop even more. I like it. "Until we decide we're done."

"That's a horrible bargain."

It's only horrible if she truly hates me as much as she says. I don't give a damn. The end result is the only thing that matters. I've bided my time. I've denied myself again and again, putting my shit on the back burner so I could keep the territory stabilized. It worked, but it won't work much longer. If Peter takes me out, a shit ton of people will suffer in the aftermath. I can't let that happen.

I *won't* let that happen.

"Take it or leave it. The offer expires the second you walk out that door."

She slaps my hand away, and I let her. Tink might know what I like, but I've been watching her, too. I've seen her get off more times than I can count, always by other's hands, mouths, cocks. She enjoys putting on a show as much as I do. More, even. She won't thank me for noticing, but all's fair in love and war, and if we don't win this fight, we won't survive. Love doesn't even enter into the equation.

Finally, she nods. "I don't have a choice."

"There's always a choice. Always."

"Not for me. Not this time." She presses her hand against my chest, and I allow her to push me back a step and then two. "How soon can you get a priest here?"

"An hour."

"Do it."

I don't give her a chance to change her mind. If I were a better man, I'd check in with her or sit her down and reassure her that she's making the right choice. I don't do any of it. I leave her sitting on Nigel's desk and send for a priest.

It doesn't take him long to show up. He's a short Black man who's worked in the church down the street for longer than I've been alive. His receding hairline has left the top of his head completely bald, and his curls have long since gone to gray. For all that, I wouldn't want to cross him. Father Elijah hasn't lived this long because he lets people fuck with him. Even Peter knew to leave the church and its parishioners alone. At least right up until the end when Father Elijah challenged him one too many times over his treatment of Tink.

Peter attacking the priest is what finally caused Tink to flee the territory. I'm sure of it. And her leaving paved the way for me to challenge Peter directly. It feels strangely like closing a circle to have Father Elijah be the one to marry us.

He gives me a long look. "Marriage is meant to be a holy union."

"Don't go trying to convert me now." I grin, my body language relaxed and open. Most people only see the charm and ignore the danger beneath. Father Elijah isn't most people, but threatening him will backfire. I need him to do this, to make my marriage with Tink official. Legally, yes, but more importantly, I need it official in the eyes of the territory. I open the door for him. "You know I'm a heathen."

"We're all God's children." He snorts. "Even the assholes."

"Especially the assholes. Pretty sure that was the sermon a few Sundays ago."

"You'd know if you ever darkened our doorstep." He walks into the office, and I can't see his face, but his voice lights up. "Tatiana."

Tink hops off the desk and pulls at the fabric of her dress to straighten it. "Father Elijah. I didn't—I didn't know you'd be here." She looks a little lost for the first time since she showed up here, her gaze flitting over his face as if tracing the injuries Peter had left there. They might be healed, but look at her expression says that their memory lives on with Tink.

The priest must see it too, because he moves first, holding out his hands. "Come here, child. Let me look at you." He waits patiently for her to take his hands and tugs her forward a step. "You look good." For any other man, those words would be lewd and crass. Hell, they were when I said them. Father Elijah actually means them exactly how they sound. "I'm so proud of you."

Her bottom lip quivers the tiniest bit before she locks it all down. "I've been working at a kink club for five years, Father. I practically have Sinners 'R Us tattooed on my forehead."

He gives an easy smile. "You got out. You've made something of yourself and you're doing good for those who don't have your resources."

A faint blush colors her cheeks and she won't quite meet his gaze. "I don't know what you're talking about."

"Of course, child. We never have to speak of those monthly donations."

I manage to school my expression before they both look at me. I had no idea Tink was sending money to the church. There's no reason I *should* know that, but, fuck, it doesn't even surprise me now that I think of it. It's exactly something she'd do.

"Shall we?" I motion Nigel and Colin into the room and shut the door. Despite there being three years between them, they could almost pass as identical twins. The only difference is that Colin wears a full beard and has a penchant for graphic T-shirts from 80s rock bands. Today's is AC/DC.

Tink narrows her eyes as she looks at the papers I lay on the desk. "You already got us a marriage license. Somehow. Despite the fact that I'm supposed to be present for that."

"Just greasing the wheels." I hand her a pen. "Sign here."

"You're such a bastard." She doesn't hesitate to sign, though, and then practically stabs me with the pen when she thrusts it back at me. I follow suit.

Father Elijah shakes his head. "I didn't want this for either of you."

I can appreciate his sentiment—I didn't want this shit for me, either—but marrying Tink doesn't even rate on the list of horrible things I've had to do over the years. It's necessary, yes, but I'd be lying if I said I didn't want it. Didn't want *her*.

Father Elijah arranges us before him. I start to tell him we don't need the full show, but he shuts me up with a harsh look. I stare down at Tink as he goes through the whole song and dance of our wedding vows. Even in her heels, she barely comes up to my shoulder. It's so easy to forget how short she is because her personality expands her presence. It's not doing that right now. She looks too pale and a little wide around the eyes as she says, "I do."

I repeat it when it's my turn, and it feels a whole lot like promising shit I have no ability to give. She knows that, though. She's walking into this fully aware of cost, the same as me. If I'm the one who forced her to this point, I'm not sorry I did it.

Father Elijah sighs. "I now pronounce you husband and wife. You may kiss the bride."

CHAPTER 5

*A*s tempting as it is to knee Hook in the balls, I am overly aware of Father Elijah watching us. He's a good man and one of the few things I found bearable during my time with Peter—at least until that was taken from me, too.

In the end, he was the straw that broke the camel's back. After Peter forbid me from attending church, Father Elijah tried to intervene. In the aftermath of that, it felt like I woke from a long sleep. I'd known I wasn't getting out of my relationship with Peter alive, even if I couldn't admit it to myself at the time. But realizing that I'd take down innocents, too? *That* I couldn't stand for.

So I ran. Took the route and resources I'd been too terrified to contemplate before, and fled to Hades, where I begged him to save me. He could have demanded anything and I would have accepted. By comparison, five years is a bargain.

Now I'm making a different kind of bargain, though it's just as driven by fear as the last.

I lift my face and let Hook press a surprisingly sweet kiss to my lips. I don't know what I expected, but this wasn't it. I have to fight not to step forward, not to close the distance between us, not to nip his bottom lip so he'll *really* kiss me.

He lifts his head and grins. "Let's do this." Then he takes my hand and tows me toward the door.

Father Elijah gives a rough laugh. "Don't be a stranger, Tatiana."

It takes two tries to form words. "I won't." Every time someone calls me by the name I intentionally left behind, it feels like they're forcibly shoving me back into a skin that's too small. I'm not that girl anymore. I don't want to ever be her again.

And yet here I am, right back where I started. Hook might not have set up his headquarters in the same house Peter dominated, but so much of it is the same. Various people, all obviously armed, moving about with purpose in their steps and violence in their eyes. One doesn't run an entire territory through charm alone. Threats must be delivered and examples must be made. And Hook does it all. He wouldn't be able to hold his power without getting his hands dirty.

Rationally, I know he's nowhere near as evil as Peter is. I'm not even sure he's evil at all. But he chose to take over this territory, and that decision more than speaks for itself.

Hook doesn't quite drag me through the halls, but I have to step fast to keep up with his longer strides. I try to memorize the building's layout, but though it seems like a straightforward business from the outside, the inside has been completely gutted and renovated into something else entirely. We move through what feel like smaller apartments, hallways, and then a living room, and then another hallway. It's really brilliant as a way of forcing an invading enemy into pinch point after pinch point, but it's discombobulating. I'm lost before we make it halfway through the main floor, and that irritates the hell out of me.

He hauls me to an elevator and ushers me inside. The

second we're behind closed doors, I yank my arm free. "Manhandling is not sexy."

"I beg to differ."

I ignore the innuendo in his low voice. I may have intentionally blocked out his presence in the Underworld whenever I could, but there was no escaping the end-of-shift reports with my fellow employees. We were information gatherers, and everything we learned went into the impressive files Meg keeps on anyone of interest in Carver City.

I know more about what gets Hook off than I have any right to. I also know that he's been paying attention to *me* this entire time. He knows my kinks. He's seen them on display. I can't think about that too hard or I won't be able to fight the blush buzzing beneath my skin. "Not like this," I manage.

"Okay," he agrees easily.

I give him a sharp look, trying to sense the shape of the trap he's letting me walk right into. Hook might fake being agreeable, but he *is* faking it. I don't know why Hook won't move on Peter without this sham of a marriage, but I can't afford to be picky right now. Not when I can still feel that bastard's fingers digging into my wrist. It will bruise, and that pisses me the fuck off. These days, the only bruises on my body are the ones I *want* there. Not from him. Never again from him.

The doors slide open, and Hook ambles out into a massive bedroom. I whistle before I can stop myself. The ceiling arches high above us, and it's made entirely of glass. I bet at night, the stars look close enough to touch. It's a struggle to drag my gaze back down to earth and the room itself. It's set up in a studio style with a surprisingly top-of-the-line kitchen taking up space on the left and a series of hardwood wardrobes on the right, half of which look like they're in the process of vomiting clothing onto the floor.

Seeing that chaos makes my blood pressure rise to dangerous levels, so I turn to the wall that appears to be made of vaguely translucent tile. The door next to it confirms it as the bathroom, and when I walk over to investigate, I roll my eyes. The entire wall is the shower, which means anyone standing there will be outlined almost perfectly for viewing from the rest of the room. Great.

Then there's nowhere else to look but at the bed. It's large enough that only the term orgy-sized would fit. Considering the scenes I've witnessed Hook participate in, that doesn't surprise me in the least.

I want to hate the whole room. I really do. But it's weirdly cozy and decadent and as long as I don't look at how he disrespects his clothing, I kind of like it.

I point at the bed. "You had damn well better change the sheets if you want me anywhere near that thing."

Hook drops onto the edge of the mattress and, good god, that's a scene right out of the fantasies I refuse to admit to having. The top few buttons of his shirt have come undone somewhere along the way, and the deep V of his medium brown skin with a dusting of dark hair actually makes my mouth water. He leans back, letting me look my fill.

To annoy him, I do exactly that. Or at least that's what I tell myself as I let my gaze roam over the strength in his shoulders and way his thighs fill out those slacks. I save his hair for last. It's almost as long as mine and thick enough that I'm envious. I need creative use of a straightener and a whole lot of product to achieve the same amount of wave in my hair. Hook's is all natural.

And then there are the piercings. I once heard Hercules describe Hook as a sexy pirate and he's not wrong. Between the long hair and the neatly trimmed beard and the rings he has on multiple fingers and … My attention snags on the labret piercing nestled below his full bottom lip. I can't look at his mouth without wanting to kiss him, which exactly the *wrong* kind of mentality to have about this shit.

"See something you like?"

"My jailer."

His grin only widens. Hook's perverse like that. It doesn't matter how many times I turn him down or how mean I am, his response is always to seem downright delighted by me.

IT'S a marked difference from the few times we interacted *before*, when he looked at me with pity and some emotion I never dared name. Peter's other men either ignored me or lusted after me—at least when he wasn't looking. Not Hook. I could always feel his attention drilling a hole through my carefully curated numbness.

I don't know what changed in those months between my leaving and his taking over the territory. He tried to see me once, but I couldn't stand the thought of any connection to Peter touching my fragile new life. Plus, I didn't trust him. Hades might have promised me safety, but if Hook dragged me back to Peter, would he pursue? I didn't know, so I went the safe route. I hid.

There's no pity in Hook's dark eyes now. No, there's just pure delight at my snark. I don't understand it, and I don't trust it. Even in the Underworld, there were Doms who saw my attitude as an invitation to break me down. I learned to avoid them, but I don't have the safety net the club offers now.

He waves a casual hand at the atrocity that is his closet area. "I'll send for your shit. Put it wherever you like."

I sift through the words for a hidden meaning but find nothing. "And then what?"

"Tonight we announce our happy union in the only appropriate way for people like us."

I know what he means even as I try to deny it. There's only one way to communicate this kind of big change to the entirety of Carver City. It's possible I'm wrong. "How?"

He pushes to his feet. "The Underworld."

"No. Absolutely not." I swipe my hands through the air as if that will make a difference. "You said no sex."

"I said *I* wouldn't fuck you, and I won't until our terms are met." He wades into the mess of his clothes and digs through the middle wardrobe while I gape at him. Surely he can't mean ... He definitely doesn't mean ...

Hook retrieves whatever he was looking for and stalks back to me. He holds out a hand, and I gingerly place mine in his. It's hard not to notice how much larger he is when his big palm is dwarfing mine. I watch numbly as he slips a ring with a giant-ass diamond onto my finger. It fits perfectly, which will piss me off later, when I'm not so shell-shocked. "What about you?" I don't mean to ask. I really don't.

He laughs. "I have one, too." He pulls a matte black ring from his pocket and slips it onto the ring finger of his left hand.

I hate that he was so sure of me that he bought rings. I hate that mine is a princess cut diamond that's simple and elegant and exactly what I would have chosen for myself. I yank my hand from his. "I'm not going to the Underworld tonight."

"You don't have a choice." He unbuttons his shirt in slow movements. "Unless you plan on hiding in this room like a coward for the rest of your life, you have to play the game. You know that, so stop wasting both our time fighting over something that you know you can't win."

I watch helplessly as he shrugs out of his shirt. "What are you doing?"

"Showering." He kicks off his shoes in the approximate direction of the rest of his clothing. "Want to watch?"

With how the shower's set up, I won't have a choice, and he knows it. I paste a bored look on my face. "I've seen the show. I'm not interested."

"Ah, but this one's different." His hands fall to his pants.

I almost lick my lips before I catch myself. "Why is this one different?"

When he speaks again, the amusement is gone from his voice, leaving it deeper. "Because this show is for you." Hook walks away before I can come up with a response to that, which is just as well because I don't *have* a response to that.

I stumble to the bed and sink onto the edge of it. The moment I do, I get a whiff of the clean scent of laundry soap, and I almost laugh. The bastard cleaned his sheets in preparation for me. Of course he did.

The water comes on in the bathroom, and I look up to find that just as I suspected, I can clearly see the outline of Hook's naked body as he steps beneath the spray and tilts his head back.

Holy shit.

I've seen him naked before. Impossible to participate in the Underworld's public activities *without* seeing others naked. It's different now. There's no one else here. He's putting on this show for me and me alone.

I bite my bottom lip as I watch him soap himself up, running his hands over his body in slow, methodical motions. All the fear and frustration and turmoil of the last couple days switches to pure lust as he takes his cock in his fist and gives himself a rough stroke. I don't have to see the minute details to know exactly what it looks like. Long and thick and perfect for the rough kind of fucking I crave.

My body goes tight and hot, and I press my thighs together. It doesn't relieve the feeling. It only makes it worse. He's teasing me on purpose, hoping to stoke me into a lust-fueled frenzy that ends with me on my knees and begging.

Depriving myself would only give him what he wants, right? The logic is hazy at best, but I kick off my heels and shift back farther onto the bed. Before I can think of all the reasons this is a terrible idea, I drag my dress up and delve a hand into my panties.

I circle my clit in time to Hook's strokes, each touch sending my pleasure spiking higher. The fact that it feels absolutely forbidden to be doing this while he's jacking his hand half a room away only makes it hotter.

"Tatiana."

I jump and press hard against my clit. I have to fight back a moan, but my voice comes out breathy when I answer. "What?"

"If I walk in there right now, am I going to find your hand in your panties?"

I start circling again. His pleasure-roughened voice only pushes me closer to orgasm. "Yes."

His curse makes me smile, just a little bit. Hook is so *much*, all the time. It can be frustrating as hell, but he's not one to play games and pretend disinterest. He wants to fuck me, and he's not shy about letting me know.

He turns and braces a hand against the glass, a perfect imprint of five fingers and his palm. With his other hand, he resumes stroking his cock. "Always the dirty girl. Always fucking teasing me."

Suddenly, my fingers aren't enough. I want more. Goddamn it, I want him, and I hate myself for it as much as I hate him for making me feel this way. I try to pull back, but I'm too close. My body has a mind of its own now, my hips rising to press against my fingers. A moan remains trapped on the inside of my lips through sheer force of will.

"Get that pretty pussy of yours ready, Tatiana." He growls my name and, for the first time, it doesn't make my chest tighten. It sounds sexy and forbidden and, holy fuck, what is he doing to me? We're not even in the same room, not really, but it feels like he's whispering directly into my ear. He curses. "Come for me, beautiful girl. Take the edge off so I can take care of you tonight."

I come before I can stop myself, responding to the rising desire as much as to his rough words. I watch helplessly as he follows, his strokes becoming rougher as he finishes with a muttered curse I can't quite make out.

I barely get my hand out of my panties before he shuts off the shower and walks in the room with a towel wrapped around his waist. He hasn't bothered to dry off and water drips down his chest in tiny rivulets that are the most tempting kind of invitation. If he was a different person, if we were in a different situation, I'd want to trace those same pathways with my tongue.

The look he gives my bare legs sends heat bolting to my core despite my orgasm. Hook's one of the only people who knew me when my body was considered "ideal" by society's standards. I gave that shit up a long time ago in my quest for *me*. I don't care what he thinks of my abundant curves and softness.

Except the way his eyes get hot and he licks his lips is really, really hot. Knowing it's because he likes what he sees … I'm not immune.

I'm an asshole in my own right, because I use a single finger to drag my panties to the side and let him see the mess I made of myself.

He moves a step closer and then another, his gaze glued to my pussy. A quick glance at my face and he kneels at the edge of the bed. "Tell me your safe word, Tatiana."

I can't quite catch my breath. "You don't need my safe word if you're not going to fuck me."

His lips curve. "Beautiful girl, you know better. There are

thousands upon thousands of things I can do to you without ever penetrating that pretty pussy."

I don't want to tell him. But changing the safe word I've used for five years because I don't want to admit it is as cowardly as he accused me of being. I grit my teeth. "Pirate."

Hook's grin is downright blinding. "Pirate," he repeats slowly. "I see."

"No, you don't."

"Mmm." He releases me from his gaze and narrows his attention on my pussy again. "Are you ready to be on your knees?"

If I say yes, if I go through with it, then he'll fuck me right now. The intent is written all over his face. He wants this as much as I do. More, maybe.

If I say yes, I lose what little leverage I have.

"No."

"So be it." He snags the wrist of the hand I used to masturbate and drags me forward. I watch with wide eyes as he sucks each individual finger into his mouth, one at a time. His tongue slides against my sensitive skin, and I can't quite stifle a whimper. Hook releases me and drags his thumb across my palm. "Your stuff will be here in the next few days. No one in the house will mess with you, but it's wise to stay in this room until we've gone public with the marriage. Once everyone knows you're mine, they won't touch you." He grins. "Unless I ask them nicely and you're down for it."

I blink. He's moving too quickly, switching subjects with ease when I'm still hung up on the way he makes my skin buzz.

But then, it's just a game for Hook. He's like every other territory leader in this city, moving the pieces about in his eternal quest for power. I'm just a pawn in another person's game. My only value to him is that Peter won't let me go.

Marrying me, rubbing our so-called relationship in the public's face, that's destined to piss Peter off. *That* has to be part of the plan. A plan I need to remember, because Hook is not for me. He's everything I very much don't want in my life. I've walked this path before, falling for a man more in love with power than he could ever be with me. If I had a single choice in the matter, I wouldn't go down it again. Peter was a monster before he was powerful, but that old saying about power corrupting a person isn't wrong. The more power he claimed, the more monstrous he became. No one is immune to the seductive temptation of *more*. Not Peter. Not Hook, either.

If he's not a full monster now, he will be in the future.

"You're saying I'm trapped here." I carefully withdraw my hand from his. "Is this another joke of yours, because you can't possibly be serious."

"I *am* serious. It's safest for you here, at least for now." He hesitates for the briefest of moments and then pushes to his feet. "Be ready at nine."

I manage to keep my temper locked down until the elevator doors close behind him. How *dare* he? I am not a toy he can use and toss away when he's not in the mood any longer. He wants a wife, but not until the right time, not until he can use me to his best advantage.

I drag my hands through my hair. I can't do this. I can't be trapped like this. It's a different house, a different room, a different *man*. It doesn't matter. Hook knows my history, and he still essentially locked me up here.

My gaze lands on the mess of clothes. That fucker wants to lock me up?

He'll have to pay the price.

CHAPTER 6

*A*s much as I'd enjoy spending the next few days playing bedroom games with Tink, the reality is that I married her to ensure I have everything I need to bring down the largest threat to my territory and people. She is the key to Peter, and all of this song and dance is carefully orchestrated to draw him out of whatever shithole he's hiding in.

Yes, I want her in my bed more than I've wanted anything in living memory. But that's a selfish desire, rather than one designed to ensure the safety of my people. I'm bastard enough to want to have my cake and eat it, too.

I stalk into Nigel's office and drop into the unoccupied chair next to Colin. "What do you have for me?"

Nigel takes a long look at my face. "Trouble in paradise already?"

"Fuck off."

He snorts and gets down to business. "We don't have eyes on Hades's blocks."

"I'm aware of that." I wave it away. We might have surveillance on our neighboring territories to the north and south—Jasmine and Malone's, respectively—but Hades is a different animal. Crossing him means losing a priceless resource. No one does it for fear of being caught. That includes me. I rub my hands over my face.

Tink didn't come here because she was so delighted by the idea of marrying me that she couldn't resist saying yes. Peter said something to her to make her think she wouldn't be safe living outside of the Underworld. I want to know what. She had resources to live on her own. I've tried not to follow her life too closely, but even I can't escape what a success she's become with her clothing shit. I'm honestly surprised Hades is letting her fly the coop. Between his club and the fact that most major players in Carver City actively invite Tink into their homes to style them, he had unsurpassed access to people and information.

Now half of that belongs to me, at least in theory. It could be an incredible resource for the territory if we live through the coming conflict with Peter. If I can convince her to stay once the threat of him has passed.

Despite myself, I think back to the scene waiting for me when I walked out of the bathroom. The little tease was fingering herself on my bed, and all it'd taken to get her to that point was a little peep show in the shower. I grin. Under other circumstances, convincing Tink I'm one hell of a catch, convincing her to stay, would be a fun little journey.

Unfortunately, we don't have time for that shit right now. I need her on my side, and I need her there now.

"I want everyone talking about this marriage. *Everyone*, Colin. We make sure Peter knows, and I want him to know as soon as possible." Rumors aren't enough, though. That's why it's doubly important to go public in the most spectacular way possible. It'll draw him out of whatever hole he's been hiding in. He knows this area better than I do, even after all this time, and he's got people hiding him from me. If

I can't come to him, I have to make him furious enough to come to me.

I stole his power. I stole his territory. Now I've stolen his woman.

I turn my attention to Nigel to find a muscle ticking in his jaw. "You have something to say."

Anyone else would pussyfoot around. Nigel is family. He sits back and narrows his eyes. "It's shitty to bring her back into this."

Ah. Here we are. "She was always in it. She never got out."

"That's bullshit and you know it. She had a chance to go straight, and you pulled her right back into the muck with us."

I should have known Nigel would fall on this side of the line. He's always had a soft spot for Tink, so much so that he took more than a few beatings as the result of trying to step between her and Peter. He never learned that trying to intervene just made shit worse for her. He still hasn't learned it.

I hold his gaze. "You either stand with me or you don't. It's as simple as that."

"You know I have your back."

Yeah, I do. Which is why I have to take care of this now. Nigel isn't one for divided loyalties. Doubting me will eat him up inside until he does something noble but ill advised. I lean forward. "I didn't haul her here over my shoulder and hold a gun to her head while she said her vows. She showed up. She took the bargain. She married me. That's the only truth that matters. We have bigger problems right now than Tink's pride."

For a second, it looks like he might argue, but he finally jerks his chin down in a movement that's almost a nod. It's enough. I push to my feet. "I'm taking her to the Underworld tonight to go public with the marriage. Tomorrow, she integrates with the rest of the household. While everyone is focused on her, you keep sniffing for the traitors who are hiding Peter. If we find them first, Tink won't have to play a role."

This time, Nigel's nod was stronger. "We still don't know there are people hiding Peter."

"Yes, we do." Our last three gun shipments into Carver City had been stolen, and every person of mine onboard killed. I knew Peter was behind it, but that slippery bastard is never where I expect him to be. Every time I go on the attack, he disappears into thin air. He's making a fool of me, and I'll be damned before I let it continue.

So I'll make *him* come to *me*.

With Tink in my house, in my bed, he won't be able to stop himself for long. And when he does, I'll do exactly what I promised and give Tink his head on a platter. In the meantime, I'll put on a show destined to get his attention.

"Double the escort to Hades's territory, but do it subtly. I don't want to deal with an attack, but we can't look like we're scared."

We get down to planning out the details and then go over accounts for the last month. Business is good, but not good enough to take the hit of another lost shipment. Only my paranoia ensured we had enough weaponry stocked to fulfill our orders. All gone now. If Peter gets to the next shipment, we'll be royally fucked.

A week. I have a week to figure it out. A fucking blip of existence and a small eternity, all rolled into one.

An hour later, we sit back. I'm not satisfied, not by a long shot, but I won't be satisfied until I send that bastard to hell. I push to my feet and stretch. A quick glance at my watch confirms that I barely have enough time to change and get ready before we need to leave. "I better check on the missus."

Nigel makes a choked sound. "Be sure to call her that

sometime when I'm around to witness the resulting bloodbath."

"I might just do it." Tink is especially beautiful—and dangerous—when she gets riled. Since she lost that haunted look in her eyes at the Underworld, I've enjoyed poking her every chance I was afforded. Now I can do it whenever I want.

I take the elevator up to my suite, but the second I step out of the doors, I freeze. "What the hell?"

"Honey, you're home." Her smug voice comes from the bathroom, but I only have eyes for my closet.

It's unrecognizable. All my shit is gone. I walk to the nearest wardrobe and touch an empty hanger. "Where are my clothes?"

"Hmmm?"

Her innocent act is ruined by how delighted she sounds. I stalk into the bathroom and stop short. Tink has her hair done up in big pink curlers, and she's expertly applying red lipstick to her full lips. She's done something to her face to amplify her beauty and, holy fuck, she's pulled out all the stops for her clothing.

Her dress is short and white, hugging her big ass lovingly and giving me a whole lot of thigh to check out. Then she turns around, and my gaze snags on her tits. "Fuck."

"What's that, *husband?*" She starts to take out her curlers, leaving her long blond hair to fall around her face in waves I want to dig my hands into.

It takes more effort than it should to circle around to the problem. "My clothes."

"Oh, that." She neatly places the pink curlers back into their container, one by one. "I sent them out for dry cleaning."

"Dry cleaning," I repeat.

"That's what I said." She blinks big green eyes at me, all

55

feigned innocence. "I assumed they *must* be dirty, being as how they were all on the floor." She presses a hand to her chest. "After all, I'm just your little wife, right? That's what you wanted when you left me up here to cool my heels."

Oh, she is downright fucking *wicked*.

"I ought to put you over my knee for that bullshit."

She smiles sweetly. "We both know I'd enjoy that too much for it to serve as a deterrent. Give it up, Hook. I win this round."

I might laugh if I didn't want to kiss her so desperately. "What, pray tell, am I supposed to wear tonight since apparently every item I own is at the dry cleaner?"

"Oh, I'm sure you'll find something." She waves that away and turns back to the mirror. I notice that the counter is covered with her shit now. Tubes and canisters and eyeshadow in every color imaginable. I kind of like it.

I leave her to it and return to the main room to search for something that might have escaped her purge. She was remarkably thorough, and she also seems to have claimed the nearest wardrobe as her own. Her clothing hangs in neat color-coded rows. I'm mildly impressed at the sheer amount of shit she had packed in that pink suitcase. I pull open a drawer and find a rainbow of lingerie. Some of it I recognize. Others are new to me, and I shut the drawer again before I can examine my reaction to that too closely.

Jealousy for those who have seen her in them. Anticipation for my own experience with her. Something infinitely more complicated.

I find a pair of leather pants shoved in the back of a drawer in the farthest wardrobe. I shake them out and sigh. Not my favorite, but they'll do.

I've barely finished getting ready when Tink walks into the room. Even having seen her a short time ago, the sight of her rocks me back on my heels. The woman is a fucking *stunner*. She knows it, too. She gives me a snarky little smile. "I see you found something after all."

I don't bother with a shirt. Technically there is a dress code in the lounge part of the Underworld, but I've found that a lot of things can be overridden if a person has enough confidence to brazen it out. The missing piece of clothing is more than worth it as Tink stares at my chest. It's nothing she hasn't seen before, but it feels different. She's actually *looking* at me for the first time. More, she's mine now. I guess that means I'm hers, too.

I spread my arms and give her a wide grin that I know will spike her blood pressure. "You can touch if you like, Tatiana."

"Stop calling me that."

"It's your name."

She props a hand on her hip. "Not anymore."

It's tempting to argue, but ultimately it's not my call what she chooses to call herself. If she sees Tatiana as representation of the person she was before, who the fuck am I to argue? "Okay," I finally say. "Not anymore."

I slowly let my arms drop. I didn't really expect her to take me up on my invitation. Our game has barely begun, and I won't lie and say I'm not looking forward to her making me work for it. She wants me. She wouldn't be fingering herself to the image of me in the shower if she didn't. She's also a prideful little asshole, so she's going to hold out as long as possible before giving us what we both desire.

I'm going to enjoy every second of it.

CHAPTER 7

TINK

*I*t feels like six months have passed since I was last in the Underworld, rather than something like twelve hours. Adem gives me a bright grin when he sees us walk through the doors. He's one of those too-gorgeous-to-be-real people, which is saying something in our world. His dark brown skin doesn't appear to have pores, and he always dresses to the nines. Tonight is no exception. He's wearing a three-piece suit that would be overdoing it for anyone else working what is essentially a front desk job. On Adem it's just … Adem. "Couldn't stay away, could you?"

"Not even if I wanted to." It's impossible to be a part of Carver City's power base without spending some time in the Underworld. Even Peter came here from time to time before I made my deal and Hook subsequently staged his coup. Though he never went beyond the lounge.

Hook and I will be playing tonight. I'm sure of it. He doesn't need to fuck me to be married to me, but he was pretty damn explicit about what he wants. My body, traitor that it is, is thrilled by the thought of the pending power games. I'm stubborn to a fault. I don't know how to be anything else. I *can't* give in to Hook. Not without a fight.

His big hand presses against the small of my back, branding me right down to my skin. He gives an easy grin. "Adem."

"Hook." Adem's dark gaze lands on the giant ring on my finger and goes wide. "Uh… Congratulations."

"Something like that," I mutter.

Hook's laugh rolls through me in the most delicious way possible as he hooks an arm around my waist and hauls me against his side. "I'm planning something special for the little woman tonight. We're celebrating."

Adem's dark brows rise and keep rising until I'm a little afraid they'll just disappear entirely. "I … see."

The impulse to explain shoves against the inside of my lips, but I stifle it. No matter the reason I said yes, this *is* a real marriage. Undermining it the second I get a chance undermines my safety and the safety of others.

Others.

I haven't had a chance to think about the implications of being Hook's wife, at least beyond the obvious. He's the ruler of his territory. Even though it's on the smaller scale, there are hundreds of people who are ready to jump to obey his every whim. There are those who would see him forcing me to get married as a sign of strength, but that puts me at a disadvantage for the rest of my life.

I start. *The rest of my life?* What the hell am I even saying? This isn't about the rest of my life. This deal only serves to protect me until the threat of Peter has passed. That's it. A shoring up of Hook's strength because I can't protect myself. Always the victim, never the partner.

I've played that part. I will never willingly go back.

So I lean into Hook and rub one hand up his bare chest. His muscles jump a little beneath my fingers, but his expression doesn't change. I smile at Adem. "We wanted to surprise everyone."

"I think it's safe to say you'll do exactly that."

Hook catches my hand and presses a kiss to my palm. "Go in ahead of me. I have a few calls to make."

I don't trust *that* at all, but arguing will undo all the work I just put in. I give Adem a wave and walk to the set of large black doors that dominate the wall behind him. This entrance is built to intimidate and transition a person from the real world to the one that lies within. Sin and decadence and power games. Only Hades's laws matter here, and anything is permissible as long as a person's safe word is honored. It's fucking heady, even now.

Especially now.

I have no idea what Hook is planning tonight. A public announcement of our marriage, yes, but I doubt he's going to be happy standing on the bar and declaring it for everyone present. No, he'll go about it in a uniquely *Hook* way. I shiver.

It's late enough that the lounge is more than half filled. I recognize Gaeton sprawled in one nook and smile a little when he raises a hand in greeting. A flash of pink hair draws my attention, and I turn to find Aurora bearing down on me. Before I have a chance to react, she throws her arms around me and gives a strong hug that belies her delicate build. "I was so worried about you!"

"I'm sorry." I don't know why I'm apologizing.

She takes a hold of my shoulders and leans back. "I didn't even know you were leaving, and then you were just gone and Hades had people packing up your room. Are you okay?" She takes me in with a glance. "You *look* great, but you always look great."

I can't help but smile. A real smile. Aurora is so fucking sweet, sometimes she makes my teeth ache. It's genuine with her. She's just a good person. "I'm okay." I nod at her outfit.

"You're looking good tonight, too." She's wearing a white underbust corset that highlights her trim waistline and a gauzy fabric draped in a way that's *almost* a dress. It highlights her light brown skin and I can see her nipples through the top of it. The folds beneath the bottom of the corset mostly obscure her around her hips and leave her legs bare. She is, of course, barefoot and wearing the collars all the submissives on staff wear while on shift.

Strange to think I'll never wear mine again.

"Thanks." She smiles, before the expression falls away. "Seriously, though. What can I do? I can't believe Hades just kicked you out."

I can't really believe it either, but the time for being pissed about it has come and gone. "You know me, Aurora. I always land on my feet."

"Still, I'm here if you need anything. Absolutely anything."

The wave of affection that rises in response to her offer nearly takes me off my feet. I've tried to hold myself separate, to drive people back with my shitty attitude, but it never fazed Aurora. Her bubbly attitude is infectious and if I was anyone else, we might even be considered friends. Maybe? I'm not even sure what real friendship looks like. Growing up, I moved homes too often to set down anything resembling roots or form lasting friendships. Then I was with Peter and anyone close to me painted a target on their chest, so people kept their distance and I did the same.

Her gaze flicks over my shoulder. "Don't look now, but here comes Hook."

I sigh. "Yeah, about that …" I hold up my left hand.

Her jaw drops. "What? No. Seriously? *No way.*"

"Yes, way." I almost manage not to tense as Hook's arms come around me, and he plasters himself against my back and props his chin on my head. His skin is warm against mine, and even as I tell myself to stand firm, I get a little melty.

"Hi, Hook," her voice is very small, and her eyes are very wide.

"Hey, Aurora. Nice dress." He gives me a squeeze. "You want a drink, wife?"

Oh, so it's like that. He wasn't even trying to be quiet when he said that. Out of the corner of my eye, I can see heads swiveling in our direction. Then the whispers start. I grit my teeth and turn in his arms to press my hands to his chest. It's a mistake—touching Hook is always a mistake—but jerking away is conceding defeat, and that's something I'll never do. I look up into his laughing eyes and have to fight the urge to jab him in the throat. "Subtle. Really subtle."

Thankfully, he lowers his voice. "You know me, Tink. I don't have a subtle bone in my body." He lowers his hands, too, and the sound he makes in the back of his throat when he cups my ass has my pussy giving an answering zing. He drags me closer yet and, yes, I can feel his very *un*subtle boner pressing against my stomach.

"Control yourself."

"Never." He grins. "Have a drink with me. If you manage not to stab me with something for the duration, I'll give you your surprise."

I do not understand this man. I don't think I ever have, no matter what I told myself. The way he relishes every confrontation with me can't possibly be real. It has to be an act, and one that will bite me in the ass sooner rather than later. I glare up at him, and my ire only seems to make him more delighted. Finally, I sigh. "Yes, I'll have a drink. I want a—"

"Seduction on the Rocks."

I blink. "You know my drink."

He doesn't answer. He just ambles off to the bar, leaving

me blinking after him. Dazed, I turn back to find Aurora staring at me like she's never seen me before. "What?"

"You married him." She shakes her head slowly. "There's no way this is a love match."

"You don't know." I'm not sure why I'm arguing. Aurora has worked with me more nights than I can count over the last few years, and she's seen me avoid interacting with Hook *a lot*. She knows I haven't given him the time of day before now.

"I *do* know." She takes my arm and pulls me toward the door that leads to Hades's public office. "I don't care what he did to make you say yes, we can fix this. If I have to threaten Hades myself, I'll get you out of it."

Oh no. I cover her hand and dig in my heels, hauling us to a stop. I'm painfully aware of the attention of the people around us. "Aurora, stop."

"It's not fair that you're put in this position. What the hell is the point of a deal if Hades hangs us out to dry the second it's finished?" She shakes her pink hair, her expression as ferocious as I've ever seen it. "No. Absolutely not. We're getting you out of this and we're doing it now."

I know I'm staring at her like I've never seen her before, but I can't seem to stop. She manages to drag me a few steps before I remember that I'm supposed to be resisting. "Why do you care so much?"

She finally stops and looks at me, anger flickering into confusion. "We're friends, Tink. Protecting each other is what friends do."

There's that word again. Friends. Apparently I don't really know what it means, after all. I can't let her confront Hades. I've made my bed with Hook, and fighting Hades will only endanger Aurora's deal. Panic flares in my throat, hot and tangled and confused. I've never had to look out for someone else before. I've been too busy trying to survive. But if Aurora gets hurt because she's trying to defend me …

"We were seeing each other in secret," I blurt. "I couldn't do anything until my contract was up."

She finally stops tugging on my wrist and narrows her eyes. "You're not lying?"

Oh, this sweet girl. Even after so long of moving through our world, she has an innocence about her that nothing has touched. I hope nothing ever does. I take a breath and work on morphing my expression into one she'll believe. "I'm not lying."

She studies me for a long moment. Finally, she shakes her head, looking more confused. "Wow. I just … Wow. I didn't see this coming."

"I don't think anyone did." That, at least, is the truth. I carefully remove her hand from my wrist. I don't know what I'm supposed to say to someone who was willing to go to bat for me. "Thank you. You don't have to fight for me."

"Of course I do." She smiles, though it looks a little brittle. "The Underworld is going to be weird without you here. I'm going to miss you."

The novelty of being *missed* is something I'll have to ponder later. The feeling in my throat only gets more tangled, and I try to swallow past it. Are my palms sweating? Because this feels more anxiety-inducing than participating in my first scene. "I, um, I'm going to be busy for a bit getting settled in." Another wobbly breath that does nothing to fill my lungs. I expel the rest of the words in a rush, already bracing for rejection. "But do you want to get coffee some-time soon?"

"Really?" The hope that flares in her dark eyes makes me feel both like the biggest asshole in existence and also so relieved I'm a little dizzy. She gives me a happy smile. "I'd love to get coffee."

I open my mouth to say—I don't even know. Maybe to apologize for being such a dick since I've known her. Hook sweeps in before I get a word out. He hands me my bright drink and slips an arm around my waist again. "I'm stealing my wife back, Aurora."

She immediately drops her gaze, her training finally kicking back in. "I wouldn't dream of keeping her from you," she murmurs, though there's an archness beneath the words that tells me she'd fight him with everything she has if she thought for a second he was forcing me to do something I didn't want to. Just like she was about to fight Hades.

Yeah, I really *am* an asshole.

Hook guides me to a booth near the door to the public playroom, and I'm still too caught up in processing Aurora's response to be irritated by him. It's only when he slides into the booth next to me instead of across from me that I refocus on Hook. Impossible not to when he's pressed against me from shoulder to knee. He drapes one arm over the back of the booth, which brings me closer yet, tucked right under his arm.

I fit. It's annoying that I fit.

I take a sip of my drink, mostly to give my hands something to do. It's perfect, but then Tis made it. She's the best bartender I've ever encountered, in my totally unbiased opinion. But thinking about her only makes me think about everything I've lost in the course of the last few days.

It's time to stop dicking around and put some honesty on the table. I look up at Hook. "You're using me as bait."

He doesn't blink, doesn't lose that charming smile, but his body tenses the smallest bit. Confirmation, not that I need it. In the hours after the farce of a wedding ceremony, I had plenty of time to think this through from all angles. There's only one that makes sense. Hook can't find Peter on his own, so he needs to piss him off enough that Peter comes to Hook.

He's likely tried other things already, so he's landed on me. He must have thought I'd say no if he told me the full truth.

Finally, he responds. "I'm using you as bait."

It shouldn't sting. I knew he didn't practically blackmail me into marriage because he was overcome by love or some bullshit like that. This was always about territory and power. *Everything* in Carver City is about territory and power: claiming it, keeping it, taking out anyone who threatens it. It was never about me.

It really, really shouldn't sting.

I take another drink, hating that my hand shakes. "Where he's concerned, I've always been a big red button."

"I won't let anything happen to you." Hook speaks so low, I can almost convince myself that I can't actually make out the words.

"That's not a promise you have any business making." Bitterness creeps into my tone, a direct counterpoint to the sweet drink on my tongue. "It's not a promise you *ever* had any business making."

"I know you had no reason to trust me then, and you have no reason to trust me now." I feel, more than hear, his exhale. "But you *can* trust me to keep you safe."

At least he's not pretending he doesn't understand. I close my eyes and strive for calm, strive to keep the past in the past, locked up in the box I created just so I could get through my days without being a sobbing mess of trauma. "I don't want to talk about *then*." The before, when I couldn't take tomorrow for granted because the threat of Peter hung over my head every second of every day.

For a moment, I think Hook will push the subject. Another of those long exhales and all the tension leeches out of his body. "One day, we'll talk about what happened the night I offered to get you out of his territory."

"No, we won't." There's no point in pulling out all the

wrongs done during those years and looking them over. Hook isn't even the perpetrator, but he stood by and witnessed, which is almost as bad. I don't exactly blame him for it, but I *can* blame him for the fact that the past is clinging to my back more fiercely than it ever has.

"Tink." He practically purrs my name, a low grumbling sound that has me focusing on him completely. Just like that, the rest of it fades away, and there's only this man who stares at me as if he can divine my thoughts right out of my head. He drags his thumb along my jaw to stop just below my bottom lip. "Would you like your reward?"

I reach for some attitude, but it slips through my fingers like water. I might be mouthy, but in my heart of hearts, I love submitting. I love the moment when I hand over control to someone who will give me exactly what I didn't even realize I need. I love that I am never *truly* at their mercy because I will always have a fail-safe, and they will always respect it. At least here in the Underworld.

There are bad Dominants. There always will be.

Hook isn't one of them. I hope.

"No, beautiful girl. Don't get that look on your face." He releases my chin and presses his finger to the spot between my eyebrows, smoothing out my frown. "Stay with me."

I shouldn't let him soothe me, no matter how good he is at it. But I am so goddamn tired. The events of the last few days cascade over me, and all I want is to forget for a little while. I press my lips together, clinging to my last bit of defiance. "I'm not crawling to you tonight." Too late, I realize I all but admitted that I *will* crawl to him, *will* beg for his cock.

"I know." His smile is nowhere near his usual shit-eating grin, but somehow it's more genuine. "I have something else in mind for you."

CHAPTER 8

HOOK

*J*t's been years since I've seen Tink look so fragile. I hate that talking about the past fucks with her like this, though I can hardly blame her for it. She survived Peter. It's more than others can say. Guilt pricks me, both remembered and current. Hearing her say the truth aloud feels different than when I was putting together this Hail Mary plan. I'm using her as bait. I dragged her back into my world in service of finishing this fight with Peter. I meant what I said about not letting him near her, but he's more than capable of hurting her without laying hands on her again.

He's doing it right now, reaching through the years to put those shadows in her eyes.

I can't take back those memories. But I'll sure as shit put some good ones in her head tonight. It's the least I can do, considering what this marriage will cost her. More, I *want* to. That's reason enough for me.

I climb out of the booth and hold out my hand, a silent command. It's a token of how off-center she is that she takes it without complaint. Eyes follow us as I lead her to the door to the public playroom. As usual on the weekends, Allecto leans against the wall next to it. Her dark gaze flicks over me and Tink and the spot where I have her hand in mine. "Interesting turn of events."

"Allecto," Tink warns.

The Fury shakes her head slowly, expression downright dangerous. "I think I'll tag along when you have coffee with Aurora."

Tink tenses. "You heard that."

"You know better. I hear everything that goes on in this place." She shifts her attention to me, and it's everything I can do not to tense, too. Crossing Allecto is a good way to lose a limb. There's a reason she's Hades's head of security, and it's not simply because she has a habit of knowing things she shouldn't. She can also take down damn near anyone in this room without breaking a sweat. She narrows her eyes. "You fuck with her, you fuck with me. You got it?"

"I'll follow the rules while I'm playing in Hades's territory."

She doesn't like that, but she can't do shit about it. This only works if Hades keeps control of his people. If they go out hunting in others' territories, we're looking at an all-out war, and no one wants that. It cuts into the bottom line and everyone will lose valuable people. Bad for business across the board.

Finally, she steps aside. "Carry on, then."

The public playroom is mostly empty, the various couches and equipment unoccupied and practically shining with invitation. More people will trickle in as the night continues, but right now there are only two scenes going on. Meg is whipping Hercules, the long tail an extension of her arm. She's completely focused on him as she draws her arm back and flicks it forward to strike. The other is a couple I don't recognize fucking on the spanking bench.

Normally, I'd linger. I like watching Meg work, and she

does it in public less and less as time goes on. But I can't tonight.

As we head into the hallways with the themed rooms, I glance back at Tink. She's still got that fragile look on her face. Damn it. I stop in front of the door leading to our destination and squeeze her hand. "Stay with me."

"I'm here, aren't I?"

Not quite her usual snark, but it will have to do. I open the door and tow her inside. She looks around and snorts. "A bed? Really? How vanilla of you."

The room is more suite than simple bedroom. Though there's a bed nearly as large as mine taking up half the room, there's also a trio of overstuffed chairs next to a gas fireplace. It's cozy and romantic and perfect for what I have planned. A wedding night to remember.

I motion to the spot in front of the fire. "Stand there."

Tink slowly walks over. The firelight plays on her pale skin and golden hair, flickering over her curves in a way I'm almost jealous of. Soon. Soon, I'll have her in every way I want her. I move to her and drag a hand down her back to her ass. "Tell me your safe word."

Her sigh is her only protest. "Pirate."

I fucking love that she picked that word. I love what it means, that somewhere in that pretty head of hers, she was thinking of me all this time. "Good girl." I unzip the back of her dress, careful with the tiny zipper. She wiggles out of it and I have to stop a minute and just appreciate the sight of Tink in white lingerie. Her bra lifts her breasts up and creates some truly impressive cleavage. Her panties are barely there. And the fucking garter belt and thigh highs. I simultaneously want to rip every single piece of lingerie off her and also keep her in it forever.

"Cat got your tongue."

I don't stop my slow perusal of her. "You dressed to impress. Give your man a second to enjoy the view."

"You're not my man."

"My ring on your finger says otherwise."

Her huff is music to my ears. Slowly, oh so slowly, she's inching back into her comfortable, confident self. I don't know if it's being back in the Underworld or bantering with me, but I'll take it either way.

I walk a slow circle around her, and *fuck*. The temptation to throw my plan away is nearly overwhelming. But the plan *is* to seduce her into my bed. Tonight is simply doing it our way. "Do you trust me?"

"No. Next question."

I chuckle and stop behind her. Her only response is a slight tensing in her shoulders. But she doesn't turn to keep me in view. Good. "I'm not talking about your heart, Tink. I'm sure as fuck not talking about your soul." I slowly drag her hair off her neck and twist the shining locks around my fist. "I'm talking about your body. Do you trust me with your body?"

"I …" She shivers. "Yes. Fine. I trust you that far."

"Good." With my free hand, I reach behind me and grab the blindfold off the mantle. I lean forward, bringing my chest against her back, and show her the silky padded fabric. "Then we can begin."

"Oh, you asshole," she breathes.

"Close your eyes." I slip the blindfold over her head, careful not to tangle her hair. It takes a few seconds to adjust it, and then I go on one knee next to her. I guide her hand to my shoulder and proceed to take off her heels. Once I'm sure her balance is stable, I nudge her hand away and gather up her shoes and dress. They're deposited in the little dresser on the other side of the bed.

I move back to stand in front of her. "Kneel."

"I really hate you."

"No, you don't. Kneel."

She sinks gracefully to her knees. I've seen her in this exact position a thousand times over the years, but never for *me*. The sheer satisfaction nearly knocks me back a step. Tink's mine. She's finally fucking *mine*. "Do not move from this spot. Do you understand?"

She wets her pink lips and finally nods. "Yes ... Sir."

Oh fuck, this woman is going to kill me. I leave before I can change my mind, stalking out of the room with heavy footsteps to let her know where I'm going. I don't bother to be quiet shutting the door. The anticipation is half the game right now, and making her be patient will only enhance the payoff for both of us.

Three people wait for me outside the door, just as I requested. I look to Gaeton first. Of the trio, he's the only one I'd call a friend—with the occasional benefits. Beast and Malone are more peers with a series of shared interests. I respect the hell out of them, but I'm very aware of the power they wield outside this club. Beast may be a general for the Man in Black, same as Gaeton, but there's something about him that keeps everyone at a distance. Malone rules her own territory, one of the largest slices of Carver City. She's also my neighbor to the south, though we've never had so much as a whisper of a territory dispute since I took over.

Really, the only thing they have in common is that they've played with Tink in the past and hold enough fondness for her to get over their issues with each other. At least for the duration of a scene.

Gaeton grins. "Interesting way to spend your wedding night." He stands several inches taller than me, and at least half a foot taller than both Beast and Malone. The man is fucking huge.

We've already gone over the details. Shared domination

of Tink for the duration of the scene. I've done shit like this before, but I'm usually one of the guests involved, rather than the Dom running the show. "You've all played with her before. You know what she likes. I want her on the edge, but don't take her over."

"We can do that." Malone idly strokes her golden riding crop. It's a ridiculous piece of equipment, the bottom of its handle encrusted with jewels that, knowing Malone, are all real. She's wearing a pair of deep purple pants that fall in carefully tailored lines to hug her ankles and show off her shiny black heels that look like they could kill a man. A black silk blouse and suspenders finish the look, and with Malone, it's always *a look*. Her short blond hair is styled back from her face. I'm still not sure how old she is. There are faint lines at the corners of her eyes that would probably deepen if she ever smiled, but that could put her anywhere between thirty and sixty.

"Lot for her to take." Beast watches me closely. He might be a few inches shorter than me and built leaner, but he's not one I'd happily turn my back on outside of this place. Having both him and Gaeton in the same room for this scene is a risk. Even now, they stand on either side of Malone, as if they need a buffer to even occupy the same space.

Fuck, am I making a mistake? I pin him with a look. "Are you two going to play nice?" If they wreck the room, Hades is going to kick my ass.

"We've put aside old … grudges … recently." Gaeton grins, but not in a way that convinces anyone standing here. "Haven't we, Beast?"

"More or less." Beast might be the only person in this place who can get away with wearing jeans and a plain T-shirt, but somehow it just works for him. He holds my gaze, his blue eyes almost eerie in the low light of the hallway. "Regardless, we'll behave tonight."

It's as good a promise as I'm going to get. "Then let's get started."

I open the door and am gratified to find Tink exactly where I left her, kneeling with her head bowed. The fire backlights her, and fuck if the view doesn't steal my breath for a second.

Gaeton bumps his shoulder against mine and waggles his eyebrows. I glare, but it's hard to maintain my distance when I'm anticipating what's to come.

I let Tink hear me walk to her as the others spread out. I guide her slowly to her feet, keeping a hand on her hip to ensure she doesn't wobble. "Tell me your safe word again."

This time, she doesn't hesitate. "Pirate."

"Good girl. Let's get started."

CHAPTER 9

TINK

There is nothing like a blindfold to change the face of a scene. I wasn't lying when I said I trust Hook with my body, but not being able to see what's coming has anticipation and a delicious lick of fear curling through me. There is only one true rule in the Underworld, but there have been times in the past when people broke it. When someone was threatened or harmed because of an ignored safe word.

I might be facing down a tsunami of fear at the thought of what the future holds, but I know right down to my bones that Hook won't do anything tonight that I'm not 100 percent into.

I just don't know *what* he's going to do.

His big hand comes to rest at the back of my neck. Not gripping, exactly. It's more of a steadying touch and hell if I don't lean back into it. He's my rock in the sea of blackness, the one thing I can be sure of in this room. His voice sounds in my ear, low and intimate. "I'm feeling particularly generous, so I'm going to give you a series of choices tonight."

It's a trap. It has to be.

I lick my lips. "Okay."

"First up—pain or pleasure?"

I strain my ears, but I can't sense anything except him at my back. I suspect he left the room when I heard the door open and shut, but I've also seen that trick set up to only *seem* like the Dominant left their submissive unattended. The agony of waiting without knowing for sure is a special kind of foreplay.

If he did leave ... What did he leave to do?

In the end, I can only answer him honestly. "Both."

His chuckle rumbles through me, and I clench my thighs together in response. I've denied my attraction to him for so long, it's as if it's been building all this time, a volcano ready to erupt in a flurry of really impulsive fucking decisions. Even knowing that, I can't stop. I'm trapped and afraid, and damn it, I'm going to take this little slice of pleasure for myself, and I'm not making a single damn apology for it.

I want Hook. It's enough of a reason to take it.

His free hand catches mine. "Greedy girl. You think I won't give you exactly what you want and more?"

"What I want is your cock." The words burst free, a truth I've been actively ignoring for far too long.

"As always, my offer stands." His mouth brushes my bare shoulder. "Providing you're willing to get on your knees and beg."

I know I'm going to get to that point. It's inevitable. I want him inside me. I want him using his body to pound away my worries until we're sweaty and exhausted and sated. I just plain want him. But I'm a prideful creature, and I can't make myself beg. Not like this. Not yet.

I shake my head slowly. "No."

Instead of sounding disappointed, his voice is downright delighted. "I thought as much. Don't worry, beautiful girl. I said I'll take care of you tonight, and I have every intention of following through on that." He pauses, the moment filled with anticipation. I can't help holding my breath as Hook releases my hand, though he keeps the heavy weight of his palm against my neck. He strokes his thumb down the side of my throat. "Since you can't have my cock, I've arranged for several substitutes."

A second set of hands land lightly on my hips, calluses pressing against my over-sensitized skin. Even knowing better, I jump. A rough laugh in front of me tells me what I already suspected from the touch. Gaeton. No one has hands quite as large as his. A moment later, his breath ghosts over my stomach, and then his tongue follows. I have to fight back a flinch. I love my body, but I'm not immune to body image issues. My stomach is soft, and there are several other body parts I'd prefer his mouth on if I had a choice.

Hook's voice in my ear drags me back to the here and now. "Cross your wrists at the small of your back."

I move slowly to obey. Too slowly, because Gaeton snags my wrists and guides them to where Hook wants. He pins them in place with a single hand and Hook tsks. "Are you planning on being difficult, Tink?"

"I'm always difficult." My voice is breathy despite my best efforts.

"That's the fucking truth," Gaeton murmurs against my stomach. He bypasses the garter belt, and his tongue dips beneath the band of my panties. Not enough touch to do more than tease with the promise of later.

"Mmm." Hook isn't quite laughing at me, but he sounds like he wants to. I've had Doms of every flavor over the years, but he's one of the few who doesn't bother with the distant power thing. He's amused and enjoying the hell out of himself already and isn't bothering to play games. At least not games of emotional distance. He *is* playing games, though. "I suppose we'll have to ensure she keeps her hands where we can see them."

Gaeton keeps stroking my hips and pressing lazy kisses along the line of my panties. Despite myself, I relax, letting Hook's hand on the back of my neck support me a little as I arch my hips against Gaeton's mouth.

Then a third set of hands touch me. Soft palms. Long nails. Feminine.

I freeze, but she doesn't seem to care if I'm at ease or not. She takes my wrists from Gaeton and presses them into a padded cuff. Every move speaks of a wealth of experience as she tests the tightness to ensure it's not uncomfortable, and then her touch disappears and reappears on my other side. A cool metal bar replaces Hook's hand at the base of my neck. I'm left wide open, unable to move my arms.

They shift around me, and Gaeton drags my panties down my legs. I put them on over the garter belt for exactly this reason, and Hook's low curse is a reward in and of itself. "What a pretty picture you make." He smooths his hands through my hair, and as the weight adjusts, I belatedly realize he's braided it to keep it out of my face. Not that I can see while I'm wearing the blindfold, but Hook has his own reasons. He always has.

A cool press of a blade at my sternum and the bastard cuts off my bra. I jerk back, but the woman catches me. She's slight, but she's strong. Between her hands on my shoulders and Gaeton's on my hips, they keep me on my feet. "What the fuck, Hook? Do you know how expensive that was?"

"Hold still."

Part of me wants to obey, but I've already spent too much of this scene cowed. "Fuck off."

I can hear his grin with his next command. "Hold her still."

Gaeton's grip changes, digging into my hips even as he

nuzzles my pussy. The woman must take hold of the spreader bar because I'm forced to bend back until I'm leaning against her. I get a faint whiff of amber, and suddenly I know exactly who she is. Malone. The Golden Queen.

Holy shit, Hook has pulled out all the stops for this scene.

I fight because I can't seem to help myself, because every time they forcibly still me, my desire spikes higher. Through it all, I track Hook's footsteps as he circles us. He's stepping heavy on purpose, letting me know exactly where he is, giving me something to ground myself with when the rest of the scene is so out of my control.

"The nipple clamps." His voice comes from a short distance, so I know it's not his hands that cup my breasts. It's not his mouth that sucks my nipples to stiff peaks.

There are three other people in the room with us. I can't quite wrap my mind around it. I know he likes to share, but this feels like something different altogether.

The third man fastens the nipple clamps and gives my breasts one last squeeze that's just shy of painful. Gaeton is still teasing me, not quite licking, not giving me the contact I need. Malone has me forcibly immobile.

I know I can stop this with a word. All of them will respect it. Ultimately, I have the power here, even if it's only in relinquishing it entirely.

I don't want it to stop. I welcome the cascade of sensations as they lift me a little and someone hooks the spreader bar to what sounds like a chain overhead. I'm not quite suspended—my feet can still barely touch the ground—but it's a precarious balance. As if to prove that truth, Gaeton and Malone release me, and I wobble. Hook catches me instantly, which tells me that he was here all along. That I was never in any danger of falling.

The thought makes me want to laugh. It's true. I've lost

the ability to fall a long time ago. I have no interest in getting it back. Not even for him. *Especially* not for him.

"Still with me?" He murmurs. For a second, I can almost imagine his thumbs brushing my cheekbones, but the touch is gone so quickly, I'm sure I imagine it.

I lick my lips. "Where else would I be?"

"Good." Another light touch, this time his lips on mine. "You get your pain before you get your pleasure."

It takes my swirling mind a few precious moments to catch up to what he's talking about, and by then his touch is gone, and he's just a disembodied voice in the near distance. "Gaeton is going to lick your pretty pussy, but you will not come until I allow it."

"Orgasm deprivation. Real original." I try to smirk, but I can't quite manage it. It takes everything I have to keep up the attitude, but I don't have another choice. We've barely begun to play, and I'm already teetering on the brink of something unforgivable.

"Let's see if you keep that smart mouth through what I have planned, beautiful girl."

I open said smart mouth to reply, but Gaeton chooses that moment to grab my thighs and drag me bodily to his mouth, lifting me a bit so my toes barely touch the ground. I'm not small, but he's built like a brick house and his arms don't even shake as he drags his tongue over my pussy. "Mmmm." Gaeton rumbles out a laugh. "Hook, you give the best gifts."

"I'm just getting started." Hook still sounds amused, but his voice is rougher, as if he's just as affected by this as I am. "Begin."

For a second, I think he's speaking to me, but then the first lash hits my back, and I realize he was talking to the other two. They flog me, strikes landing just so, as if they're standing at different angles at my back. It doesn't *hurt*, exactly, but the sting morphs into a hot delicious burn that has me writhing just as much as Gaeton's mouth does. "Hook," I gasp.

"Everything they do to you is an extension of me." He sounds directly in front of me. He must be standing at Gaeton's back. "Gaeton's tongue between your thighs." The man in question groans against my skin, and then I feel the back of Hook's hand touching my inner thigh. It takes my pleasure-pain drugged brain a moment to understand that he's got his fingers in the other man's hair, that he's using his touch to guide Gaeton's mouth, urging him up to my clit.

I try to roll my hips, but Gaeton's got me in too tight a grip. Hook's laugh goes a little mean. "*Everything* in this room happens at my whim. That includes your orgasms. Not yet, beautiful girl."

The strikes against my back pick up, and I can't hold a whimper down. It feels like my back is on fire. "Please."

"That's a start."

Pleasure winds and winds, the pain buoying it into something beyond comprehension. My toes curl with it. Each exhale comes out more like a sob. I can't hold my orgasm back. Fuck, I don't want to. I'm so close, I can feel myself tipping over the edge...

Everything stops.

Gaeton gives my thigh a nip and carefully sets my feet back on the ground. The flogging stops as suddenly as it started. I'm left weaving on my toes, half hanging from the bar shackling my wrists. It's not comfortable, exactly, but I'm too over sensitized to care. I gasp in a breath, but the oxygen only makes my brain and body meld into a cascade of sparks. "You *fucker*."

"There she is." Hands unclasp the cuffs around my wrists, and then Hook's arms are around me. I'm too out of my mind to question that I know it's him. It simply is. He guides me over his broad thighs and carefully places my hands on the floor. The position leaves my ass in the air, and I already know what's coming when a paddle descends and pain reverberates through me.

"Holy shit." This pain play is still on the light end of the spectrum, but it's a carefully orchestrated dance Hook's overseeing to keep me on the edge. It's working.

"Does it hurt, beautiful girl?"

I try to relax into the strikes, but he's started playing his fingers along my still-smarting back. The sensation is too much. My thoughts scatter like marbles. "Yes. Is that what you want to hear? *Yes*, you asshole, it hurts."

He squeezes my ass, right on the spot where the last strike fell. I cry out and writhe, but I can't begin to say if it's to get away from his touch or press closer. "I suppose that's enough for now."

I frown behind the blindfold. Things feel hazy and indistinct, and I can't quite focus. "That's enough?"

"Mmmm." Another squeeze, and he trails his fingers down to cup my pussy. "Drenched. Tell me a truth, and I'll reward you."

I can't keep up with his jumps in conversation. I don't know if I'm supposed to, but it's impossible to stay focused with him touching me like that while my entire body is lit up with remembered pain and pleasure. "Yes?"

His clever fingers barely brush my clit. "Did you pick your safe word with me in mind?"

Some distant part of me demands I lie. I have every intention of following through on it, but when I open my mouth, the truth spills free. "Yes," I breathe.

His touch stills and I could almost swear that his hand shakes a little as he guides me carefully back to my feet. His thighs bracket me in, steadying me as much as his hands on my hips. "Scream if you must."

It's the only warning I get before he releases the first nipple clamp. Blood rushes back into the denied space, and the pain bows my back and draws a whimper from my lips. Then Hook's mouth is there, his tongue soothing and tormenting in turn. The pain barely fades when he repeats the process with my other nipple.

"One last question before we continue."

Each Dom has their own style. I've mostly seen Hook work from a distance, have only heard the reports from the other subs he's scened with after the fact, so I'm honestly a little surprised at how verbal he is. I probably shouldn't be. He always had a mouth on him, same as me. I lick my lips. "Okay."

"How many cocks do you want tonight?"

One sentence to strip away the last of my barriers. I open my mouth, but a whimper escapes instead of words. Hook strokes my hips, a touch that might soothe if it wasn't so full of promise. When I don't immediately answer, he leans in until his breath brushes my lips. "I'll give you a hint, Tink. The number can be between zero and three." He chuckles. "If you want more than three, we'll see what we can do."

"Three." The answer bursts forth with all the grace of a belly flop. "I want three."

"Greedy girl." He brushes a kiss across my lips. "Do you trust me?"

No. Not even nearly out of my mind in the middle of a scene. "With my body."

The barest hesitation. "That will have to do."

CHAPTER 10

TINK

Several minutes later, Hook moves me to the bed to straddle a man. Gaeton. I'd recognize those thick thighs anywhere. His rumbling laugh only confirms it. "A shame you can't see the show, Tink."

"Another time," Hook says before I can speak.

For the first time in a very long time, I don't know what to say. It's just as well that I don't *have* to say anything. I'm not the one running this show. Hook is. And it's *his* hand that brushes my thighs as he fists Gaeton's cock, as he rolls a condom onto it, and *his* grip on my hip that guides me down. I know it's Gaeton filling me almost uncomfortably full, but tonight he's not in charge any more than the others are. His cock, his mouth, his everything is an extension of Hook's will.

Hook's will includes giving me three cocks on my wedding night.

I might love him if I didn't hate him so much.

I shift, trying to adjust to Gaeton's size, and Hook's fingers find my clit. "Relax."

Relax. As if that's even remotely in the cards right now.

My earlier denied orgasm teases me in time with the pad of his finger circling. I shift, but that only has Gaeton rubbing deliciously inside me. "Fuck."

"Such a mouth on you." Another chuckle. "Lean forward and brace your hands on Gaeton's chest."

Gaeton helps me along, pressing my hands where Hook instructs. He's tall enough that the position has me stretched out over him. Hook smooths a hand down my spine, stopping at the small of my back.

Feminine hands squeeze my ass, spreading me. I tense before I can stop myself. Malone's low laugh joins Hook's. "Are you sure this is a present to your wife, rather than us? I'm feeling rather fortunate at the moment."

Wife.

The word brands me more than any action any of the people in this room could take. Nothing they do to me can match that Hook has fundamentally changed my role. That I let him.

"Malone is eager to take your ass." Hook's voice is pure temptation in my ear. "Would you like to guess what color strap-on she chose for tonight?"

Malone has a whole rainbow of strap-on dildos that she uses at her pleasure. Each has a different size, shape, or feature. The collection is just as notorious as the woman herself.

I swallow hard. "Purple?" A nice middle-of-the-road size and shape. Nothing too fancy.

"Close. Blue." The next size up. He nips my earlobe, making me shiver, which sends a cascade of pleasure through me when the move vibrates Hook's fingers and Gaeton's cock.

Gaeton curses. "Fuck, but your woman feels good, Hook."

I've fucked Gaeton before. He's fun, and he's mean, and after his last relationship went down in flames, he had just as much anger to work out as I did. As I *do*. It's never been like this before. I'm a toy to be played with, and they're all tools used by Hook for my pleasure. Both things are true, and yet I can barely wrap my mind around it.

"Hold," Hook murmurs. I'm not sure if he's talking to me or Gaeton.

In the end it doesn't matter, because Malone ensures there's no forgetting about her. She spreads lube over me, and then the dildo is pressing against my ass. Blue isn't anywhere close to her largest strap-on, but it's still no joke. I whimper as she breaches my entrance and presses deeper, inch by slow inch.

Hook stops playing with my clit. His hands seem to be everywhere. Stroking down my spine and back up again. Over my arms. Cupping my breasts briefly before repeating the cycle. Soothing me. "Relax, beautiful girl. You can take it. Don't fight it. Just breathe."

My breath hisses out as Malone sinks the last inch and her narrow hips meet my ass. With Gaeton's giant cock taking up so much space, I feel impossibly filled. I shift, but there's no relieving the sensation. "I need ..."

"I know." Hook's hand lands on the back of my neck, grounding me even as he guides me up. The new position pushes the other two even deeper, and I can't help restlessly moving against them.

"Jameson." I don't mean to say his name. I really don't. It comes out more like pleading than anything that's crossed my lips thus far.

"Soon, Tink." He drags his thumb over my bottom lip. "Will you let Beast in? He's been rather patient, don't you think?"

Oh. My. God.

I nod slowly. Dazed. Needy. "Yes, Sir."

"Good girl." He nudges my mouth open and shifts me slightly to the side, and then Beast's cock is there. My tongue plays over his piercings as he pushes past my lips. Deeper and deeper, until he nudges the back of my throat and breathing through my nose is something I have to concentrate on to accomplish.

"If you need to stop for any reason, slap Gaeton's chest." He picks up my hand and demonstrates. "Do you understand?"

Speaking is out of the question, so I moan a little. Beneath me, Gaeton laughs, the sound as strained as I feel.

"If you could see the picture you make." Hook's thumb strokes the spot behind my ear and down my neck. "You'll take everything they give you, and you'll thank me afterward for the pleasure of the experience." His voice goes hard. "Begin."

They start fucking me slowly, each working to figure out my limits. I can't focus on any one penetration. Gaeton shoves deep and grinds against my clit. Malone is working my ass in steady strokes. Beast wraps my braid around a fist to hold my head immobile while he fucks my mouth.

He finds his rhythm first. Or maybe he just knows what he likes and fully intends to use me to accomplish it. It makes me feel a little dirty and a little used. I love it. I open wide to allow him as deep as I can take him.

"Harder." Hook's command flips a switch in the other two.

Gaeton grips my thighs and spreads me wide. Then he begins fucking me in rough strokes that shove me back against Malone while pushing Beast's cock deep enough into my throat that I gag and tears spring from my eyes to soak the blindfold.

Finally, blessedly, my brain clicks off completely, the last of my defenses sliding away. I relax into everything they're doing to me, relax into the pleasure beating my body in vicious waves that are almost too much.

Through it all, Hook's hand on the back of my neck keeps me from floating away entirely.

Wait.

This isn't right.

I keep on hand on Gaeton's chest like I've been ordered, but I reach for Hook with my free hand. He lets me touch the muscles lining his stomach, lets me grip the waistband of his pants, lets me undo the fastenings with fumbling fingers. I can barely focus, but I manage to get his cock out. I give him a stroke, but it's not ... I can't ...

"Hold."

Everything stops.

My jaw aches as Beast eases from my mouth. Hook gives the back of my neck a squeeze. "Tell me what you want." No amusement in his voice now. Just harsh command.

"I want Gaeton to suck your cock." It's not the only thing I want. But even blitzed out of my mind, I can't quite speak the words that will have the cock I *really* want inside me.

"Mmmm." Despite his low words, I'm *sure* I'm not imagining his hand shaking on the back of my neck. It's the slightest tremor, but I'm suddenly sure I'm the cause. "What do you think, Gaeton?"

"What the fuck do you think I think? Yes."

There's some shifting around, though Hook doesn't relinquish his hold on me. I appreciate that more than I can put into words. He's my tether, the contact that will see me through this.

"It's a shame you can't see Gaeton take my cock deep, wife. It's quite the sight to behold."

"Maybe next time," I repeat his earlier words back to him.

Hook's laugh is harsh. "Yes. Next time." The barest pause. "Continue. Don't stop until she's coming or you are."

Beast gives my braid a yank, and then his cock fills my mouth again. This time, there is no pausing, no hesitation. The three of them simply resume fucking me as if they never stopped.

I can't move, can't think, can't do more than take what they give. Take and take and take. The pleasure is so acute, it edges on pain. And through it all, even though I'm half sure it's my imagination, I can *hear* Gaeton sucking Hook's cock. The low sound in the back of his throat when Hook shoves deep. Hook's harsh exhale when Gaeton does something with his tongue. All of it.

And then Hook's voice, reaching across the darkness to show me the way home. "Let go, Tink. I've got you."

My orgasm catches me entirely by surprise, shattering me down to my base parts and grinding them further to dust. Until I am nothing, and there is peace in that nothingness.

It only lasts a moment, and then I'm slammed back into my body as Beast pulls from my mouth and hot come lashes my breasts. Malone eases out of my ass mere seconds before Gaeton hooks me around the waist and flips us, sending me to the mattress on my back and driving into me once, twice, a third time. He pulls out, yanks the condom off, and comes across my stomach with a low curse.

"Look at the mess they made of you," Hook murmurs approvingly. His hand touches my temple, and it's the only warning I get before he eases the blindfold from my eyes.

The room is only lit by the firelight, and even then it's glaringly bright after so long in the dark. I blink rapidly, trying to force my eyes to adjust. Things come into focus one at a time. Gaeton kneeling between my thighs, his skin shining with a faint sheen of sweat. He's got freckles. That always surprises me.

Standing behind him on his left is Malone. She's dressed in an outfit I designed for her and looks like she just came from a business meeting or a runway, aside from the blue cock strapped to her hips. She gives me a faint smile, though her eyes are warm enough.

On Gaeton's other side, standing back near the wall, is Beast. He's got the most flawless cheekbones I've ever seen on a person, and the faint flush to his pale skin only makes him more attractive. He's already tucked his cock back into his jeans and leans against the wall as if he wasn't just fucking my mouth.

Finally, inextricably, my gaze is pulled to Hook. He's on one knee at my side, still bracing the back of my neck. He studies my face with dark eyes, and I can't begin to guess what he sees there. Whatever it is brings a slow smile to his lips. It's a little crooked, a little imperfect, but it's the realest one I've seen on him to date. "You've pleased me, Tink."

Something flutters in my chest in response. I don't have the strength to convince myself that it's the same weightless sensation I always get after a good scene. It's different. Not just because this whole experience was so intense. It's different because it's *him*.

"You're welcome to stay if you'd like." He lifts his voice a little bit, obviously talking to the others.

Malone's taken the time to remove the strap-on, and she steps around him to ruffle my hair. "I'll see you later, Tink."

Beast meets my gaze for a long moment and nods. He hasn't said a single fucking word this whole time, which is both painfully sexy and also weird as shit.

Then they're gone, leaving only Gaeton. He stands and stretches, his fingertips nearly touching the ceiling. "I'll stick around for a bit."

Hook snorts. "You're just looking to get your ass pounded."

"Guilty." He gives a charming smile and suddenly the

room seems several shades brighter. "You know your little wife will like to watch."

In fact, I *would* like to watch. Gaeton was a switch, but he doesn't submit in public, so I've never gotten the opportunity to witness it. Watching Hook dominate him?

Yes, please.

Hook's watching me closely. "Yes, it appears she would." He picks me up and climbs easily to his feet. "I'll get to you presently, Gaeton."

"By all means, take your time." He flings himself down onto the couch and grins. "She's a dirty girl. Better clean her up."

I have to bite down the impulse to tell Hook to put me down, that I'm too heavy. He's obviously got things well in hand, and it's just my fool brain being an asshole.

He sets me down on the bed and steps back to look at me, his eyes warm. "My little cum slut." As I hold my breath, he drags a finger through Beast's come on my chest and down to where Gaeton marked my stomach.

It takes me a full second to realize that his meandering path is not, in fact, random. I frown down at my body. "Did you just write *mine* in the come of two other men?"

"Yes." He reaches past me to pull the comforter up around my shoulders. "I'm going to get something to clean you up with. Try not to menace Gaeton too thoroughly in the few minutes I'll be gone."

I can't stop looking at the mess they made of me. "I'll try."

"Good girl." Then he's gone, shutting the door softly behind him.

My shakes start, and I pull the blanket more firmly around my shoulders. Gaeton kicks the leg he has draped over the arm of the couch, his eyes on me. "So, you and Hook."

"Shut up."

"An old married couple."

"Shut up."

"Next thing you know, you'll be three kids in and won't come play with me anymore."

I force myself to hold his gaze, to banish the queasy feeling his words bring. "Gaeton. Shut up."

He finally shuts up.

I can't think about kids. Surely Hook won't ask that of me in this sham of a marriage? I mean, yes, I always wanted a family. I still do, though my confidence that I won't fuck up some new human isn't particularly high at this point. Still, a family that loves unconditionally is all I ever wanted.

It's the lure Peter dangled in front of me in the first place. All smiles and promises that family really doesn't have anything to do with blood relations, that he's built up his very own that he plays king over. Spinning a dream of being queen at his side and mother to this family, something I couldn't quite comprehend at sixteen, but was attracted to all the same.

For a while, it was really, really good. He showered me with attention and I soaked it up like the starved thing I was. Then the sanctions on my appearance, words, and time started, cutting me off from anyone who wasn't Peter so slowly that I didn't realize it was happening until it was too late.

I shake my head, trying to dispel the memories, but it doesn't help because my body is shaking now. Before I can figure out a way to hide it from Gaeton—he's a dick, but he's still too good a Dom to let me suffer while he's sitting in the same room—the door opens and Hook returns.

He takes one look at me and curses, crossing the room in several long strides. Seconds later, I'm in his lap with his strong arms holding me close. "I've got you."

He doesn't though, not really.

I close my eyes and accept the aftercare. I'm distantly aware of Hook speaking to Gaeton in a low voice, but the words glance off me, unable to find traction. It's just as well. When I open my eyes again, we're alone. "Poor Gaeton."

"Please. He got your pussy *and* my cock tonight. More is just him being greedy." Hook rests his chin on top of my head. "Do you want to go home tonight or stay here?"

Home.

The word doesn't apply. The Underworld *was* my home until today. Hook's fortress is his, not mine. Marriage or not, I feel displaced and adrift. I lean my head against his shoulder and sigh. "I don't want to stay here." It would hurt too much to occupy one of the overnight rooms, and I doubt Hades will allow me access to my suite.

He eases me off him and moves to kneel at the edge of the bed. It should be a subservient position, but it isn't this time any more than it was back in his room. He pulls open a little cooler-looking box and proceeds to pull out a warm, wet cloth to clean me up.

I stare.

There are clean up kits in each room. Getting dirty goes with the territory, and most people won't necessarily want to wander the club with various messes on them. Hook took it one step farther. Not only did he get wet cloths, but he ensured they'd still be warm when he got back to me.

I don't...I don't know how to slot this new information.

"You did well tonight." He's taking his time, seeming to enjoy touching me as much as I'm enjoying this strangely intimate moment.

"I didn't do anything except take it."

He shoots me a look. "You know that's not true."

Yeah, I suppose I do. I try for a laugh, but it comes out a little hoarse. "You know, if you're trying to convince me that

I need your cock, having me filled with three other people probably isn't the way to go."

"Mmmm." He presses the cloth to my pussy, making me jerk. I look up to find him watching me with that cocky grin on his face. "None of their cocks are mine, Tink. For all intents and purposes, they were tonight, but we both know who you were really craving."

"I don't know. Gaeton is pretty stacked. Malone has more cocks than anyone else I know. And there's Beast's pretty jewelry. A girl likes options."

His smile doesn't so much as flicker. "And yet you called *my* name when you lost control."

Jameson.

CHAPTER 11

HOOK

*T*ink doesn't want to stay here. It doesn't mean anything. There are dozens of reasons for that to be true, and none of them reflect on how she feels about me. I don't give a fuck. Tonight she'll be in my bed. Tonight, and every other night, stretching out into the future.

At least until this ends.

She climbs to her feet, and I reach out to steady her. She shies away before I make contact. "I'm fine."

Of course she is. She's always fine, always determined to do it on her own. I understand, at least in theory. For years, she had no independence of her own, her will crushed under Peter's thumb. She gained plenty of strength while living here. It stands to reason that she won't want to give any of it up, even on the small battles. "Letting people help you isn't a sign of weakness."

"Isn't it?" She steps back, her eyes downcast, and pulls the blanket more firmly around her. "Let's just go."

I broke down barriers with this scene. I fucking know I did. But here she is, building them back up as fast as she can.

If we leave now, she'll retreat. By morning, we'll be farther away than we started today.

"Tink." I love the way her name feels coming out of my mouth. Like a secret, sinful and dark.

I love her reactions even more.

She spins on me, a finger raised to poke my chest. "You heard me when I said—"

I catch her wrist and bring the offending finger to my mouth. Her jaw drops as I suck hard for a moment before releasing. "We're not done."

"The hell we aren't!"

I walk to the couch and drop onto it, watching her all the while. Her glare is something truly outstanding to behold. I motion to the door. "You want to leave? Leave. I'm sure you'll find somewhere to go." It's more than a little cruel to remind her that she needs me, but I'm feeling more than a little cruel right now. If Tink would take a moment to look around and gauge the situation, she'd see that I'm not the enemy. I've *never* been the enemy. Not hers, at least.

Fuck, for once, I just want her to see *me*.

She gives a truly impressive snarl. "I'm not crawling to you."

"Not tonight. But you will—and soon."

"How is there any space left in this room with your ego?"

I crook a finger at her, enjoying the way her brows slash down in response. "Come here."

"Fuck off." Despite her words, she crosses the distance between us in hesitant steps, as if her body and mind are at war.

I take her hand and give a tug. She rolls her eyes, but allows me to pull her down to straddle my lap. I hold her gaze as I smooth my palms up her thighs to her hips. She looks like she wants to tell me to fuck off again, but she's already going soft beneath my touch. I press my fingers to the small of her back, urging her closer until her hips are flush against mine. "Tell me your favorite part of tonight."

"I'm not really into recaps."

I nip her bottom lip, hard enough that she gasps against my mouth. "Don't make me repeat myself."

"Fine." She shifts against me, rubbing against my cock and shivering. "I ..."

The truth wars with lies, all of it right there on her face for anyone who cares to look. It's a testament of how rattled she still is, because normally she hides her thoughts better than this. "Close your eyes." I wait for her to obey to continue. "Now. Stop thinking so hard and tell me what you favorite part was."

"Your hand on the back of my neck." Her voice comes out soft and slow. "Knowing that you directed everything they did to me. The fact you kept me tethered even in the midst of it all." Her eyes fly open. "I mean the three cocks. The three cocks were my favorite."

"Mmmm." I resume my slow stroking, enjoying the ability to touch her however I please. She's rocking against me, ever so subtly, but I doubt she's aware of it. "It strikes me that you had three cocks and only one orgasm."

She narrows her eyes. "It was one hell of an orgasm."

"Yes. It was." It had been downright fucking glorious to witness. Tink, shattered to pieces between three other people. Even with my cock shoved down Gaeton's throat, it'd rocked me to my core. Knowing I was the cause, the one who'd orchestrated her pleasure ... That was what drove me over the edge to my own orgasm.

I nudge her up a little and slip a hand between her thighs. "Tender?" Gaeton isn't a small guy, and he wasn't holding back earlier. None of them were.

"I can take more."

Her eyes flutter as I slide three fingers into her pussy.

"You will. Not tonight, though." I stroke her slowly, watching her expression as I explore her. "Tonight was a special occasion for obvious reasons." I press the heel of my hand against her clit. "The next cock you'll have is mine. All you have to do is ask."

She braces her hands on my shoulders, her nails digging in the tiniest bit as she rocks against me. "I'm never going to ask."

"Yes you are." I ignore her restless moving, a silent demand that I pick up my pace. "And when you do, I'll let you ride me. Or I'll bend you over the nearest piece of furniture and fuck you until you see the face of god."

Her breath hisses out in a sound that's somewhere between a laugh and a sob. "Bold words."

"True words." I still my touch.

Now she truly does whimper. "Please. Don't leave me hanging again. I can't stand it."

I use my free hand to move us, toppling her down onto the couch and settling on top of her. "I won't leave you hanging for the rest of the night, beautiful girl." I don't usually like playing the orgasm deprivation game, but it has its purposes. Like tonight, blending with the pain delivered by Malone and Beast, prepping Tink to take all three of them.

I can't help kissing her. I don't even bother to try to resist the impulse. I simply take her mouth. Part of me expects her to fight this like she's fought everything else up to this point, so I'm surprised when she digs her hands into my hair and wraps her legs around my waist.

Maybe that's why I forget myself and sink into the feeling of her tongue tangling with mine. Kissing her feels like coming home, which doesn't make a damn bit of sense, but I'm too drugged on the taste of her to question it.

With her heels digging into my back, I thrust against her.

I'd give anything in this moment to not have these fucking leather pants on, but a promise is a promise, and letting lust drive me is a mistake. Tink will try to top from the bottom if I give her an inch of leeway.

That's why I break the kiss. I could spend hours memorizing the taste of her, the feel of her, but every second pushes me closer to forgetting myself.

I can't allow it to happen.

Her whimper is music to my ears, and I waste no time sliding down her body and pressing her thighs wide. She's wet and pink and perfect, and my first lick is heavenly.

"Oh *fuck*." Her fingers touch my hair, but she hesitates.

She's waiting for permission.

I lift my head enough to hold her gaze. "Hang on to me, beautiful girl. You're going to need an anchor before I'm finished with you."

She doesn't need to be told twice. She digs her fingers into my hair and lifts her hips to my mouth. My second taste is even better than the first. I let myself sink into exploring her, my entire being focused on what touches draw that breathy little gasp from her lips. And then I keep doing it until she's shaking and trying to wrap her thighs around my head. I keep her spread open and pinned in place, loving the way she pushes against me as she tries to ride my mouth.

When she comes, it's with a soft cry that's so vulnerable, I want to gather her up and shield her from the harshness of the world. A foolish desire, even if it wasn't concerning this woman. No one is safe from the world, especially if they're in my bed. Tink least of all. *I'm* part of the reason she's not safe. *I'll* hurt her. Not physically—I'll cut off my right arm before I raise a hand to this woman—but I'm intentionally putting her in a position where she's in danger.

Some days I wonder if I'm actually better than Peter, or just a different shade of monster.

I move away from her clit, gentling my touch and letting her come down. I'm not finished yet. I need to escape from the shadows flicking through my mind as much as she does tonight. From the way her fingers flex in my hair, she's more than willing to meet me every step of the way.

Good.

I wait for her breathing to settle a little, and then I begin again. I play with her pussy until she's sobbing and writhing, until she's not thinking of anything but me. Not fighting. Not the future. Nothing but the slow slide of my tongue against her clit.

"*Jameson.*"

There she is.

I move up her body and shift so I can cup her pussy. It's not meant to drive her back up again. It's a claiming, pure and simple. "Every time you fight me, I'm going to make you come so hard, you can't see straight."

She blinks those big eyes at me. I'm gratified when it takes her two tries to speak. "That's a really shitty punishment."

"Is it?" I trace her opening with my middle finger. "I don't care where we are, Tink. I don't give a fuck who's around. I'll shove up your skirt and suck that pretty little clit of yours until you're a sobbing mess."

Another of those slow blinks. "You wouldn't."

"Test me." I have no shame, and she should know that by now. Playing this game with her is more than worth it.

"I ..." She frowns and licks her lips. "We're going to fight about this later."

"Then you'll be riding my face later." I press a soft kiss to her lips, tracing the path her tongue just took. "Let's go home."

She tenses, but relaxes as if deciding it's not worth the effort of arguing. "Okay."

I climb off her and take a second to adjust my cock. Her gaze follows the movement, but I shake my head when she opens her mouth. "Don't even think about it."

"Think about what?" She sits up and hell if the sight of her doesn't take my breath away. She's naked, her hair a tangled mess from all the fucking, her pale skin flushed from desire. She's perfect. She catches me checking her out and spreads her legs a little, giving me a good look of where I had my mouth just seconds ago. Tink's hand drifts down. "Think about how hard your cock is? About how good it'll feel to be filled by you? About you fucking me until ... What was it you said? Until I see the face of god?"

"Tink." I sink enough warning in my tone for her hand to stop its descent. "You touch your pussy without permission and I'm going to put you over my knee and paddle your ass."

She freezes. "You're shitting me. You don't get to decide when and how I touch my own goddamn pussy."

"You heard me."

"You bastard." She says it slowly, almost wonderingly. "What if I decide coming is worth a little spanking?"

I'm on her before she can react. I grip the back of her neck and shove three fingers into her. "This pussy is mine, Tink. *Mine.* I will take care of it—take care of you—for as long as that's true." I fuck her ruthlessly with my fingers, and her eyes flutter as she fights the pleasure. "If that means I pass you around until you're covered in other men's orgasms like the little cum slut you are, then I will make that happen. If it means fucking you morning, noon, and night until you can't see straight, I will do it happily. If it means strapping you to a sex saddle until you come so many times, you pass out, I'll enjoy the fuck out of it."

"Oh shit." She loses her battle with desire and grabs my biceps, holding on as she comes again.

I force myself to still, to not keep going until I've worked out my frustration on her pussy. It takes a few seconds longer than it should, but I finally release a pent up breath and ease out of her. "I will take care of you, beautiful girl. But you will follow my orders. Do you understand?"

"Yes, Sir," she whispers.

"Good girl."

I dress Tink in leggings and a black sweatshirt that has a picture of Krampus printed on the front, both provided by Meg when I left the room earlier. Tink just watches me like a deer looking down the barrel of a rifle at a hunter, unable to quantify the threat.

I could save her the trouble and tell her my plans. I won't. As unsure of me she is ... The truth is that I can't trust her either. Not beyond her hate of Peter and her lust for me.

Socks and boots follow, and then I stand and pull her to her feet, keeping a hand on her hip to ensure she stays there. She's still a little wobbly, which satisfies a deep, dark part of me. I won't deny that I want to stamp my name on her ass so she remembers who owns her, but this is the next best thing. I take a moment to grab the dress and shoes she was wearing earlier and then it's time to go.

The second we walk out the door, I scoop her into my arms. Tink goes rigid. "Put me down."

"No."

"I'm too heavy." She flinches as soon as she says the words, but I ignore both as I stride down the hallway to the public playroom. People are in various stages of scenes and fucking, but at least a handful of eyes follow us as I pick my way through the space to the door on the other side. Good.

Let them look and know that this is real.

No matter what else is true, no matter what other lies we tell, this *is* real.

It just may not be till death do us part.

CHAPTER 12

TINK

*M*y world has gone topsy-turvy in the last twelve hours. Marriage. One of the hottest scenes I've ever participated in, and I'm not talking about the five-some. Being the center of Hook's attention—and when we're together, I truly am the center of his attention—is exhilarating and terrifying. He makes me want to push against the line he draws in the sand just to see what he'll do.

He makes me want to obey without question.

I'm still spinning when the car pulls up in front of his building. He opens the door and helps me out, every inch the courteous rogue, as if an hour ago he wasn't finger fucking me while he threatened a gang bang. I still haven't decided if it was meant as reward or punishment. I get the feeling that Hook enjoyed scening with the other Doms as much as I did. That he likes to watch as much as I like to be in the spotlight.

Between one blink and the next, we're inside the elevator. Another blink and we're in his room. I'm weaving on my feet, the events of the last few days catching up with me.

I make a beeline for the bed, but he hooks me around the

waist and turns us toward the bathroom. "You'll sleep better this way."

"Your shower is amazing, but I don't want to sleep in it."

"Smartass." But he says it fondly. "You have two minutes, and then we're getting ready for bed." He nudges me into the bathroom and shuts the door.

I take care of business and peek out the door to find him standing there … naked.

I stare. I can't help it. I know I should be aloof and unaffected, but holy shit, he's so gorgeous I can barely stand it. His lean body is carved with muscle from his shoulders to his calves. I nibble my bottom lip as I eye his thighs, lightly dusted with dark hair. I'm not a biter, but I have the sudden impulse to become one.

And then there's his cock.

He's perfectly sized. Long and thick, and I just know he'll fill me in exactly the way I crave.

I take a step forward before I catch myself and look up to find him watching me with a single raised eyebrow. I manage to dredge up a glare. "Shut up."

"I didn't say anything."

"You're saying it with your cock. Knock it off."

Hook snorts. "For someone who says she doesn't want my cock, you're staring at it awfully hard."

"It's pretty." Whoops. Didn't mean to say that aloud. But now that it's out there, I can't help wanting to make one thing clear. "You said my pussy was yours."

He goes still. "I did."

"That's some archaic misogynistic bullshit, but it works for me, so don't stop."

He barely seems to breathe. "And?"

The words stop up in my chest, but I've gone too far to back out now. This is part of the negotiations I didn't think to include when we were rushing to the altar and then to

Hades's club tonight. I lift my chin. "If my pussy is yours, then your cock is mine."

"Agreed." He says it far quicker than I anticipate. "Are you saying you don't want to share it?"

Am I saying that?

I shake my head before the thought reaches completion. We covered this before. I know we did. But it was barely theoretical at that point, and now it's all too real. "I liked Gaeton sucking your cock. I would have *really* liked watching you fuck his ass. The group sex stuff is fun." I give myself another shake. "I don't know what I'm trying to say."

He smiles slowly. "My cock is yours, beautiful girl. I won't touch anyone else unless we're in a scene and the boundaries are clearly defined." His smile widens. "Naturally, you don't get to ride my cock until the terms are met. But you have my consent to touch to your little heart's delight."

I narrow my eyes. "You're just looking for a hand job."

"Maybe I'm just looking for *you*."

I don't know what to say to that, so I back into the bathroom before my mouth can betray me yet again. Then I stand there, feeling out of sorts, while Hook works his truly impressive shower. It's got six shower heads—two on each side and two overhead. He leaves the overhead ones off but turns the others on. Standing in there will be a bit like standing in a really sexy car wash. I can get on board with that.

I reach for my sweatshirt, but he gets there first. "Let me."

"I'm twenty-five. I've been dressing and undressing myself for a very long time."

"And yet I've only been dressing and undressing you for a few hours." For all that, it doesn't take him long to get me naked. When I agreed to this, I expected down and dirty fucking. I didn't expect the gentleness and ... care. I don't know what to do with the latter. It's not within my frame of reference. Aftercare is one thing. I know how to handle *that*. This is something else.

He nudges me into the shower, and I let him, still muddling over why this feels so damn different. It's not until he's pouring my shampoo into his hand that it registers. I jump back, nearly slipping on the wet tile. "Stop that."

"Stop what?" He sounds so mild, it makes me feel like I'm overreacting.

I *know* I'm not overreacting. "You're trying to tame me."

His eyebrows damn near disappear into his hairline. "You're not a horse."

"No shit, I'm not a horse. You can't just fuck me and take care of me and expect me to fall all over myself to please you."

Just like that, his expression crinkles, and he loses it. His laugh booms through the space, bouncing off the tiled walls. "You have some funny ideas about the ownership of a horse."

"You know what I mean!"

"Yes, beautiful girl. I know what you mean." He steps to me, and I freeze, but the only place he touches me is my hair, gathering it carefully in his big hands and massaging the shampoo into it. "I'm not taming you. I'm taking care of you."

"I know aftercare. This isn't it."

"Isn't it?" He tilts my head back to rinse my hair, his expression contemplative. "Call it what you want. I like to do it, so I will. That's reason enough for me."

I might strangle this man. I truly might. "You don't get to just decide that you want to do something and then do it. That's not how the world works."

"That's exactly how the world works for the powerful. You know it as well as I do." He studies the bottles I stashed in the shower earlier. "Conditioner?"

"I can—" I sigh when he ignores me and repeats the same process he did with the shampoo. "I don't want this."

"Then use your safe word." He takes longer with the conditioner, working it through my wet hair until all the tangles are smoothed out.

I realize I closed my eyes without intending to and open them. "That's for scening."

"Wrong. That's for us." He's silent as he rinses my hair. "I like my lines blurred, Tink. All except for that one."

I can't believe what I'm hearing. "So, what, you want me to submit all the time? We already talked about this, and you damn well know that's not what I signed up for."

"I want you to communicate." He contemplates me for a moment and then steps back to begin his own washing process. I try to tell myself that the sinking feeling in my chest isn't disappointment. I watch his muscles bunch and move as he soaps his hair and beard. He ducks under the spray and drags his hand over his face when he's rinsed. "Since you're incapable of talking without biting and snarling, your safe word is the only no I'll listen to."

"Get ready to hear it a lot."

He grins, and I hate that my stomach gives a happy little jump at the mirth on his face. "Guess we'll see, won't we?"

We finish showering in silence. By the time we dry off and brush our teeth, I'm so tired, I don't have the energy to fight him when he pulls me into his massive bed and tucks his big body against my side.

I stare up at the stars visible through the thick panes of glass overhead and listen to Hook's breathing even out. His arm is heavy across my waist, but for once, I don't mind.

There's one lie I never let myself believe; the lie where I tell myself that I'm finally safe. I'm not. I've *never* been safe. Not in foster care, no matter how seemingly kind the household. Certainly not with Peter, when every breath felt like it was on borrowed oxygen, an increasing price that I'd never be able to pay. Even in Hades's household, there was always the deadline hanging over my head. I'd let myself believe the expiration date might not matter so much, and look where that left me.

I can't afford to believe the lie here.

Hook fully intends to use me as bait. The whole point of bait is that it gets plucked right before the trap springs shut. He cannot guarantee my safety, even if he is inclined to try. Letting the fucking and weird aftercare go to my head will only backfire.

I'm so goddamn tired. The kind of exhaustion that spans years, rather than days and months. Decades, even. Sometimes, I feel like I've been exhausted from the moment I drew my first breath and the woman who birthed me promptly gave me away.

As if sensing my mood, even in his sleep, Hook draws me closer and nuzzles my temple. The heat of him steals through my body, relaxing me muscle by muscle despite myself. I only intend to close my eyes for a moment, but the next time I open them, dawn steals across the sky overhead.

It's beautiful, like a painting made just for me. I didn't expect this kind of romantic thing from Hook, though he didn't create this room with me in mind. He must have done it for the sheer joy of sleeping under the night sky. It's frivolous, but I appreciate it all the more for it.

I roll over to find him on his back, his face and body still relaxed in sleep. He's beautiful in the way a lightning storm is beautiful. Gorgeous and deadly and overwhelming. He'll level me if I give him half a chance.

The smart thing to do after last night is put as much distance between us as possible. Hook isn't offering me anything beyond revenge. Getting my emotions mixed up just because he happens to be a good Dom and seems invested in my pleasure and emotional well-being—at least where fucking is concerned—is a mistake. Once the threat

Peter represents is eliminated, Hook will have no more use for me.

I don't know how annulling a marriage works. We haven't had sex by the most Catholic of definitions, which I'm pretty sure is a requirement. But even if an annulment isn't an option, divorce always is. I've survived this much. A divorce is barely a speed bump.

It still leaves me feeling unsettled. Maybe it's because divorce seems like a flavor of failure, and that's not something I've ever had much peace with. Yes, that must be it. I can't change my nature, even when it's concerning a sham of a marriage.

Hook shifts, and the sheet slips lower on his waist. Dark hair dusts his bellybutton and trails south. I saw him in all his glory last night before, during, and after the shower, but that doesn't stop me from tugging the sheet down, inch by inch.

Now that I have more time to study him, I notice faint scars. Small circular ones on his chest that I recognize as cigarette burns. A jagged scar on his thigh that must have been horrifically painful when it happened. My attention turns back to the burns. Those are from his father. I'd bet my last dollar on it. Hugh Hook had an unfortunate name and an even more unfortunate temper. He'd worked for Peter's father and then for Peter when he took over the territory. I remember bloodshot eyes and a temper that warned me to keep my distance, though even the most foolhardy person in Peter's territory wouldn't touch me for fear of reprisal.

No, that privilege was Peter's and Peter's alone.

I shudder. Like Hook, I have my own scars from the time I spent helpless in this territory. Unlike him, mine are all internal. Scars on my very soul, wounds that still bleed at the most unexpected times.

I desperately don't want to think about that. Not now. Not ever. In the dark of the night, sometimes I lie awake and fear creeps in. Fear that I'll never be free of Peter. Fear that the abuse he dealt during those four years will continue to poison anything good for the rest of my life.

He took those years from me. I desperately don't want him to take my future, too.

I close my eyes and take long, slow breaths. One after another, until the frantic circling of my thoughts eases, just a little. The fear isn't gone. It's never really gone. I've just learned to live with it.

I don't examine my motivations too closely as I climb to my knees and shift to kneel between Hook's legs. I want to do this, so I'm going to do this. As simple as that. I run my hands over his thighs. His breathing stays deep and even, but his cock twitches. I almost laugh. The man is nothing if not consistent.

"Hook." He doesn't move, so I brace my hands on his thighs and give him a squeeze. "Jameson."

He opens those dark eyes still fogged with sleep. "Morning."

"It's about to be." I stroke his cock. "I want to suck your cock. Now." It's framed as a request, but from the way he narrows his eyes, he knows it's anything but.

Still, he doesn't move. "I'll allow it, Tink. This one time."

He's not talking about the blowjob. He's talking about my topping from the bottom. Instead of answering, I lean down and drag my tongue up the underside of his cock. He lengthens beneath my touch, and I allow myself one last look before I take him into my mouth. There are times when a hard and fast blow job is the name of the game. Not now. I explore him with my mouth the same way he explored me with his last night. Learning him. Memorizing his taste and feel against my tongue.

He laces his fingers through my hair and pulls it back from my face. I open my eyes and look up his body to find him watching me. His smile is nowhere in evidence. No, he looks at me like he's the big bad wolf and I just wandered into his forest.

I suck him harder, and his grip tightens in my hair. I hold his gaze as I work his cock, and I'm not even sure what I'm trying to convey. Pure lust, maybe.

Hook gives a deliciously deep growl. "You've made a mistake, beautiful girl. Waking me up to that hot, wet mouth. You'll be lucky if I don't command you to be my alarm every single fucking day."

I'd do it. I don't even know why, but I'd do it. Seeing him like this is almost like seeing him without his mask. He's not the charming, boisterous man who moves through this city, hiding everything behind that fucking smile.

The truth of him is that he's just as much a survivor as I am. That he'll fight until he can't fight any more in order to never go back to feeling helpless again. That he's mine. At least in this moment.

"Suck me harder, Tink." His voice is low and almost angry. "You want this? Fucking finish it."

Though part of me wants to keep teasing him, I obey. I give myself over to sucking his cock. Taking him as deep as I'm able to, using my fist to make up the difference. My jaw aches, but I welcome the pain. It means I'm still alive, still *here*.

His fingers tighten in my hair, and he curses as he orgasms. I drink him down, watching every expression play over his face. He looks fucking *wrecked*, staring at me like he's never seen me before, like I'm some kind of phantom who wandered into his room to give him one hell of a morning blow job.

I give him one last long suck and sit up. "Thank you for last night."

"Don't thank me. It was driven entirely by selfish desires."

He moves faster than I anticipate, grabbing my arms and hauling me onto him. I squirm, but he bands his arms around me, keeping me in place. Hook's dark gaze flicks over my face before finally settling on my mouth. "Good morning."

I feel like I've been stripped bare, which doesn't make a damn bit of sense. *He's* the one who just showed me far too much. I should be feeling secure in my power, at least for the moment.

Instead, I'm fighting not to shake.

This time, when I thrash, he releases me. I bolt from the bed, practically running to the bathroom and closing myself in. I lean against the door, breathing hard. What the hell is *wrong* with me? I press a shaking hand to my chest. My heart feels like it's trying to break through my rib cage. I can't catch my breath. Is this what dying feels like?

A knock on the other side of the door. "Tink."

"Leave me alone." I sound just as desperate as I feel. Worse, there's a thickness to my voice that mirrors the feeling clogging my throat. *Oh no.*

"Open the door."

"No!"

I actually hear his sigh over the blood pounding in my head. "We need to talk about this."

"The fuck we do."

Another pause, longer this time. Finally, he says, "I'll give you thirty minutes. When I come back upstairs, you either open the door or I break it down."

I hear him walk to the elevator, hear the doors whisk shut. Only then do I slump to the floor. What the hell is wrong with me? Hook systematically broke me down last night and then swaddled me in tenderness while I recovered. There isn't a single damn thing he could do this morning that would top that scene. *I'm* the one who initiated things.

My body isn't listening to logic, though. My fight or flight responses are all tangled, pushing for me to act and act now, screaming that I'm in danger. I can't combat it because I *am* in danger.

For the first time, it's not what Peter might do to my body that I'm afraid of.

It's what Hook could do to my heart.

CHAPTER 13

"*You're* not focusing."

Nigel isn't wrong. Twenty minutes into this meeting to go over anything pertinent that went down last night and my mind keeps wandering back to Tink up in my bedroom. How she woke me up with a demand to give me a blow job. And then promptly bolted and locked herself in the bathroom.

I shouldn't have left her like that. She was obviously out of sorts and fucked up, but I can't be sure that staying would have helped more than it hurt. Which is why I'm sitting here, listening to my cousin go over information that I can guarantee I won't retain. I drag my hand over my face. "Sorry."

"How are things coming with her?"

I huff out a rough laugh. "How do you think? Fighting or fucking. Those are the only two modes we have." Fucking isn't on the menu right now, either. I've laid out my terms, and I'll be damned before she convinces me to walk them back. I'm the unstoppable force to Tink's immovable object, and I have to be the one to win. Too much rests on it.

Though I'd be lying if I said fucking her had anything to

do with securing the territory against further coups. The marriage was enough to get that ball rolling. No, I want Tink on her knees for me. I want her. Full stop. That's reason enough for me.

"You could try talking to her."

I give him the look that deserves. Nigel sighs. "Fine. Fuck. Do what you want. I've already put out the news of your wedding. Had some of the kids talk it up on social media, too, in case he's monitoring that."

Hard to say. Peter was always a traditionalist, though I suspect it's because he doesn't trust new technology. Social media makes the rules more fluid and can get the unwary into trouble, especially when they move through the shadows like we do. Illegal activities and the publicness of the internet do not go well together.

"He's got people watching us. One way or another, he'll know she's here soon." If he doesn't already. The knowledge gives me a petty level of satisfaction. Everything of his is mine now. His territory. His people. Even his woman. Tink having belonged to Peter at one point doesn't make the list of reasons why I want her, but the truth is less important than perception.

A challenge of one monster to another.

Nigel leans back and stretches his arms over his head. "I've already reached out to Hades to negotiate having our people pick up her stuff."

"Good." It might make her feel more secure to be surrounded by her shit. And she's got her clothing business to take into account. That won't stop just because she's living here. She'd gut me if I so much as suggested it, and I'm not cruel enough to carve away one of the things she fought so hard to establish in her independence. Especially when it's presents an opportunity to be such an asset.

That doesn't mean she'll be able to move around with the

same ease she used to. She's no longer an employee of Hades and in possession of a neutral place as a result. She's mine, and there are legions of strings that come with that new role.

I file that away as one more thing we have to talk about. Fight about. The same fucking thing.

"Hook!" Colin comes skidding into the room, his eyes too wide.

Instantly, I'm on my feet. "What's going on?"

"It's her. Tink. She's …" He looks over his shoulder like he expects her to appear there and rip him a new one. When he finds the hall empty, he tenses further. "She's trying to leave. Edgar is holding her off, but it's not looking good."

Considering Edgar is six-five and nearly three hundred pounds of muscle, I don't want to know what Tink's doing to make it look *bad*. I share a glance with Nigel, and we both decide speed is the best option because when I sprint after Colin, he's right on my heels.

The scene I find in the entrance of the building would make me laugh if I didn't have the intense desire to throttle everyone involved. Edgar is blocking the double doors as best he can, using his body as a shield. Tink stands in front of him, holding a truly impressive knife. It looks like something a hunter would use, large and serrated. Where the fuck did she get *that*?

"Tink." I put enough snap in her name that she actually looks at me. Apparently the time apart has not calmed her down any. She looks just as panicked as she did when she ran from me earlier. It makes me want to go to her, but there's the knife to consider.

And the fact that she's threatening one of my people who is simply doing his job.

"Put the knife down." I hold her gaze as I say it. "Now."

She bares her teeth at me. "Make me."

"Oh baby, you do not want me to do that." Wife or not, I

can't let her undermine me in front of an audience. I start for her. Her eyes go wider yet, and the little asshole takes a swipe at me. It's a good strike, fast and low. If I were anyone else, she might have actually succeeded in gutting me.

I grab her wrist and wrench her arm away from both of us, holding it wide so she doesn't cut herself by accident. "Drop it."

"Die in a fire."

My patience, already worn thin by too much stress over too short a period of time, snaps. I twist her wrist, and the blade clatters to the ground. She's still fighting because of course she's still fucking fighting. The woman will come back swinging as long as she draws breath and, while I admire that part of her as much as the rest, it doesn't change the fact that I cannot let her challenge me. Not like this. Not when I'm holding on to the power in this territory by my fucking fingertips.

I grab Tink and haul her over my shoulder. She's kicking and punching and hissing like a pissed off cat, but I ignore her as I turn and stalk back through the building to the elevator. I ignore her demands to be put down the entire ride back to my suite. I stalk to the bed and toss her onto it, careful to ensure she lands on her ass in the middle of it.

"You dickwad!"

I'm on her before she has a chance to do more than push up onto her hands. I press my palm to the center of her chest and keep her from sitting up farther, but I don't force her down. I'm not even really holding her down, just exerting enough pressure to stop her from rushing the exit again. "What the fuck is wrong with you?"

"You don't get to ask me that after manhandling me like I'm some kind of ... I don't even know what! It's unforgivable!"

She's worked herself into a frenzy, and under different

circumstances, I might be able to dredge up some sympathy for how fucked her life's become. A part of her has to see recent events as representation of her being right back where she started—the woman of a territory leader. A pawn.

I can't afford sympathy right now, because I *am* a territory leader. If I was just a man, the rules would be different, but I am so much more. The responsibility of it threatens to break me on the best of days and this is hardly that. I press her back to the bed and try to keep my voice tight and contained when all I want to do is roar in fury and frustration. "You pulled a knife on my man."

"He wouldn't get out of my way."

As if that makes it okay. I glare down at her. "Don't pull that twisted logic bullshit. Not with me. You are my *wife*—"

"Yeah, you keep reminding me. Maybe you should tattoo your name on my ass."

"Don't tempt me." The threat is heavy in my voice. My name on her ass would satisfy a primal part of me that I don't make a habit of letting out to play. I've learned better than others there's little this world gives me it won't take away again. Food. Shelter. Even family. It's all temporary when it comes right down to it. If you don't have power, someone else who *does* have power will determine if they're in the mood to allow your very survival. I've been the former. Now I'm the latter, and I'll fight tooth and nail to never go back again. If it was only me ...

But it's not. It hasn't been since I took over the territory and it never will be again.

Losing my place as its ruler means hundreds of people at the mercy of a monster like Peter. If not him, then another who's willing to kill their way to the top. I've done unforgivable things to ensure I remain on top. Things that have stained my soul in a way I'm not sure I'll ever recover from.

When I was a kid, I didn't have a choice. I was born into

this world, and I did what it took to survive. Same as Peter and my father, when it comes right down to it. When we were kids, everything was outside of our control The choices we make as adults? We have no one to blame but ourselves. *I* have no one to blame but myself.

It doesn't matter. It *can't* matter. I'll keep doing them because there are too many people who depend on me not shying away from making hard choices. Better that I bear the scars than stand by, unharmed, while innocents are victimized.

Innocents like Tink was when Peter first drew her in.

And that's the kicker. I don't want to hold Tink with a loose grasp the same way I have with relationships in my past. Fucking and fun is all I was ever down for, and every single person knew the score before they came to my bed. This is different. *She* is different. When I'm with her, I want to strip her down, clasp a collar around her throat, brand her ass—do whatever it takes to ensure she'll never leave me.

I take a slow breath and remove my hand. I haven't hurt her, but overwhelming her with my larger body is inexcusable.

A lot of shit I've done to get my ring on Tink's finger is inexcusable.

Her mouth opens, and her brain finally seems to catch up with her emotions because she shuts it without firing back some additional impulsive threat. *Finally.* I sit back. "You are my wife. Your actions are an extension of mine. Threatening my people—our people—is out of the question."

"You can't trap me here."

"What the fuck do you think is going to happen the second you walk out on the street? Peter got to you in Hades's territory. How much more likely is he to get to you here, where he still has plenty of people who remember the good old days when he let them run rampant? Where those same people only remember you as the woman who belonged to him?" I want to shake her. "*Think*, Tink. Stop panicking because you realize you're falling for me and get your head on straight."

She sits up so fast, she almost smashes me in the face with her forehead. "I am not falling for you."

Fuck, but this woman can drive me up the wall quicker than anyone else in existence. "I see," I say evenly. "You feeling emotionally vulnerable after sucking my cock this morning has absolutely nothing to do with your erratic and dangerous behavior downstairs."

She narrows her eyes at me. "I was *not* acting erratic or dangerous."

"Yes, you were. You know the last person to threaten Edgar with a knife in what was supposed to be a safe space? Peter." She flinches, but I keep going, drilling the point home. "*He* threatened the people who pledged their loyalty. *He* bullied and used his power to get what he wanted and let his every whim decide his actions."

"Stop it," she whispers. "I'm nothing like him."

I don't know why I expect her to include me in that, to set me apart from the man who terrorized her for four long years. I don't know why it stings like a motherfucker that she doesn't. "No, you're not. He's a monster." *Like me.* "You're in over your head and scared." I have to get her to listen. Her safety and the success of my plan both hinge on her obeying me. "The people in this house, the people who are under *our* protection, don't care about your motivations. All they care about are your actions."

She inches back from me. "I hate you."

Another sentence that strikes right to the heart of me. How the fuck can she *not* hate me after everything? I give her an arrogant grin to keep the truth buried deep—I don't know if I can ever win Tink's trust in any lasting way. "Try saying that with some conviction next time." I have to get out of here. Fighting with Tink might be satisfying in a very particular kind of way, but I need to go undo the damage she just caused and keep Peter from doing damage of his own while I'm distracted with my new wife. He'll be coming, and soon.

It's certainly not because part of me is sure that I'll turn around and find her staring at me with real fear in those big eyes. I climb to my feet. "I'm having your shit brought here as soon as we can manage it. Try not to burn down anything in the meantime. I'll be back for dinner."

"*Dinner*." She looks at the large clock hanging just to the side of the cabinets in my kitchen. "It's barely eight."

"Yeah."

"You said I was going to integrate with the household today."

I'm holding onto my temper through sheer force of will. "You were, Tink. Right up until you threatened one of my people with a knife and created a mess that I have to go clean up. I'll see you tonight." I head for the elevator. I have to. Staying here will mean sitting down and talking through what the hell is going on in her head and … I want to know. I really, truly want to know. I want to ease her fears. To build trust. To make a whole list of promises I have no business making.

Instead, I walk away.

CHAPTER 14

TINK

I'm not cut out for captivity. Hades discovered that early on and loosened my leash, saying I was no good to him if I fought him every second of every day. Hook apparently hasn't gotten the memo. Or he flat out doesn't care about my mental health.

Not that I blame him. Not after the scene I caused earlier.

If I'd been thinking clearly, I wouldn't have tried for the front door. I sure as hell wouldn't have pulled a knife on a guy who was big enough to make even Gaeton look like a normal sized person.

But when I finally worked up the courage to leave the bathroom, all I could see was evidence of Hook everywhere I looked. I mean, I'm in his bedroom. Of course he's put his stamp on every single surface. But it was too much and my brain short-circuited.

The elevator doors open, and my heart leaps for a moment before I recognize Colin striding into the suite. He's like a cute younger version of Nigel. Where Nigel has the sort of poise that his name brings to mind—even if I've seen him beat a man bloody more than once—when Colin isn't trying to project *badass*, he's as bouncy as a puppy.

Or he used to be. I don't know this new version of him with the hardness in his dark eyes and the scar marring the light brown skin of his left cheekbone. He stops short when he sees me, and the way his gaze flicks over me isn't sexual in the least.

More like he's checking to ensure I don't have any weapons handy.

Colin holds up a phone. "Hook's orders." He steps just close enough to hand it to me before retreating again.

I look at the carefully curated space between us. "Are you scared I'm going to pull a knife or afraid that Hook will gut you if he thinks you touched me?"

Colin coughs out a laugh. "I'm being perfectly respectful of my cousin's wife, who apparently has a deep and abiding love of knives."

I don't have a good response to that, so I examine the phone. It's already got a number of contacts keyed into it. I raise my brows as I read through them. Hook. Meg. Hercules. Aurora. Even Nigel is in here.

A text comes through, and I snort. Hook's already put a selfie of himself in his contact information and, damn, it's a good one. He really has the smolder thing down. I click through to read the text.

We talk tonight.

No telling if that's a threat or a promise, so I send him a gif of a cartoon flipping the bird and slip the phone into the back pocket of my jeans. "Why are you still standing there?"

"I'm your protection detail for the day." Colin looks like he'd rather be anywhere but here, and I can't really blame him.

I laugh. "You drew the short straw, huh?"

"You have no idea."

I want to snarl and snap, but Hook's earlier words still linger in the back of my mind. I am *not* like Peter. He knows that. He only said it to give me a verbal slap I more than deserved. It's not Colin's fault I'm in this situation. Hell, it's not even Hook's. He took advantage of my misfortune, but he didn't orchestrate it.

Finally, I exhale the tension threatening to creep up my shoulders to my ears. "What are the parameters that Hook set?"

Colin's looking at me like I might try to bite. "You have free range of the house, provided that you don't pull a repeat of the earlier attack."

"But no limits on guests?"

"No," he says slowly. "He didn't mention anything like that, though I'll have to get anyone you want vetted."

I wave that away. I expect nothing less, though I'll be damned before I invite someone over simply to spite Hook. No matter how tempting the thought. "He said my stuff will be here soon."

"That's the plan."

"When?"

Colin shrugs. "I don't know."

Yeah, that's what I thought. I can appreciate Hook ensuring I get my possessions quickly, but ultimately he's got other things on his mind. Other priorities. I've already lost too much work time in the last two days. I have a dress due to Isabelle Belmonte in a week, and I've only begun to sketch it. She's got a particular style, and while I normally enjoy the challenge of working with her, it's not something best left for last minute.

"Well, thanks for this."

He picks up the clear dismissal and sighs. "I'll be at the elevator doors downstairs if you need anything."

More like to ensure I don't do anything impulsive. I nod.

"Thanks." This time, it actually sounds like I mean it. I barely wait for him to leave before I find Meg's contact and call her.

Despite the relatively early hour—most people who live in the Underworld are on a mostly nocturnal schedule—Meg answers rather quickly. "You know, if I'd realized you were desperate enough to marry Hook, I would have fought Hades harder on letting you stay."

I release a silent breath, something loosening in my chest. So she *had* fought for me. I'd thought so—I didn't believe Meg would offer to let me stay on without having some intention of following through on it—but hearing her state it in her dry tone makes me believe it.

It's tempting to spill everything. To tell her about the threat Peter still represents and Hook's plan to use me as bait to remove him once and for all. I open my mouth to do just that but stop before a single word escapes.

We're not on opposite sides. Meg's not on *any* side but Hades's … which is the point. Sharing the dirty details with her means sharing them with Hades, and I'm not willing to do that. Not when he could use it against Hook. Hades deals in information, after all. He's not technically supposed to meddle in leadership shit with the territories, but if he's not caught, who would know the difference?

I clear my throat. "I'm doing okay. I chose this."

Meg's silent for so long, I check to see if the call got disconnected. Finally, she says, "If you change your mind, all you have to do is tell me. I'll get you out."

Shock has me rocking back on my heels. She says it as if it's fact; if I ask her, she'll get me out. End of story. It unsettles me the same way Aurora's defense did. Neither of them hesitate to defend me, to offer me a way out. I don't know what I'm supposed to do with that. "What about Hades?" I ask weakly.

"What *about* Hades? I have resources of my own, and you

of all people know I'm not beholden to him beyond our relationship."

In my opinion, that's plenty beholden, but I don't point out lots of people have committed atrocities because they fell in love with the wrong person. Even I'm not immune, though the only person hurt when I was with Peter was me.

I realize that Meg and Hades hardly have a relationship like Peter and I did. Hades is a cold bastard, but he sees Meg as a partner and has no intention of grinding away the things that make her *her* to ensure she never leaves him. I don't really understand their relationship, but I know it's nothing like mine and Peter's.

Still, it's a big deal for her to challenge him on something concerning a deal. It could potentially have consequences that would spin out through all of Carver City. I can't shrug off the offer because it *means* something. I swallow past my suddenly tight throat. "Thank you."

"If you're not calling me to orchestrate an escape, why *are* you calling me?" Before I can register the sting of that, the reinforcement that my attempts to keep everyone at a distance for the last five years has more than paid off, Meg keeps going. "Did you want to grab a drink? Somewhere *not* in the Underworld?"

"Yes." The word startles me as much as how much I actually want to do exactly that. I *want* to get drinks with Meg, and coffee with Aurora and Allecto. Or, hell, drinks with all three of them. I haven't been gone very long, but I miss them in a way I'm not prepared for. I tried so hard to keep myself separate, but the more distance I get from the Underworld, the more I realize I didn't actually do that good of a job with it. That knowledge should frustrate me, should be yet more evidence of my failings.

It doesn't. I press my hand to my sternum. It feels good.

Weirdly good. I glance at the elevator doors. "I have to take a raincheck, though, until we get a territory issue handled."

"Another time, then."

"I'll hold you to it." I clear my throat. "But the real reason I called was because I need a favor."

"Whatever you need." The fact she doesn't put qualifiers on it staggers me. Everything about this conversation is staggering me.

Heavy emotions settle in my chest. Did I make a mistake trying to hold people at a distance? It seemed like the only choice available to me, the only one that would ensure I wouldn't end up in a situation identical to the one I'd just escaped. I couldn't trust my instincts because my instincts had said Peter was a good guy. His promises of a family that would love me without reservation—They weren't worth the air he used to make them.

I never stopped to think that trying to stay separate meant perpetuating the damage he did to me. It seemed smart at the time, but now I have a tiny amount of distance, I feel almost sad at the missed opportunities to deepen my friendships with Meg, Aurora, and Allecto. I didn't even realize I *was* friends with them until two days ago. "I really do want to get drinks. And I really, really appreciate the offer to get me out —and Aurora's offer to go head to head with Hades over me."

She doesn't seem fazed by my circling back to that. But then, Meg's always seen a bit too much when it comes to me. Proof of that is her almost gentle tone when she says, "We're your friends, Tink. You'd do the same for us."

She's right. The implications never even occurred to me. I give a tentative smile. "I would."

"Took you long enough to realize it." She laughs softly. "But back to what you need from me …"

Right. The initial reason for this call. "Hook has people

coming for my stuff sometime soon, but I was hoping you could like, courier over some things today. Everything on my desk, specifically, and the green and gold bolts of silk."

"Tink … Have you *seen* your desk? It might be organized, but there is a truly fearsome amount of shit on it."

"Yes, Meg, I've seen my desk. Every time I sit down to work at it. Just throw everything in the extra suitcase in my closet. The sewing machine has a special case, so be careful with that. But I have a commission I really need to work on, and this asshole isn't going to let me leave."

Something dangerous filters into Meg's cool voice. "Isn't he?"

I realize what I just said and curse. "Not like that. Look, Peter's on my ass. I thought he would have lost interest by now, but the second I left the Underworld, he was there."

"Yes, Hercules mentioned it." She sounds so cold, I shiver. "You should have come back to the Underworld."

I couldn't guarantee Hades would support me, but I can't say that to her. It hadn't even crossed my mind that Meg would go to bat for me, and I might be new to this whole friendship thing, but even I realize that telling her that would hurt her. "Hook will handle Peter."

"He damn well better." She huffs out a breath. "Okay. I'll get your desk packed. I can have it to you by early afternoon."

"You're a goddess."

"No, I'm a Fury."

That draws a laugh from me. "Hell yes, you are."

"Maybe I should deliver these personally."

Alarm flares. If Hades is the distant lord of the Underworld, Meg is the one who is neck deep in everyone's day-to-day bullshit. She manages all the employees, the books, and is usually the person who issues the initial threats and punishments when patrons get out of line. Some of those responsibilities have shifted to Hercules since he arrived and made their couple a throuple, but Hercules is a human-shaped teddy bear. Meg's the muscle, even if she's built like a goddamn bird. If she comes here, I can't guarantee Hook won't say something to piss her off, and then it's a city-wide incident.

I work to keep anything worrisome out of my tone. "No need for you to take time out of what's no doubt a busy day. You're looking for my replacement, right?"

"Yes," she says slowly. "You're one hell of an act to follow. Everyone is too nice, too timid, or just too not you."

Warmth fills my chest, even as sympathy rises. No matter what else is true, I found myself in the Underworld and Meg's one of the people who helped me get there. "You'll figure it out."

"Without a doubt." A deep male voice in the background and, when Meg speaks again, her voice has gone husky. "I've got to go. Your stuff will arrive this afternoon, and don't think for a second that I'll let you get out of getting that drink. Even if I have to come to you myself."

"Deal." I manage a smile. "And thank you."

"Don't thank me, Tink. If I was more on top of things, you wouldn't be married to Hook. He's not a bad guy as such things go, but he's exactly what you've tried to avoid for years."

There's no denying that, so I don't bother. Five years of running and I'm right back where I started—the main squeeze to the man who rules this particular slice of Carver City. The ruler of a territory. "Talk to you soon." I hang up before she can say anything else. I recognize the voice in the background. Hercules. Meg's probably off to bang her sexy younger man—seriously, they can't seem to keep their hands off each other, and Hades can't keep his hands off *either* of them. They're like a trio of teenagers, fucking all over the place.

And I'm over here, not fucking anyone.

I walk to the kitchen and set my phone on the counter.

As much as I'd like to pretend I have options, I don't. I tied my star to Hook's, and that means falling in line, no matter how strong the instinct to dig in my heels and fight with everything I have. I agreed to this. He didn't force me. Fighting me means he's fighting on two fronts.

Or maybe I'm just looking for an excuse to give in without damaging my already bruised pride.

I dig through the fridge and am mildly surprised to find it fully stocked with fresh produce and a variety of other things. I didn't know he could cook. It's not numbered among my skillset, so I dig around until I find an apple and some peanut butter. There are also protein bars in the cabinet, protein shakes, and some tubs of powder with vaguely fitness looking labels. Of course there are.

I ignore all those and slice up the apple and dab a metric shit ton of peanut butter on the plate. It works for a snack but less so for a meal. Maybe I can order out? I stare at my plate. Focusing on food and work seem all well and good, but what they're really doing is failing to distract me.

Approaching this situation haphazardly and without committing isn't doing me any favors. The risks are too high to ignore; it's why I'm here in the first place. More, my feelings for Hook aren't as straightforward and negative as I had convinced myself they were. I care about him. I want him. Denying us both that pleasure when the threat of Peter's shadow stretches over our every move …

I sigh. All those things are true, yes, but they aren't why I'm contemplating how I'll play tonight. No. The truth is I want Hook. That's it. Which means there's only one course of action to take.

I need to crawl on my knees and beg for his cock.

My stomach gives a weightless little flip that isn't entirely pleasant. Humiliation isn't my kink, but I have a feeling meeting Hook's terms will be anything but humiliating. And the reward for the little sting to my pride? Worth it. More than worth it.

It's official.

Tonight I'm fucking Hook.

CHAPTER 15

*A*nother day wasted with no sign of Peter. I see evidence of him in the reports of my people finding chilly responses from small business owners in the southern portion of the territory. I collect two percent of all profits. Not a huge amount in the grand scheme of things, not with the services I provide. And I sure as shit *do* provide services beyond keeping all the other problematic players out of this area. My people have a problem, they come to me or Nigel, and we ensure it's handled. Whether it's an unexpected fire or some issue with inheritance or even that they need some shit moved around and don't have the employees to handle it.

We're multipurpose like that.

What we don't do, the thing that's fucking us right now, is put the fear of god into these people.

I don't lead by love. That shit is for the birds. Love can sour and go cold and any number of bad outcomes. Fear works. And they do fear me, just not as much as they fear Peter. Because I have lines that Peter will happily cross whenever he feels like it. He's got to this portion of the territory. I don't know how, because we've had people watching that area specifically, but the proof is undeniable.

I'm so fucking furious, I want to charge through the streets, bellowing his name until he meets me for the final battle we both know is bearing down on us. If I thought for a second it'd work, I might actually do it.

But no, I have to stay the course. Peter *has* to come to me, and I have to deal with him once and for all.

First, I have to deal with my wife.

I find her working over a desk that definitely wasn't in my suite when I left earlier. She's got several colors of fabric draped over the open wardrobe doors and a dress form thing with thin white fabric pinned in place around it. I can almost see the shape of the dress she's working on, but the blue marks on it might as well be Latin for all I understand them.

Sap that I am, I stand there and watch her work. Her brows are furrowed in concentration as she circles the dress form with pins carefully held between her full lips. A tuck here. A fold there. Each deftly held in place in the span of a heartbeat, though I would have stuck my fingers several times by now.

Tink is always beautiful. Always fierce. Always a woman I'm drawn to, often despite myself.

Seeing her so lost in creating a piece of clothing? It's like seeing through a tiny window into her soul. She's more than the submissive with a snarky attitude and a quick mouth. More than the strong person who survived shit no one should have to survive. She's a shining goddamn star barreling through the heavens and fuck if I don't feel privileged to watch her trajectory.

"Stop staring at me."

Apparently she's more aware of her surroundings than

she seems. I walk to the bed and drop onto it. My whole fucking body aches after today, and I can't even blame the workout I snuck in before lunch. It's stress, pure and simple. I still manage to dredge up a grin for her. "I like watching you."

"Creeper."

"Voyeur," I correct.

She finally lifts her head to glare. "Pretty sure we both already knew that."

"Indeed." I allow myself to take her in fully, to let her see how much I appreciate the view. She's wearing a pair of jeans that look worn and comfortable and hug her ass and hips in a way I truly appreciate. A fluttery green crop top gives flashes of her stomach beneath. She looks as fresh-faced as a college girl, and it's like viewing the woman I know through a lens of what-if. If things had fallen out differently, she'd have already graduated college. She'd be exactly as wholesome and innocent as she looks right now, standing there with her bare feet and toes painted pink.

Tink narrows her eyes. "What's got that look on your face? You look almost … wistful."

I could lie, but I'm curious about how she'll respond. "You look like the horrors of our world have never touched you."

She snorts. "Shows what you know. Appearances are deceiving. That's literally my job now; helping my clients accomplish the image they're trying to project, all without saying a word."

"If you hadn't met Peter—"

"Stop." She carefully sticks the remaining pins into a cushion that looks remarkably like Hades's head. "I can't afford to play the what-if game. There's a reason he found it so easy to get to me. My life wasn't as bad as a lot of kids' experience in foster care, but it wasn't easy, either. Whatever rose-tinted vision of this alternate universe you're looking at, it's not what would have happened." She shakes her head. "I can't look back, Hook. I can't. It's what he wants, it's why he's trying to show up and fuck up my life all over again. I won't let him win."

The thought of Peter winning anything, of what it would mean, leaves me cold. "I won't let him."

Her attitude melts away, and she gives a sad little smile. "It's not like he's going to ask your permission first."

I push to my feet and cross to her. Without her heels, she barely hits my shoulder. Tink gives the impression of being bulletproof now, but I know better. I've seen her broken and terrified. I'd do damn near anything to avoid seeing it again. "I won't let him touch you," I repeat.

"Don't make promises you've already broken."

She keeps saying she doesn't want to talk about the past, and then she nails me to the fucking cross and crucifies me based on shit that happened in that same shared history.

If not for the frustration riding me hard, I would never let my control slip enough to say, "You don't get to lay that sin at my feet. I tried to get you out. The first chance I got, I offered to get you away."

I can still remember that night, how fucking scared shitless I was. Both my father and Peter were out of the building for the first time in months. I had a truck parked on the corner, and Nigel had risked his neck by stashing enough cash to at least get her out of Carver City. To get us both out if it came to that. We hadn't interacted more than a scattering of words over the years, but she *had* to know I had the best of intentions. I wasn't one of Peter's men. I never had been, for all that I was trapped in the territory, same as her.

When I laid it out for her, Tink stared at me with lifeless eyes out of a wasted face sporting a new bruise on her cheekbone, and told me to take my escape and go fuck myself.

I still don't know *why*.

135

She doesn't look lifeless now. No, she looks like she wants to knee me in the balls. "That's not fair."

"It sure as fuck isn't; just like you blaming me for shit like I didn't try to help."

"You call that *help?*" She laughs hoarsely and moves away from me, charging into the kitchen and hauling out a bottle of vodka. "You idiot. Do you really think Peter didn't have little spies who reported my every move, my every conversation to him? That he wasn't ready to take any sign of disobedience and punish me until I wished I was dead?" She flashes me a dark look. "We never would have made it out of the building. And we wouldn't have survived the night."

"You don't know that."

"I sure as hell *do* know that."

I follow her into the kitchen and snatch two glasses out of the cabinet. "No matter your reasons for saying no, don't fucking pretend like I didn't *try.*"

"Trying doesn't mean shit when it's done so recklessly!"

"Then stop punishing me for it!" I realize I'm yelling and try to moderate my tone. "Either you blame me for not getting you out or you realize we were both trapped in dangerous situations."

"Didn't stay trapped, did you?"

Ah. There's the crux of the issue. Not what happened while she was still in the territory. No, it's what went down after she left. "You have something to say. Might as well get it out."

Tink dumps vodka into each glass. I hate that her hands shake, but she won't take comfort from me. We need to get this out now before it undermines our ability to work together.

Yeah. Sure. That's why I want the air cleared. For the endgame. Not because I can't stand the way she looks at me

136

sometimes, like I'm the enemy. Like I'm a monster akin to Peter. Even if I am.

She downs her glass and flinches. "Should have had a chaser," she gasps.

"For fuck's sake." I stalk to the fridge and yank out the first thing I find—orange juice. I pour a second glass of it and pass it over while she watches me with wide eyes. When she doesn't immediately drink, I give her the look, the one primarily reserved for Dominants when their submissive has pushed back too hard and is edging over into disrespect.

Tink drinks the orange juice.

When it's halfway gone, she sets the glass aside. Her voice has lost its hoarseness. "You say you hate what he did, but here you are, squatting in his territory."

"It's *my* territory now."

"That's exactly my point." She waves a hand. "You're occupying the same space he did. If you really loathed everything he and your father did, why didn't you leave? You could have gotten out. Your trying to get *me* out proves it. But you chose to stay, and you chose to fight him and take his place."

The truth is there, edging my tongue. Speaking it means peeling away parts of myself I never show anyone. Oh, Nigel and Colin get pieces of me no one else does because they're the kind of family a person actually craves, rather than one linked by miserable accident of blood. I got lucky with them. Everyone else?

I've seen what this world does to people who expose their vulnerable centers. I might respect the hell out of Tink, but I don't trust her. She only accepted my bargain because she has nowhere else to turn. She didn't choose *me*. For the last five years, she's been pretty damn clear that she never would if she had another option.

I take my vodka as a shot and don't bother to flinch. "I need you on my side, Tink. If not behind closed doors, then in public. You need something, you tell me. As long as it's reasonable, I'll do my best to make it happen. You pissed at me? You wait until we're up here to rip me a new one. I cannot have you threatening my people and ignoring my orders out there." I jerk my chin at the elevator.

I expect her to yell, to snark, to do anything but look at me as if I'm a math equation that she can't quite puzzle out. "I don't understand you."

The problem is that she understands me all too well. She's right. I *could* have gotten out. I could have convinced Nigel and Colin to come with me and blown out of Carver City without looking back. Even now, we could be holding down normal jobs that don't stain our souls and worrying about 401ks or whatever the fuck normal people worry about.

I didn't. I chose to stay with eyes wide open. I knew exactly the price it would extract from me, and I decided it was worth the cost. Peter had to go, had to pay for his sins, and then there were too many people who looked to me to lead. Walking away meant abandoning a whole territory where I was suddenly sure I could make a difference. Arrogant? Delusional? I still don't know the answer to that. "You don't have to understand me. Just agree to keep shit behind closed doors."

She looks away, a faint blush coloring her cheeks, and I can't tell if it's the alcohol or embarrassment. "I'm sorry about earlier. You're right. I shouldn't have drawn a knife on him."

I clap slowly, mostly to break the tension of our fight. "So it *can* be done."

"Shut up."

"I'm just saying."

"Yeah, well, say something else."

"You're the most beautiful woman I've ever seen."

She blinks. "That's not what I meant."

I know, but I never did like playing by the rules. I shrug. "It's the truth. The first time I saw you, I tripped over my feet like an asshole."

"I don't remember that."

No, she wouldn't. It had been where Peter held court. It must have been a week or two after he got to her, because it was the first time he'd brought her out publicly and claimed her for himself. She stood at his side, a foot or so behind him, her hands clasped in front of her, her head bowed. "You had on a hideous white dress that covered you from neck to wrists and looked like it had to be held for you to manage to walk." *Probably so she couldn't run away*, I think darkly.

"I hated that dress," Tink murmurs, looking at me like she's never seen me before. She opens her mouth and seems to reconsider whatever she was about to say, because she closes it without continuing.

"Whatever you just thought—say it."

Finally, she says, "If you were that affected by me then …" A line appears between her brows, but she's not glaring at me, exactly. It almost seems like she's pissed at herself. "I don't look like that anymore."

Now it's my turn to blink. "What are you talking about?"

"I'm fat." She motions at her body as if I haven't spent far too many hours fantasizing about exploring every inch of her.

"Okay," I say slowly. "What's your point?"

"I wasn't then. If you wanted me then—"

Realization washes over me, and I might laugh if I didn't think she'd lob her glass right at my head for doing it. "I want you. That's the sum of it. You were gorgeous when we met, and you're gorgeous now." I almost don't continue, but she still has the tiniest bit of vulnerability lingering around the edges. "You're sexier now. You've …" I consider how to put it into words. "You know who you are now. That confidence, that attitude, the drive. It's fucking devastating."

I step closer and grip her hips, ignoring her narrowed eyes. "That might sound like I want you despite the package, but you *are* the package, Tink. If you think I haven't jacked myself thinking about your ass, your thighs, your tits, *you*, then you're out of your damn mind."

She wets her lips. "You know, most dudes would have stopped with telling me how badass I am. They wouldn't have gone into all the bits of me they've jacked themselves to."

"You know I'm not most guys, beautiful girl." I want to strip her down and show her *exactly* how much I want to worship every inch of her, but there are still the terms to be met. Fuck, I hate when I paint myself into a corner, no matter how vital it was to draw that line in the sand for us.

"That's the damn truth." She grabs the front of my shirt, and I'm caught off guard enough that I allow her to tow me down to her mouth. The kiss surprises the hell out of me, but my shock only lasts a beat before I take control.

I tighten my grip on her waist and lift her onto the counter. She immediately opens her thighs to me, and I close the remaining distance between us. We're not close enough. We won't be close enough until my cock is sheathed in her to the hilt. But it's still so fucking *good*. Tink is soft and strong, and it feels like she was made just for me.

I dig my fingers into her silky hair and tilt her head back so I can get better access to her mouth. She tastes of vodka and the sharp bite of citrus, and I drink her down. This woman *kills* me.

She runs her hands up my chest and fists them in my shirt as if trying to keep from wandering. Fuck that. I break the kiss long enough to lean back and yank my shirt off, and then I take her hands and press them to my bare chest. "Touch me."

"I'm going to do more than touch you." She pushes me back a step, and I let her.

Then Tink slides off the counter and sinks gracefully to her knees.

CHAPTER 16

TINK

*N*ow that I'm on my knees, the doubt falls away. This is the right course, the *only* course. Hook stares down at me with those dark, dark eyes. His hair is tangled from my fingers running through it, and his piercing glints against the black of his beard. He starts to say something, but cuts himself off before he gets the first word out.

Finally, he steps back and keeps moving back, holding my gaze, until he reaches the bed and sits carefully on the mattress. I wait for his Dom persona to flicker over him, for the arrogant smile to appear, for the swagger.

Instead his voice is hoarse as he beckons me forward by crooking a single finger. "Crawl."

If I'd planned this better, I'd be crawling to him naked instead of in jeans and a crop top. No time to think about that now. I move slowly, sinuously, giving him a show. The cool wood floors bite into my palms and knees, but the faint ache only heightens the desire.

He's utterly still, drinking me in as I move closer, inch by inch. If not for the tension in his shoulders and the way he fists his hands, I might be foolish enough to think he's unaffected. As long as I don't look at his eyes, that is.

Hook stares at me like I'm the most treasured possession he's ever acquired and he looks forward to examining me at length. That earlier flicker of insecurity, of wondering if he prefers me as I was instead of as I am, dies under that gaze. There isn't a single doubt in my mind that Hook desires me exactly as much as he says he does. More, even. He holds himself so tensely, it's almost as if he doesn't trust himself to see this through, to allow me this game, before he falls on me like a starving man.

"Hook." No, that's not right. Not here. Not now. I lick my lips. "Jameson."

His hands unclench and clench. "Tell me what you want, beautiful girl."

There's no going back now. Maybe there never was. I stop just short of touching him. "I want your cock. I *need* your cock." Maybe I'll regret this later, but I don't care. I sit back on my heels and run my hands over his knees and up his thighs. "I might die if I don't have it."

I half expect him to topple me to the floor right then and there, but I should know better. Hook is made of stronger stuff. He catches my hands before they reach the front of his slacks. "No going back if we cross the line. You'll be mine in truth."

Part of me flinches away from the honesty ringing in his tone. I belong to no one but myself. I can't go back to that, not ever again. "I'm yours in bed. Nowhere else."

"Tink," he says my name like he can already taste me on his tongue. "We've covered this already. You were mine from the moment you put that ring on your finger and said 'I do.' Crossing this last line only cements something we both already know."

I'm terribly afraid that he's right. "I'm scared." I want to take the words back as soon as I voice them. The tenderness on his face isn't enough to combat how vulnerable I feel.

"You should be."

Before I can process *that*, he urges me to my feet and takes his time stripping me. Shock leaves me placid and malleable. Or at least that's what I tell myself. It's certainly not that I crave Hook's hands on my body, crave the way he touches me as if every brush is a gift I've given him and that he's taken as his due.

I finally find my voice as he slides my panties down my legs. "What the hell do you mean I *should* be afraid?"

"The very best pleasure is spiced with fear. Do you deny it?"

I start to do exactly that but force myself to stop. We crossed the threshold into a scene the moment I hit my knees. I chose this. If honesty is all but a detriment in the rest of life, it's vital during this flavor of play. "No, I don't deny it."

He nudges me away from the bed. "Your safe word?"

It might be protocol to check in like this before every scene, especially with a new partner or new relationship, but I can't help feeling like that's not what this is. I speak through gritted teeth. "Pirate."

"There it is." He grins. "Can't say I get tired of hearing it."

"You're insufferable."

"Without a doubt." He rakes me with a rough gaze I can almost feel. "Stay put."

He moves behind me, and I can hear him rustling around in something, maybe the locked cabinet near the wardrobes. I poked at it a bit when I was initially doing my explorations, but there was no key in evidence, and even I draw the line at breaking open something that obviously cost a fortune just for curiosity's sake. Especially when I already had a good idea of what it contained.

A few moments later, he reappears with a long length of

black rope hanging from his hand. Hook raises his eyebrows at me, but I clamp my mouth shut before I can give him the satisfaction of a response. I love bondage as much as the next kinky asshole, but Shibari is something beyond slapping a pair of cuffs on someone's ankles or wrists. It's a study in patience and slow-roll foreplay. I've played that way once or twice, but there's a lot more trust involved than people expect. If I need to safe out, it's not as simple as unclasping cuffs. It can take *ages* to get free, and Doms can be really freaking precious about anything that might damage their ropes.

My breathing picks up despite my determination to keep my reaction under control. Hook's brows draw together, and now he's *really* looking at me. "You're not claustrophobic."

"Not particularly."

Another of those long looks, and he nods, almost to himself. "I see."

I'm terribly afraid that he *does* see. I open my mouth, but can't quite find the words. What am I supposed to say? That as much as I get off on exploring all the strange corridors BDSM can take a person down, that part of me is always held in reserve? When I worked at the Underworld, it was easy to hold back that final piece. I was just an employee, after all. A professional submissive who rose to whatever occasion the schedule demanded. Yes, I played for fun, too, but it was different.

This is different.

There are no cameras in this room, no emergency button to push, no team of security people to rush in if things get out of hand. We have nothing but trust to keep us from going off the rails.

I don't know if it's enough.

"Tink." Hook's firm voice stills my thoughts. The intense look in his dark eyes stills them further. He waits for me to focus on him fully. "Would you rather I put the ropes away?"

A tiny, cowardly part of me wants to grab the escape he offers me with both hands. Easier to do that than take ownership of what I truly *do* want. It would be so much simpler if he steamrolled over me. I could pretend I didn't really want exactly what he gave me. How am I supposed to keep fighting when he carefully extracts my desires and lays them before me?

I clear my throat. As much as I want to look away, I can't quite manage it. "No, I don't want you to put the ropes away."

He doesn't move. Doesn't give me anywhere to hide. "You have nothing to prove."

"That's rich coming from you." I shake my head. I *hate* that he keeps orchestrating emotional confessions. We haven't even fucked yet, and I can't deny the way he builds intimacy around us. I feel seen. It's not comfortable, not even a little bit, but there's a part of me that soaks up his attention like the roots of tree long thought dead from drought. "The ropes..." Fuck, why is this so hard? "Most other scenes, I say my safe word, it's over immediately, you know? The action stops, the curtain comes down, then it's just negotiating the little bit of fallout. This kind of thing ... It *can't* stop that quickly. Saying yes to this feels like saying yes to more."

"Trust." He speaks the word like it's fine wine on his tongue. Like it's *me* on his tongue. "It requires trust that I won't take us too far."

"Yes."

He still hasn't moved. "If you're not ready for that ..."

I could kiss him. I could definitely kill him.

I run my fingers through my hair, but the little movement does nothing to quell the growing feeling in my chest. "If I wasn't ready for anything you can give me, I would haven't just crawled across the floor and begged for your cock. You said a little fear is a good thing, so stop dicking around and give me that little bit of fear." I *have* to look away to say the next part. I can't handle what I might see in his eyes. "I trust you, okay? Don't make a big deal out of it."

His low chuckle has me glancing at his face, and I almost whimper with relief at what I see there. The vulnerability is gone, replaced by the arrogant asshole I'm more familiar with. "Very well." He loops the rope carefully around my neck and begins.

I only manage to stay tense for the first five minutes or so. I don't know what I expected, but he's fully concentrated on his work, his big hands winding the rope around my body and creating careful twists that slowly bind me. There's no rushing this process. Subspace creeps up on me somewhere around the point when he finishes the ladder down my torso, a row of perfectly neat twists that start on my upper chest and descend to my waist. He checks each one and the tension before moving to guide my arms behind my back.

Only then does he begin to speak, to slowly, devastatingly, draw me back into my body as he binds my arms together. "One day, I'll do both arms and legs and add one careful knot right here." He brushes his hand against my pussy, right over my clit. "Every time you struggle, it will grind that pretty little clit against the knot. How many times do you think you'll come before I release you?"

I lick my lips. "Maybe I won't struggle."

"Yes, beautiful girl, you will." He does something that cinches my arms together more firmly. It's not uncomfortable, but Hook still checks in with me just like he has at every other point during this process.

I pull on the bindings. I can't seem to help myself. Logically, I know I won't be able to just shrug these ropes off, but the physical reminder has my heart beating faster. My skin tingles in a way that is entirely too pleasant, and I clench my thighs together.

"There she is." His hands close around my shoulders, and he pulls me back against him. My hands brush against his hard cock, but with my palms pressed against each other, there isn't a damn thing I can do about the proximity.

Hook palms my breasts. The ropes crisscross above and below, leaving my breasts to hang freely without restriction, but it suddenly feels like he put them on display on purpose. Of course he did.

His rough palms drag over my nipples, and I fight down a moan. Every part of me feels overly sensitized, as if the calm during the binding only masked a growing desire I have no way to control now that it's been released.

He rotates us to face the full-length mirror near the wardrobes. This time I can't hold back my moan. I look—I don't have the words to describe how I look. The dark ropes contrast my pale skin, and the lines frame every dip and curve of my body. Parts of me that I love and am self-conscious of, depending on the day. It's a relatively simple pattern, but it still feels like he turned me into art.

Behind me, Hook is watching me with dark eyes that are so hot, I might combust on the spot. He holds my gaze as he plucks my nipples, the sensation so acute, it's almost painful. "I'm going to bend you over my bed and fuck you until you can't do anything but come."

I suck in a harsh breath. I knew this would happen, of course. But the dark intent written across his face truly highlights how helpless I am in this moment. He can bend me over any surface, and I won't be able to do anything but take what he gives me. Hell, even if I lost my mind and tried to run, it's not as if I can work a doorknob with my hands bound like this.

The flicker of fear the thought brings only heightens my desire. I'm well and truly at his mercy. "Do it."

"Not yet." He steps away from me, and I almost stumble from the absence of his warmth at my back. I watch him in the mirror as he moves to the foot of the bed and flips up the comforter to pull out a bench that had been tucked beneath the frame. He hauls it over and sets it down behind me. "Sit."

The command is deceptively simple. With my arms pinned, my balance isn't quite what it should be, and I have to move slowly to avoid toppling over as I sink onto the bench.

Hook runs his fingers through my hair, slowly, methodically. I want to make a joke, but I can't quite find the breath to do so. Not with him touching me almost reverently. This shouldn't be enough to count as foreplay, but with every motion, I have to fight not to nuzzle against his palm like a cat seeking pets. His touch finally shifts, and I force my eyes open to watch him braid my hair back from my face.

"Why do you keep doing that?" I don't mean to ask the question, but I don't mean to do a lot when it comes to this man.

"There's little more annoying than getting hair in your face when you can't do a damn thing about it." He finishes the braid and smooths a hand over his work. "And it's impor- tant to me to see every single reaction on that expressive face of yours, especially when we scene."

"Oh." Suddenly I feel a whole lot more naked. "Do you normally put this much thought into a scene?"

"Yes."

That makes me look at him more closely. I've ... mis- judged him? I always knew Hook hid a lot behind that arro- gant charisma, but I'm only beginning to realize *how* much.

He stops in front of me and sinks to his knees as grace- fully as any submissive. The thought makes me snort. "You're supposed to be the Dom. On your knees for no person and all that."

"You know better." The look he gives me has me squirming on the bench, though I can't say for certain if it's because I'm ashamed of my shit talking or simply a sheer bolt of lust. He pushes my knees wide and makes a sound as he looks at me that confirms... Yep, sheer lust. That's what I'm feeling right now.

Somehow, my mouth keeps going even though my brain has long since shorted out. "Do I?"

"I do what pleases me, beautiful girl. Right now, it's seeing you all wrapped up in my ropes, and your pussy wet with desire for *me*. You're better than a birthday present."

Before I can blurt out a response to that, he grips me under my thighs and tips me back. I'm still squawking at the sudden shift in balance, at being utterly at his mercy, when his mouth descends on my pussy.

CHAPTER 17

TINK

I don't know where to look. At the image in the mirror of this man kneeling between my spread thighs, my body on display from the rope work. At the man himself, exploring my pussy with his mouth as if he wasn't doing the same thing fewer than twenty-four hours ago.

The logic gets twisted up in my head, but I can't help it. There's no space for thinking clearly. There's only his touch and the ropes holding me as helpless as his hands bracketing my thighs.

If he lets go, I'll fall.

I'm terribly afraid that I'm falling despite that.

He sucks hard on my clit, and my frantic mental circling thoughts morph into a high keening sound. I'm only partially embarrassed to realize it's coming out of my mouth. I thrash, but even I can't say if I'm trying to get closer to his wicked tongue or put more distance between us.

It doesn't matter. I'm completely at his mercy. I won't be going anywhere until he allows it.

The knowledge spins beneath my skin, gathering strength and heat. Trapped, yes. But not helpless. A fine line we're treading. Too far in either direction and he'll trigger a response I have no control over. One of true terror.

"Tink." He doesn't look up, barely lifts his head enough to speak. "Tell me something." He doesn't give me a chance to answer, which is just as well. I can't quite find the breath in my lungs to form words with his lips ghosting over my clit. "How often did you watch me scene in the Underworld?"

He resumes circling my clit with his tongue slowly. Not quite teasing but also not getting me where I need to be. More like he wants to memorize the exact shape of me, to file away every involuntary shake and shudder and moan.

Like this means as much to him as it's starting to mean to me.

"Every time." The truth bursts from me before I have a chance to call it back. "I didn't want to but … Every single time."

"Mmm." Another of those slow licks. "You have a favorite?"

My favorites are all more recent, all involving *me*. "You and Alaric," I gasp. Alaric is one of the few switches on staff at the Underworld. "I love watching you top him."

His dark chuckle curls my toes. "Dirty girl. It's a shame he's traveling for the near future. I suppose you'll have to do with Gaeton as a substitute." He glances up. "You really do want to watch me take his ass, don't you?"

"Yes." It's not even a question.

"I'll give you everything you want, beautiful girl. Everything you need." He moves before I have a chance to register his plans. My view goes topsy-turvy as he scoops me up and throws me over his shoulder. I curse, but he just laughs and smacks my ass. "I'm not interested in having in him in bed with us right now, though. Tonight is about us."

Us.

How can he disarm me with a single word? It's not fair,

but I can't quite manage to dredge forth anger as he dumps me onto the bed, careful that I don't land on my bound arms. Hook flips me onto my stomach and catches my hips to drag me to the edge of the mattress. He kicks my legs wide, the height of the bed ensuring I can barely touch the floor, and palms my pussy. "I'm taking what's mine now."

"Can't take something I served to you on a silver platter," I grind out.

His laugh licks up my spine. "True enough." A crinkle of a condom and I turn my head to the side to watch him roll it over his cock. He doesn't give me a show; he's too intent on our destination. He notches his cock at my entrance and that's the only warning I get before he plunges deep, sheathing himself to the hilt.

I whimper, but he doesn't give me time to adjust. He palms my ass, squeezing and spreading me, and making a faint growling sound as if he can't help himself. "The things you do to me."

Something goes melty inside me despite my best efforts. I'm not even *doing* anything, and he's so fucking undone by me. Hell if that isn't as intoxicating as any drug I've ever tried. More, even.

He leans over me and gently guides my face to the other side. I see his intention immediately. From this position, the mirror gives a perfect view of us. He hasn't taken off his pants, and the sight of him partially clothed against my nakedness and rope does things for me. It does a whole lot.

He pulls out almost all the way and slams into me. This time, there's no stopping, no slowing down, no checking in. He's sure of me. He damn well should be. I'm on my toes, trying to angle my hips to take him deeper, trying to move with his thrusts, trying to do *anything* but simply take it.

Impossible. I'm immobile and held steady by his big hands on my hips, by his ropes binding my upper body. The thickness of them rubs against my skin with every rough stroke, a slick slide that has me moaning almost as much as the feeling of his cock stretching me.

"*Jameson.*"

"That's right, beautiful girl. See me." There are layers to his words, depths I'm afraid to sink into for fear of drowning. This should just be fucking, but it doesn't *feel* like only fucking. It feels like he's reached into the very core of me and now he's pulling out bits and pieces with every thrust, exposing the weak and terrified part I keep hidden.

My throat burns, and my eyes go hot. What the hell is happening to me? "I don't … I can't …"

"Let it go." His soft command lashes me with more finesse than any flogger.

I come with a sob. I fight the orgasm the same way I fight the bindings, but the struggle only seems to make the pleasure go higher. The last shudder works through my body as Hook carefully turns me over and sits me up. He studies me, his dark eyes seeing too much. They *always* see too much.

I think I'm crying. I can't be certain. I can't be certain of *anything* anymore. My gaze drops to his still-hard cock, and for some reason that makes the horrible heat clogging my throat so much worse. "You didn't come."

"Not yet." He frames my face with his big hands and strokes away my tears with his thumbs. I try to pull away, but he holds me immobile. "Tears don't mean weakness, Tink. Even if they did, there's no shame in weakness with those you trust."

"You're assuming a lot," I whisper.

"No, I'm not." He moves onto the bed and pulls me onto his lap. I hate that I feel self-conscious on top of everything else, which only makes my emotional response that much stronger. I can't stop the tears. I can't even use my own hands to wipe them away.

I can't do this.

Why did I think I could do this, that anything would be simple with Hook? He's always asked too much, demanded I act against my instincts. Defend. Run. Hide. He won't let me do any of it. If I wasn't a goddamn coward, I'd let him as close as he seems to want to be. I would see this sham of a marriage as a chance to maybe have something I've wanted since I was a kid, a burning desire that has been used against me time and time again. I might even love this man with his wicked charm and wounds that are far too similar to mine.

But I am a coward.

"Pirate," I gasp.

He's moving before the word is completely out of my mouth. I can't see what he's doing but then the bindings are gone, and I suck in a breath as if I'm drowning. Hook yanks the ropes away from my skin, and I can barely process that he *cut* them before he's wrapping his arms around me and holding me close.

"Take a slow breath, Tink. Deep inhale, deep exhale." Hook wraps me in his arms, and even though every part of me wants to run, to put as much distance as possible between us, I can't do anything but sit there and shake. And cry, goddamn it, because I never stopped once the first tear fell.

"You're safe." He somehow gets the comforter up around us, creating a cocoon of warmth.

"Not that. Never that."

His grip tightens on me before he seems to make himself relax. "Yes, *safe*. Right here, right now, you are fucking safe."

Even as my mind spins in increasingly frantic circles, my body melts into him. I cannot reconcile the two, cannot understand how I can be so afraid and so comforted at the same time by the same man, so I close my eyes and rest my forehead against his shoulder. My body continues its efforts

155

to shake itself to pieces. Even knowing it's a result of the adrenaline crash, I resent the weakness.

Or maybe I resent the truth I can't escape. My weakness goes soul deep. No matter how strong, how fierce, how mean I am, at my center, I'm still the scared teenager who fell for a monster's false kindness. I'm so, so afraid to repeat that same mistake with this man. My instincts tell me he's nothing like Peter. But then, history proves that my instincts aren't to be trusted.

Especially not where my heart is concerned.

I still can't make myself leave Hook's embrace. I take the comfort he offers, soaking it up like a flower seeking the sun. I can't seem to help myself.

Seconds tick by into minutes. I keep expecting him to ask me what triggered the safe word. I really should know better by now. Hook is too smart. He planned too carefully, was there easing me from step to step, studying every reaction and adjusting his course accordingly. There isn't a single damn reason for me to have safed out, and we both know it.

"I'm sorry." He murmurs against my temple. "I pushed you too hard."

The words burrow beneath my skin, leaving sick guilt in their wake. My shakes have subsided, but I make no move to leave his embrace, and he holds me just as firmly as he has from the moment we assumed this position. If I'm smart, I'll let *him* shoulder this guilt, deserved or not. Hook isn't heartless, no matter what I fear. If he thinks he edged into harming me, he'll back off. A desperately needed reprieve and …I can't do it. I can't be that cold, even if I'm the one who will pay the price in the end. "No, you didn't." My voice sounds as if I've smoked a pack of cigarettes.

"Tink—"

I know better than to speak truths into this delicate space, but I can't seem to stop myself. It's becoming a horrible habit around Hook. "I'm so afraid."

He goes rigid beneath me for the span of a heartbeat. A tensing and then it's gone, and he's as relaxed as he's ever been. I recognize it for a lie now.

I close my eyes. "It's not your fault, not really. I can't trust you. You see that, right? Except I kind of want to trust you when you tell me I'm safe, and *that* is the scariest thing of all." *I think I care about you. I think it might be even worse than that. I might be falling for you.* Words I can't—*won't*—speak. If he knows my heart is teetering on the brink, nothing will stop him from a full-scale siege. If the last few days have taught me anything, it's that I don't stand a chance if all the brakes are gone.

"I'm not him," he speaks slowly, softly, but no less intensely for it. "You are not the same person you were. Fuck, Tink, you were sixteen when he got his hooks into you."

"I obviously haven't learned my lesson."

"I'm not him," he repeats, though this time there's something else in his deep voice. Something like … hurt.

Fuck.

Fuck.

I am messing this up, and I don't even know what *this* is. Fake marriage. Revenge plot. A whole lot of lust. I worry my bottom lip. Even my mental list feels a bit like a lie. I finally shift back enough that I can see Hook's face.

For once, he isn't offering me a single damn thing. He's shut up tighter than the vault in Hades's office. Only the faint tension in his body gives him away. I open my mouth, but I don't know what I'm supposed to say. I don't comfort. Hell, I don't even communicate that well unless it's snark. Negotiating a scene is a whole hell of a lot different than navigating this emotional minefield.

"I know you're nothing like him," I finally manage. If I

were a better person, I'd leave it there. An acknowledgement of our shared trauma, a nod to the fact that this *thing* is nothing like anything I've experienced. I'm not a better person. I'm a scarred creature who only knows how to strike out, again and again, until it's left alone. Until there's no one else. "But you're no Prince Charming, either."

I expect Hook to set me down and walk away. It's the only rational response. He's handled my aftercare. If I'm not *fine* now, I'm recovered enough to handle the rest myself. Only a masochist would want to keep spending time with me, and that's not his kink.

He smooths back the few tendrils of my hair that have come free of the braid. "And you're no pure princess locked in a tower. We're alike, you and me. We'll survive whatever life throws at us, no matter the cost. There's no place for innocence in our world, and there's sure as fuck no place for chivalry, either." He presses a soft kiss to my forehead. "For better or worse, Tink. We have time to figure it out."

But he's wrong.

Time is the one thing we don't have.

CHAPTER 18

*T*ink seeks me out in her sleep. It might amuse me that she's a cuddler under different circumstances, but with the mountains currently left to scale, the taste of what we *could* have is almost painful. It doesn't stop me from holding her close and breathing in the unique scent of her shampoo. It's something floral I can't place, a note of sweetness against the spikes she so carefully hones to keep the world at bay.

I don't blame her for that. I also won't allow her to maintain them against me.

I could spend hours going over where the scene took a turn, but in the end, no matter what she says, the truth is I pushed her too hard. Not in kink, exactly. Having her blindfolded and filled with cocks while I direct the action is a whole hell of a lot more intense than a few ropes and bound arms. Or it would be if I'm only looking at the surface. Things shifted for us last night. It started when she crawled to me. I should have fucked her then and there instead of demanding more.

But, fuck it, I want *more.*

159

I want everything.

My phone buzzes where I left it on the nightstand, and I have to stretch to reach it without disturbing Tink. *Unknown Number*. Only one person would be calling me at four in the morning from an unknown number. I take a slow breath and lock everything down. "Yeah?"

"Wide awake and up to no good."

Peter.

Even anticipating that it would be him on the other end of the line, I go cold. "One could say the same for you. Normal business hours are between eight and five. Try calling back then." I hang up. A calculated risk, just like everything I've done for the last month since Peter started making moves. I can't root him out. I have to force him to come to me, to meet me on my home turf, so to speak. Otherwise, it's guerrilla warfare in my own territory; a conflict that can stretch on for years with my people paying the ultimate price. No fucking way.

The phone buzzes again. I count slowly to five and then answer. "Yeah?"

"Hang up on me again, and I'll slit your whore throat."

There you are. His public persona has never been quite as good as mine, but he's adept at charm when he puts his mind to it. I don't want him that controlled. I want him in a fucking freefall. "You're interrupting my night, Peter. It's rude." I let amusement filter into my tone, knowing it will drive him up the fucking wall. "I'm entertaining."

"Entertaining." He sounds like he wants to crawl through the line and strangle me. Good. But when he speaks again, he sounds almost calm. "I knew you were a fucking rat, but I didn't expect you to be so content with sloppy seconds. My territory. My men. Even my woman. It's beneath you."

"She was earlier, yes."

Dangerous silence for a beat. Three. Five. "I hear you married her."

"You heard right." Now to drive it home. "She wasn't even free a day before she had my ring on her finger. Practically begged me for it. Said she wanted a real man in her life instead of a pissant bully who can't get it up." Tink's gone tense against me, awake and listening, but I can't retract a single damn statement. Too much is at stake. "You say sloppy seconds, Peter. Tink and the rest of the fucking territory call me an upgrade."

"Whatever you have to tell yourself, Hook. She might be fucking you right now, but she never stopped being mine." He says it idly, and a thrill of true fear goes through me. Peter's the most dangerous when he's calm. "But it seems my darling Tatiana needs a firmer hand to correct her."

This is what I wanted, but fuck if I can stand hearing him threaten her. I open my mouth, but Tink's hand lands on my chest. I glance down, and she's staring at me, her green eyes a little too wide. She shakes her head and mouths, *Keep going.*

I hold her gaze, trying to tell her that it will be okay. I'll kill this fucker before I let him touch her again. I force mirth into my tone. "You can call her yours all you want, Peter. But it's *my* name she's screaming when she's coming on *my* cock. See you around." I hang up and turn the vibrate function off the phone before I toss it aside. It immediately lights up as he tries to call back, but I have eyes for only her. "I'm sorry."

"Why? This is what we both wanted."

I shake my head slowly. "This is what's required. *Want* has nothing to do with it."

She looks like she wants to argue with me, and I welcome it. Anything to chase the shaken look off her face. I've consoled myself over the years that I do what's necessary, but I don't hurt anyone who doesn't deserve it. I can't make that claim any more. Not with this woman in my bed, trying not to shake.

Not knowing what's coming.

She must see something on my face, because she sits up. "I'm fine."

"It's okay if you're not."

"Even if I'm not, it isn't *your* job to clean up the mess. I have it handled." She starts to move away.

I touch her wrist, stopping her. "We're married."

"It's hardly worth the paper they printed the certificate on. We both know what this is." She still won't look at me. "It'll last as long as we need it to, and then it's over."

No.

I have to concentrate to keep my body relaxed, my expression even. Bundling her up and telling her that I'll never let her go is the surest way to get her to bolt. "What if it's never over?"

Finally, finally, she turns back to me. She's stopped shaking, but her eyes are still too wide. "What the fuck are you talking about?"

"Come now, you have to know. All I needed for this plan was you as my wife. The rest isn't required." I smile a little at the way her jaw drops.

"You mean the rest like me screaming your name while I come on your cock?" She arches her brows, though something vulnerable still lingers on her face. "Pretty sure you just told Peter that."

I snort. "Beautiful girl, it's only a bonus that it's true. I'm not so pure that I am incapable of lying when it suits my purposes." I can actually *see* her shutting down and rush on. "Not to you."

"Please." She yanks her wrist out from under my hand. "Don't act like I'm someone special. I used to be *his*, and now I'm *your* willing pussy. That's all."

I sit up straight. "Don't you fucking dare."

"Don't I dare *what?*" She shoves off the edge of the bed and spins to face me. "Don't speak the truth? You just got done telling me how you lie to suit your purposes. But apparently not with me?" She laughs bitterly. "You already fucked me, Hook. You don't have to play the sweet card now."

I drag my hands through my hair and strive for calm. It's a lost cause. It's *always* a lost cause where this woman is concerned. "How about this for some truth? I love you, you infuriating, amazing woman."

She freezes. "That's not funny."

"Who's laughing?"

"You can't just …" She's blinking too rapidly. "You just said… What the *fuck*, Jameson?"

It hasn't slipped my notice that she only uses my first name when she's completely undone. I'm not sure that it's a good sign she's using it now, but at least she's listening. I move to the edge of the bed but don't try to touch her. "I love you."

"No, you don't."

"Tink." I wait for her to meet my gaze. "You are mighty and fierce enough to get your way at anything you set your mind to, but even you can't change the way I feel just by telling me not to feel that way."

She points a shaking finger at me. "I don't know what game you're playing—"

"Yes, you do. You've known it from the start." It takes effort to hold still, to maintain my position instead of launching to my feet and pacing like I want to. "I want you. I've always wanted you."

She looks like she wants to strangle me. "You don't even like me."

"Wrong again."

"What kind of sick fuck gets off on fighting all the damn time?"

I give her the look that statement deserves. "There are two of them in this room right now."

She makes an angry teakettle noise. "I don't love you."

"Okay."

"I don't."

"That's fine."

She practically vibrates with rage. "Stop being so calm."

"I don't know what you want me to say, beautiful girl." I'm provoking her, and I don't care. She's not thinking about Peter right now. She's right here in this room with me. Nothing I've said is anything but the truth. I don't particularly like this truth any more than she does, but I'm not one who will shy away from it. She's mine. I love her. I don't know what the future can even look like with the two of us, but we'll figure it out. One way or another.

Tink takes a menacing step forward. "You ... *You* ..."

I smirk. "I'm right here. No reason to mince words. Tell me what you really think." I love it when she's like this. A warrior woman who will take down anyone in her path with a few choice words. I must have a bit of a masochistic streak when it comes to Tink, because the meaner she is, the more I love it. The more I love *her*.

I am so fucked.

She marches up to me and presses her hands against my bare chest. "I can*not* believe your cock is hard right now. What the hell is wrong with you, Jameson?"

I cover her hands with my own, careful not to press down so she doesn't feel like I'm trapping her. "You're the only one who makes me like this."

"Lies," she hisses. Tink places one knee on the bed next to my hip. "You've been lying to me from the very beginning. You didn't need to fuck me. You just needed to marry me."

"Yes."

She straddles me, using her hands on my chest to push me back onto the bed. I allow it, though all I want in this moment is to touch her. To trace the pink flush of anger across her skin with my mouth. To hear her whispered threats as I plunge into her. I truly am twisted for this woman.

Tink presses her hips down against mine, and I barely stifle a curse at how wet she is. I catch her thighs. Not trying to still her. Just enjoying whatever the fuck she's up to. "Someone likes fighting just as much as I do."

"It doesn't mean anything."

"Whatever you say, beautiful girl."

Her nails prick my chest. "Stop being so fucking agreeable, Jameson!"

I shift my grip to her hips and catch her gaze. I let all the charm and bullshit fall away, leaving only *me*. My voice gains a growl. "Stop teasing me, and get on my cock, Tink."

She reaches between us and fists my cock. "I'm only doing this because I want to, not because you told me to."

"Bullshit. You get off on obeying my commands as much I get off on giving them to you." I lean up and kiss her. A hot, brief tangling of tongues. I set my teeth against her bottom lip, and she shivers against me. "Ride my cock, beautiful girl. Fuck me like you're mad at me."

"I *am* mad at you."

"Then do as you're told."

She slams down on me, and we both freeze. She's hot and tight, and it's everything I can do to hold still and not drive up into her. Tink doesn't take long to find her footing, though. She grinds down on me and then begins to move, rolling her hips in a way that damn near makes my eyes cross. "Yeah, just like that."

Tink bares her teeth at me. "Shut up."

"Make me."

She curses long and hard and snags the back of my neck to pull me up to her breasts. I don't need a single fucking word of encouragement. I palm her, pressing her breasts together so I can suck one nipple and then the other. I use the flat of my tongue to touch her in a way that has her hips jerking against mine. So I do it again.

"Don't stop." She digs her fingers into my hair, holding me to her. She keeps fucking me, intent on her pleasure. Selfish girl. I love it.

Despite my best efforts, I can't keep still. I thrust up as she descends, and she moans, low and throaty. It doesn't take us long to find our rhythm. But then, I've always moved with Tink as if we were meant for each other. "Touch yourself."

"Fuck off." But she shifts back enough to slide a hand down her soft stomach and finger her clit. Her pussy clenches around me, and it's everything I can do to hold myself back from the edge.

Tink's gaze is so hot, I have the distant thought that it might actually set me aflame. Her strokes become slower, working my cock over that one spot inside her as she circles her clit. When she comes, it's hard enough to bow her back. "Jameson."

My name on her lips.

I'll never get enough of it. Not as long as I live. It's the only time Tink ever sounds sweet.

I grip her hips and pound into her, chasing my own release. "Tell me where you want it."

Her smile goes wicked. "All over me."

I roll us and take up a position between her thighs. She's gone soft and limp with pleasure, and the sight of her spread out for me is enough to blast through the last of my self-control. I yank out of her and fist my cock, stroking hard as my orgasm bears down on me. I come all over her pussy, making even more a mess of her. She shivers and moans, and I grin. "Dirty little cum slut."

"I'm not sorry."

"Neither am I." I drag my fingers through my mess and circle her clit. Then I push two fingers deep. "Mine."

"No."

I shrug. "Admit it or not, Tink. You belong to me." I slowly pump my fingers, enjoying the way her thighs relax and fall wide. "And I belong to you."

"You can't just say shit like that," she whispers.

"Mmm." I press my thumb to her clit. "I think you'll find that I do whatever the hell I want."

Tink sucks in a breath. "Shit, we didn't use a condom." She props herself up on her elbows as I go still. "I'm sorry."

I can't quite make myself withdraw my fingers, but I stop fucking her with them. "I was tested recently and haven't been with anyone since."

She presses her lips together. "I, uh, I've been tested, too. And I'm on birth control."

Relief courses through me, but she's still frowning, so I fight not to let it show. "We can keep using condoms. Whatever you're comfortable with." I start to move back.

"No." Tink catches me around the wrist. "If you're willing to trust me on this, then I'm willing to trust you. No more condoms." She presses my fingers deep. "Finger fuck your come into me, Jameson. Make me messy."

Jesus fuck. I lean down and kiss her hard, and then I do exactly as she wants. She lifts her hips to take my fingers deeper. Wanton woman. She'll take whatever I give her and demand more. Loving this woman will never be easy. I can't think about any of it too closely.

Admitting I love her is easy, as simple as exhaling after holding my breath. Dealing with what that looks like in life? Accepting she's now a target for every single one of my enemies? Acknowledging how fucking *vulnerable* this makes me?

I can't handle it. I don't want to. Not with her riding my fingers as if she didn't just have an earthshaking orgasm a few minutes ago. So I shove it away. I'm good at that, at not thinking too closely about things I'd rather not.

Instead, I focus on making Tink come again.

And again.

And again.

CHAPTER 19

Somewhere between orgasm four and five, I almost forget Hook's damning words. *Love.* He can't possibly love me. Yes, we've known each other for years at this point. Yes, there *might* be more than just white-hot attraction between us. But ... love?

Impossible.

He presses a kiss to my lips and disappears into the bathroom. A few seconds later, the shower turns on, but I don't have the energy to try to join him. I'm not even sure my legs will hold me if I attempted it, and the thought of him walking out to find my naked ass sprawled on the floor in some testament to his virility is too much for my pride.

The buzzing of my phone distracts me, and for one heartstopping moment, I'm sure it's *him.*

But no, when I crawl to the nightstand and pick it up, I see Meg's name flashing across the screen. Grateful for the distraction, I answer. "Hey, Meg."

"I need you to come in."

I blink. She sounds almost ... worried. "What's going on?"

"Bring your strapping new husband, too. This concerns

169

him as well." She doesn't even put an ironic tilt to Hook's new title. That's how I know it's serious. That and the fact she's calling me before ten in the morning.

"Okay, we'll be there."

"Good." She hangs up.

Apparently my plan to avoid Hook for the foreseeable future while I get my head on straight isn't going to happen. No one refuses a call to the Underworld—not even the leader of a territory. Especially one potentially in contention like ours.

Ours.

I sit up. This isn't my territory. Not really, wedding ring or no. Feeling possessive of it when I've spent the entirety of my time locked in one room or another. Even before, Peter only trotted me out when he wanted to show off or prove a point. Hook might not share the same motivations, but it doesn't change the end result.

I'm a figurehead.

The thought doesn't sit well with me. I press my hand to my chest, but naturally the physical move doesn't alleviate the strange ache beneath my ribcage. I know better by now. Wanting something of my own—it's what got me into this mess to begin with. Promises of safety, of family, of a home. None of those things are for me. Wanting them is a weakness I can't afford.

And yet …

And yet.

I manage to get my legs in gear and walk into the bathroom to find Hook standing in front of the mirror, a towel wrapped around his waist. I stop short. I'm not shy. Even before this marriage, he's seen me naked more times than I can count.

He never told me he loved me before, though.

Just like that, it's back. The panic fluttering at the base of my throat. I can't do this. Why did I think I could do this? I start to turn for the door, but his low voice stops me. "Who was on the phone?"

I mentally lunge for the lifesaver he just threw me. Easier to focus on this than on what went down in our bed not too long ago. "Meg. She wants us to come in to the Underworld. It sounded important."

His mouth goes flat. "I'm not Hades's lap dog."

Save me from the male ego. I understand his point of view on this. All leaders in Carver City engage in a delicate dance of power with Hades. One wrong step can mean complete ruin for everyone involved. I give Hook a long look, holding his gaze in the mirror. "Are you willing to let the appearance of power potentially keep you from important information?"

"Appearance of power *is* power, Tink. I'm already balancing on a knife's edge. You know that better than anyone."

He's not wrong. Still … Ignoring this summons is a mistake. I know it down to my very bones. I take a careful breath. "Then I'll go in your stead."

He finally turns to face me. "Absolutely not."

"Either I'm your wife and partner or I'm a pretty little trinket you bought to keep locked up in this room. Which is it?" I'm holding my breath. It's a mistake, and I can't stop. I never should have voiced this question, never should have dared hope that he'd answer the way I suddenly very much need him to.

Hook crosses his arms over his chest. "If you do this, there's no going back. Are you sure it's what you want?"

My head goes a little fuzzy. I fully expected him to shoot me down. There's no frame of reference for this unexpected question. "What?"

"With you acting the part of my prize, you have a chance

to escape when this is all over." His gaze is steady, no smile in evidence for once. "If you start playing my wife and partner in truth, you're making a choice to take this. This territory. Power." A significant pause. "Me."

The fluttering in my throat transforms into a whirlwind of blades. "You're trying to trap me."

"I'm laying out the potential outcomes. It's your choice, Tink. It's always been your choice."

The two paths forward spin out in front of me. I don't know if he'll really release me, but Hook has never gone back on his word before. There's no reason to believe he'll do it now, no matter how high the stakes.

With Peter dead, I could finally be free. Truly free, without a single threat dogging my heels. The possibility leaves me breathless. I've been entrenched in this life for nearly a decade. If I could leave it behind …

Where would I go?

All my clients are here. My …friends, though I've barely come to terms with the fact they exist. A new city means starting from the bottom and scrapping my way to the top. I can do it. I *know* I can do it.

The question is if I want to.

As for my other option … Do I really want to be responsible for more people than just myself? To fully embrace the darkness, even if it's more like shadows than true night in this place? Hook has lines, but power has a habit of taking people to places they never anticipated. What's to say he won't cross his lines when push comes to shove?

What's to say he won't drag me down with him when he does?

That's fear talking, but I don't know how to silence it. I see the way his people look at him, as if he's a god who wandered down to live amongst them in this city. There's fear there, but they worship him in a way most leaders can only dream of. In return, he bears the weight of their safety around his neck. Do I truly want a share of that burden, even if the potential outcome is everything I've been too afraid to reach for on my own?

A home. A family. The kind of safety I'm not sure I believe in any more.

I look at Hook, really look at him. I can't be sure, but I think he's holding his breath, too. Waiting for my answer, for me to cut him down or embrace him wholeheartedly. I don't know if I can do either. I'm too tangled up inside. "I want kids."

He doesn't even blink. "I want kids, too."

Somehow, it makes me feel worse. It's like standing in a snowstorm and seeing the perfect life laid out before me, except I'm separated from it by a thick pane of glass. I can press myself to it in an attempt to get closer, but it doesn't have the power to chase away the cold eating at my bones. "I can't be trusted to make this call. I'm flip-flopping so hard, I'm giving myself emotional whiplash."

He sets his hands on my shoulders. It's all the invitation I need to take that last step and let him enfold me in his arms. I hate how good it feels, that I can't stand on my own when he's right here to stand strong for both of us. I press my face to his chest and inhale deeply. "This will never work."

"Not with that shitty attitude." He strokes a hand over my hair. "But you're right. It's too soon to make that call. We'll go to the Underworld together."

"Thank you." I sound subdued, but I don't know how to change that. I can't help but be grateful for the way he's handling me, too. I feel fractured, held in place by the thinnest of layers, as if one wrong touch will send me crashing to the ground in pieces. In a different world, I'd be strong enough to hold myself together. But I don't live in a different world; I live in this one. And in this one, I need all the help I can get.

I make myself take a step back and then another. "I need to get dressed. *You* need to get dressed."

Hook starts to speak but gives his head a sharp shake. "Be quick."

I make it work. I pull my hair back into a slick ponytail and dress in a high-waisted midi skirt, a fitted green blouse, and flats. It's a little blah for my tastes, but it works in a pinch. Plus, I can run in this skirt and these shoes if I need to —something that needs to be considered with any outing in the near future. At least until Peter is dealt with.

I head down to the front door and find Hook there, talking in low voices with Colin and Edgar. Edgar looks up, and his gaze immediately goes shuttered when he sees me. Fuck, I've seen that look before. He's not sure if I'm going to fuck his day up again, if I'm a threat to him. The very idea would be laughable under normal circumstances; I barely hit his armpit. But one thing physical size can't take into account is power, and I was an asshole who punched down by bringing him into my spat with Hook.

I lift my chin and stride over to the trio of men. Colin starts to say something, but Hook nudges his shoulder, silencing him. Apparently he trusts me to handle this. I bite back a sigh. "I apologize for yesterday, Edgar."

Edgar takes a step back, hands lifting like he wants to ward me off before he catches himself. "No need to apologize. We're good."

He's scared of me.

Something heady and ugly takes wing in my chest. It is *so easy* to see how someone starts down this path, craving the security that others' fear brings. Shame muffles the feeling before it can take hold. I've been on the other side of this kind of interaction too many times to relish it like this. I don't want it. I *refuse* to want it.

I paste a smile on my face. "All the same, I'm sorry."

Hook takes pity on us and shifts, drawing our attention. "We're ready. We're combining this trip with the one for collecting your things. Colin will lead the team."

I want to argue. Colin is so young. Putting him in charge of anything seems like a mistake. But I've only been back a few days. Hook has led this territory for years now. Either I trust him or I don't, and it's not worth arguing with myself because I already *know* I trust him. No matter how uncomfortable it makes me. "Okay."

He arches an eyebrow. "I had five whole minutes allotted to argue with you about this."

I snort. "Someone's overcompensating."

Colin makes a choked sound and slaps Edgar on the shoulder. "See you when we get back." He heads down the hallway toward the back entrance, leaving us to follow at a slower pace.

I know we're not alone, that there are bound to be eyes and ears everywhere on the main floors of this place, but wading through all the emotional shit for the last twelve hours has left me out of fucks to give. Hook's seen me shattered, he's systematically dismantled my defenses, and even more importantly, he's done the same to himself in my presence. He says he loves me. I don't know if I believe it. I don't know if I *can* believe it. But the rest is fact. "Thank you for doing this."

"You didn't give me much choice."

I match his tone, voice pitched low so as not to carry beyond the two of us. "As you keep reminding me, there's always a choice. You made this one. So ... thank you."

"It's entirely possible that you're not going to like what you find when we get there." He takes my hand and places it in the crook of his elbow like some kind of old world gentleman. "Hades is only loyal to himself. If Peter made a deal—"

"No." I'm already shaking my head. "Meg wouldn't let him do that."

He shoots me a look. "You're that sure of her?"

"Yes." And I am. If she's willing to fight Hades to get me out of Carver City, there isn't a chance in hell that she'll let him endanger me like that. She's my friend.

Hook releases a long exhale. "Okay."

It doesn't hit me until we're in the car, working our way to the center of Carver City. Hook took my surety as truth. He trusts me enough to walk into a potentially dangerous situation because I said we wouldn't be targeted. The knowledge rocks me. I press back against my seat and focus on breathing.

He means it.

He truly means it when he says he wants me for keeps. That he … loves me. He'd never let down his guard this fully outside the bedroom if it wasn't the truth.

I twist in the seat to look at him. "It's a bad idea to love me."

"Maybe." He shrugs a single shoulder. "But I don't think so."

I want to shake him. How can he sit there, so at peace with the emotions that have to be raging inside him? How can he *possibly* be okay with loving me? With cutting himself open for a woman who might walk away the first chance she gets? "What if I leave you and then you've shown your entire ass to your territory? It will weaken your position to make a fool of yourself over a woman, even one you married. Your enemies will use it against you. People could *die*, Hook. What the hell are you thinking?"

"You know what I'm thinking."

His arrogance leaves me breathless. "You can't possibly be that sure of me. I'm not even that sure of myself."

He shrugs again. "Time will tell. We have larger things to worry about now."

That's the damn truth. Larger things like Hades.

And Peter.

CHAPTER 20

*W*ith every step into the Underworld, Tink's tension rises. With every step, I become more fluid, more relaxed. It's easier to respond to a threat when you're not locked in place; a lesson I learned the hard way from my old man a very long time ago.

Meg meets us in the bar. I didn't know what to expect when she called Tink here and had my wife require my presence as well. Pride, maybe. The kind of arrogance I have in spades. None of it is in evidence. Meg looks tired. Really fucking tired.

She glances at me and zeroes in on Tink. "I'm sorry."

"Why are you sorry?" Tink shifts closer to me. I don't think she realizes she's made the move.

Meg sure as shit notices and narrows her eyes. But instead of commenting, she responds to Tink's question. "Our security was bypassed. They wouldn't have been able to do any damage on the upper floors, but we'd put all your packed possessions in the storage room off the garage."

Understanding hits me. The shit we intended to pick up this week. *All* of Tink's shit, aside from the stuff she has stashed at our place. I press my hand to the small of her back, the only support I'm sure she'll allow. "How bad?"

"They destroyed everything." Fury and sorrow comes off Meg in waves. Her hands clench and unclench, and she holds herself just as still as Tink does; as if she wants to offer comfort but knows it won't be accepted. "I'm so sorry. We're working on finding the responsible party, but—"

"There's no need." Tink takes a shuddering breath. She's shutting down, tucking herself behind her massive walls, piece by piece, until there's nothing left but a curious blankness I still sometimes see in my nightmares. She hasn't worn this expression since she was still trapped under Peter's thumb. "It was Peter."

"You can't know that."

"I do know that, Meg." A thread of anger in her voice, but she shuts it down immediately. "He'll come at me in any way he's able to. Since I haven't been available as a target, he went after something that matters to me."

I stroke my hand up her back. I can't help it. She's shuddering the tiniest bit, the only indication of how deep this cut goes. "We'll replace it."

"Don't be absurd. That's five years' worth of investment. Not to mention the commissions I'm going to lose because of the works in progress lost." She shakes her head. "No, this is a blow I won't recover from."

Meg glances at me. "It happened on Underworld property. We failed to protect it, so *we* will replace it."

"Some of those fabrics were custom dyed. It's impossible."

"Tink." I put enough snap in my voice that she finally looks at me. The emptiness in her eyes scares me more than anything to date. It's exactly how she looked at me when I desperately offered her an escape. I keep my tone abrasive. "Stop being such a fucking martyr and accept help that's being offered. This is important to you. We want to help, so let us help."

"It's my problem."

Meg makes a sound perilously close to a snarl, but I'm already talking. "That's bullshit and you know it. We're married, remember? What's yours is mine, baby, and that means he stole from *me*, too. That can't stand, so sit down, shut up, and make a list of what you need to fix it."

Anger flickers across her face, shattering the numbness into a thousand pieces. "Fuck off."

"Get off your ass and make me."

"Children," Meg murmured.

I hold up a hand without looking at her, keeping my focus on Tink. "Don't test me, Tink. I'll have you on your knees and choking on my cock before you can finish the next sentence."

She presses a single finger to the center of my chest. "Try it and see what happens." She bares her teeth at me. "I'm a biter when I'm riled."

I'm aware of Meg watching us closely, ready to step in. I could tell her that her interference is unnecessary, but I won't waste my breath. In the end, I don't give a shit about Meg's comfort. I only care about Tink's.

I can bring her back from the edge. We've already started, though I'm certain she'll slide right back into that numbness the second her mind wanders. Dominating her now will help, but it's a Band-Aid, and it also runs the risk of her checking out completely. No, inciting her to fight me is just as likely to harm as it is to make anything better.

"Give us a minute, Meg." I still don't look over.

Meg hesitates but finally takes a step back. "Mind the cameras." With the reminder that someone will be watching should things get out of hand, she turns and leaves the room.

I barely wait for the door to swing shut to pull Tink into a hug.

Tink goes rigid. "What the hell are you doing?"

"It's called comfort." I don't let go. She's not fighting me; she's fighting herself. I lean down a little and speak directly in her ear. "No one's here but us. You don't have to be strong right now. Let it out."

"Fuck … you." The last word comes out as a sob. Then her arms are around my waist, and she buries her face against my chest.

I hold her as she shakes. She was right before. There's no fixing this completely, even if everything is replaced. What Peter did is a violation as surely as if he reached across the distance and struck her. He'd made her feel *unsafe*.

She fists the fabric of my shirt at my back. "I hate him."

"I know, beautiful girl." I hug her tighter. I might not always say the right thing, but I sure as shit know how to comfort with my body, even when fucking isn't on the table. Sex isn't what she needs right now. She needs someone to lean on, just a little bit, until she gets her feet under her again.

Heaven help Peter once that happens.

I press a kiss to her temple. "We're moving up the timetable."

"I didn't know there *was* a timetable," she says against my chest.

"Give me a little credit."

She hesitates and gives a tiny, pathetic chuckle. "A tiny smidge of credit."

"I'll take what I can get." I don't know what the fuck is wrong with me, but I keep talking. "You can stay here while I handle this."

"*What?*"

I roll right over her protest. "You're safe in my home, but you're safer here."

"Did you miss the part where Peter got to my things *here?*" She clings tighter to me, still twisting the fabric of my shirt. "You asshole, you can't honestly think I'm safer here than I am with you."

"We both know that Hades *and* Allecto are taking this breach personally and will do everything in their considerable power to ensure that it doesn't happen again." Peter wouldn't risk coming here again. *That* I'm sure of.

"You didn't answer my question."

I force myself to take her shoulders and nudge her back a step so she can meet my eyes. "No, Tink. I don't think you're safer anywhere more than you are with me. Because I know for a fact that I'll do whatever it takes, no matter the cost, to keep you that way." I should have stopped ten minutes ago, should have had the control to keep my mouth shut when she's already reeling from me dropping "I love you" this morning. Too fucking much, too fucking soon. I can't seem to help myself when it comes to this woman.

She licks her lips. "You really meant it this morning, didn't you?"

No need to ask for clarification. She's thinking about the same thing I am. "Yes."

"Wow." She huffs out a sad little laugh. "We are so fucked up."

I can't exactly argue the point, but ... "What makes you say that?"

"You insist on seeing parts of me I'm not willing to show anyone, on seeing *me* as a whole. And no matter how often or hard I push you away, you bounce back like a goddamn frisbee."

"Pretty sure frisbees don't bounce."

"I'm not finished." She reaches up and traces her thumb

along my bottom lip, pausing at my piercing before continuing. "I should want a normal person. Maybe not the white picket fence dream, but stability. Someone who isn't a criminal."

"Probably." I can't argue this either. This woman deserves the world. I know I'm not good enough for her. I made my peace with that a long time ago. "But that normal person isn't going to understand you the way I do."

"That's the crux, isn't it?" Her smile turns bittersweet. "When the wolf comes howling for blood at my door, you're the one who will meet him there with an ax. Only a monster can kill a monster."

It stings that she recognizes me as a monster, even if it's the truth. "Yes."

I won't say I wish there was another way. It's worthless to wish on stars. The only thing that matters is action, and I can't bring down Peter through legitimate means. I've tried. Fuck, I tried. He had too many important people on his payroll, people he ensured looked the other way when it came to both his illegal activities and his abusive treatment of the people under his control. The only thing those assholes respect is power and money, so I ensured I had both when I went to take over paying them to look the other way. It makes me no better than he is, but it's a burden I'll have to live with.

I *am* a monster.

Tink nods. "There's no way out but through."

The same conclusion I came to years ago. "Yes." I have to ask, though. I may want her chained to me in every way I can, but I don't want Tink broken. That was never the plan. "If you need to go, I'll find another way."

She looks at me, really looks at me. "So you're going to, what, put me on a train and send me out of Carver City? Maybe give me a pat on the ass for the good fucking in the meantime?" She snorts. "Please. We both know that's not an option."

"Do we?" Why do I keep asking her this shit? I should take her words at face value, but that's the fucking problem. I tied her to me, but I want her to *want* to be there. "I have enough money to get you a fresh start."

She gives a sad little smile. "Haven't you figured it out yet, Jameson? There is no fresh start for me. Wherever I go, whoever I interact with, I'm still *me*. I'm still hauling around all the scars from my past." She presses her fingers to my lips when I start to argue. "I'm staying. Stop wasting time trying to convince me to go and focus all that impressive will of yours on fulfilling your promise to provide me Peter's head on a platter. The sooner the better."

She's still raw, still shaking, but she doesn't look lost any more. I smile against her fingers. "As my lady commands."

CHAPTER 21

TINK

*A*fter ten minutes of arguing, Meg finally allows me to see what Peter did to my things. They were stored in one of the rooms off the garage that the club uses for large shipments before they're organized and sent up to their appropriate destinations.

My belongings are entirely ruined.

I stand in the doorway, conscious of Hook's comforting warmth at my back, and take it in. Peter—or, more likely, his flunkies—went through the space with a vengeance. My backup sewing machine is in a thousand smashed pieces. My chest gets tight just looking at it. It was the first purchase I made for myself after I saved up from working at the Underworld. The first thing in this world that was truly mine that no one could take away.

Except Peter has done exactly that.

I drag my gaze away, taking in the bolts of fabric. They didn't bother ripping or cutting them. They simply dumped some kind of chemical all over everything. It looks like Drano; something thick and blue and impossible to clean.

My actual clothes ... They set them on fire.

Hook takes my shoulder. "Enough."

I want to fight him out of the sheer perversity of doing it, but he's right. Standing here a second longer will only be flogging myself with what I've lost. I can't focus too closely on that. Not if I want to keep moving. "Let's go home."

"Tink." A new voice behind us. I knew he was coming at some point. No way could something like this go down in Hades's place without him making an appearance.

I take a slow breath and turn to face him. He's as perfectly put together as ever in his black on black suit. Hercules stands at his shoulder, and a distant part of me is proud to see that the guy is finally taking my fashion advice and dressing in a way that shows off his impressive physique instead of baggy T-shirts and jeans. He's wearing a suit I designed for him, slate gray over a lighter gray button-up shirt. Hercules opens his mouth, but Hades speaks first. "We will make amends."

Not this again. "It's fine."

"Tink." He sinks enough warning into my name that I have to fight back a shudder. Hades raises his brows. "You know how this works. Pick a fight with your husband if you need to assuage your bruised pride. It's not my concern. This insult done on *my* property is."

His rebuke stings exactly as much as he meant it to. Worse, he's right. Hook's offer to replace everything is surprisingly sweet, no matter the motivation behind it, but I know exactly how much money will be required to balance the scales. Hook has it. No question there. But if I'm really staying, that means looking out for the good of the territory the same way he does. That money can be used in a variety of different ways to benefit the people we protect.

Which means letting Hades foot the bill.

"Fine. I'll send you an itemized list."

"Much obliged." He studies my face before his gaze flicks

to where Hook's hand rests on my shoulder. It's an innocent enough touch, though it's the only thing keeping me anchored in the here and now. Hook's presence is a flame against the night that continues to seek hold inside me. I don't *want* to check out, but the self-defense mechanism isn't something I can fully control. It was the only thing that got me through being trapped with Peter, being able to disassociate enough that he didn't break the last piece of me I held close.

Being in proximity to physical evidence of how he plans to punish me ... I shudder.

Hook squeezes my shoulder. The barest press of his fingers against my skin, but it gives me the strength to meet Hades's gaze. "If that's everything?"

He nods. "Allecto will provide an escort to the border of the Underworld's territory." He turns and heads back toward the elevator.

Hercules steps forward and pulls me into a hug. "Good luck." He releases me immediately as if he's sure I'm going to bite.

Two hugs in one day, three if I'm going to count the one in Hook's bathroom earlier. What the hell is this world coming to?

Meg gives me a brief smile. "Take care of your business, Tink. I expect to hear about it *very soon* over drinks." Then she links her arm through Hercules's and follows Hades through the parking garage to the elevator.

I barely wait for it to close before I turn to Hook. "Let's go." I have to keep moving or I'm going to fall apart. I may be farther from that breaking point than I was thirty minutes ago, but it's still close enough to taste on the back of my tongue.

For once, Hook doesn't have a snarky comment to offer. He simply falls into step next to me. We head to the waiting

187

car and slip into the backseat. Colin's driving, and he takes one look at our faces and apparently decides that conversation can wait.

Hook leans forward between the seats. "They'll provide escort."

A calculated risk—an escort could be translated into us being too weak to protect ourselves—but as long as we're on Underworld territory, we don't have the ability to refuse Hades. Especially when it's a reasonable request.

Still.

The thirty minutes it takes to navigate the traffic back to Hook's building are some of the tensest in recent memory. It's everything I can do to keep my eyes forward and not rubberneck around, looking for an attack. I know it's coming. Peter destroying the majority of my worldly possessions is as much a declaration of war as sending a signed letter. Not knowing when he'll strike? It's enough to drive a person mad.

I jump as Hook laces his fingers through mine. He's not looking at me, his dark gaze intent on the street outside his building. We make it into the parking garage without issue, but he still doesn't relax. Why should he? Peter infiltrated *Hades's* parking garage just hours ago.

Hook waits for Colin to shut off the engine. "Sweep the place starting from the ground up. I don't want anyone in the building who isn't meant to be here. No girlfriends, no boyfriends, no fuck buddies, no delivery people. No one."

"Will do."

He squeezes my hand, and I obey the silent command to follow him out of the car. It's not until the elevator doors slide silently shut that I realize he kept his body between me and the entrance to the street the entire time. Protecting me. I look at our linked hands and tell myself to release him, but my body isn't obeying my mind.

Or maybe I just flat out don't want to.

"This is going to get ugly."

He finally looks at me. "It was always going to get ugly. The only way to eradicate an infection is to lance the wound and dig it out so it can heal cleanly. Peter is a wound in this territory, and I have to bear the burden of letting him live five years ago."

I'm not sure what I'm supposed to say to that. He *did* let Peter live and, yes, that's put a number of people in danger now. But what's the other option? "You're not a cold-blooded killer."

"I wasn't then." His smile is empty and cold. "People change."

The doors open before I can come up with a response to that. We barely make it a single step out before Nigel waylays us. "There's someone here to see you."

"Now's not a good time." Hook shakes his head, already turning away. "Colin is organizing a sweep. I want everyone who isn't ours out."

But Nigel doesn't budge. His expression is more serious than usual. "It's Gaeton." The barest of hesitations. "The Man in Black is dead."

"*What?*" The word escapes before I can wrestle control of my mouth. The Man in Black rules—ruled—the largest slice of Carver City. He's the only one strong enough to manage that much territory without incident, and he's sure as hell the only one capable of holding both Gaeton and Beast's leashes. He's also Isabelle's father.

Hook touches the small of my back. "Send him up in five minutes."

I manage to keep my mouth shut until we're in his room, and then I spin on him. "This is a mess. He's a cornerstone of Carver City. Knock out that leg and the entire thing topples. If someone gets it in their head to test his untried eldest daughter—and they will—it could be a domino effect to send us *all* to war." The only reason the power structure works in this city is because it's perfectly balanced. The small internal squabbles and changing of leaders doesn't make a difference in the overall city because it doesn't affect the overall territory boundaries, so everyone has approximately the same amount of power. There hasn't been a territory grab or a war in … I don't even know. Decades, at least. Since the Man in Black fought and killed the leader of the territory to his eastern border, and brokered with Hades to create the neutral territory in the city center. If someone decides to get greedy now, none of us are safe.

For the first time in a very long time, Hook looks tired. Well and truly exhausted. He scrubs his hands over his face. "We should send Gaeton on his way. We have enough to worry about without getting pulled into whatever the hell is going on in that territory with the old man's death." The words seem to bring him no pleasure. He speaks them because it's the smart thing to do.

Neither of us has been all that good at doing the smart thing.

I cover Hook's hands with mine and lace my fingers through his. "He's your friend. He's my friend, too." Admitting that someone is my friend gets easier every time I do it. Gaeton may not be on the same level as the ladies in the Underworld, but he *is* a friend.

"Yes." The word comes out as a sigh.

I squeeze his hands. "The Man in Black was like a father to him. He'll be grieving."

"*You're* grieving right now."

He's not wrong but focusing on Gaeton's pain is so much easier than dealing with the fight barreling down on us. I manage a small smile. "Then it sounds like comfort is the name of the game tonight."

Hook frowns, but there's no time to question me further, because the door opens and Gaeton walks in. He barely looks around, just walks straight to the kitchen and finds the liquor cabinet. He's been here before, that Hook trusts him enough to let him into this inner sanctum of sorts. It confirms I'm right about what we need to do.

Gaeton considers the bottle and apparently decides that he's not quite gone enough to drink without a glass. He pulls out three and sets them on the marble counter with a clink. "You heard."

"We heard." The exhaustion is gone from Hook's face. He doesn't quite have his charming rogue mask in place, but he's pulled back. I didn't realize how much he allows me to see until I watch him tuck away bits of himself.

He pauses to give my hand a squeeze that could mean absolutely anything and then tows me to the kitchen. Gaeton pours steep shots into each glass and sets the bottle down hard enough that I fear it might shatter. "We knew he was sick, but we'd half convinced ourselves that the old bastard would outlive both of us."

No need to read between *those* lines. Gaeton and Beast. Beast and Gaeton. A hostile and yet strangely symbiotic relationship if ever there was one. I can't pretend to know Beast's mind, but the best I can tell, Man in Black looked at both of them as the sons he never had.

"I'm sorry." I don't know what to do with my hands. I might have crossed into being a person that accepts hugs as comfort, but I don't know how to offer them. I'm not even sure Gaeton will accept that from me. Or if it would actually help.

Hook doesn't have my confusion. He simply takes the shot with Gaeton and pulls the big man into a hug. "I'm sorry, too."

I stare at them, at this man who cares *so fucking much*

about the people he considers his. It might not always be the right thing, but the way Gaeton holds him, It's the right thing right now. My heart lodges in my throat and, yes, no matter how strange it feels to admit it ... This is love, isn't it?

I love Hook.

I don't know what I'm supposed to do with that information, so I shove it down deep to inspect later and take my shot.

Hook shifts away to take Gaeton's face in his hands. "What do you need?"

Gaeton tries for a smirk, but it doesn't quite stick. "You sure I'm not here for political reasons?"

Hook's lazy grin has my heartbeat picking up. He traces the other man's cheekbones with his thumbs. "You're here because you need to stop thinking, and you trust us to make that happen, so stop dicking around and answer the question. What do you need?"

Gaeton's breath catches. "I can't turn my fucking head off, man. I just want some peace for a little while."

"Tell me your safe word."

"Rose."

"Good boy." Hook releases him and turns to me. Tenderness filters into his dark gaze, and he takes my left hand and presses a kiss to my knuckles next to my ring. "And what do you need, beautiful girl? Watch or participate?"

I can't quite take a full breath. "You're asking what we need. But what about you?" I don't know if I've ever asked a Dom that question before. It never occurred to me that I should, but Hook isn't just any Dom. He's mine.

He gifts me with a soft smile. "I want to fuck Gaeton's ass while he eats your pussy, and then I want to sleep." He lifts his voice the smallest amount. "You're invited to stay until morning, of course."

"No promises. Let's just see where the night takes us." He glances at me. "Depending on if Tink is cool with it."

Fondness wells up in my chest. Gaeton might be a full-fledged asshole most of the time, but he truly is a friend. What a novel concept. I lean around Hook to shoot him a look. "Only if you're not a cover hog."

He grins, a little of his normal arrogance appearing. "I'm as hot as a furnace. You won't need any fucking covers with me in your bed."

"Promises, promises." I switch my attention to Hook. "I want what you want. I trust you to get us there." Does he understand the implication of what I'm telling him? I've always trusted him within a scene, but this feels different. Because it *is* different.

He's silent for a long moment, studying me as if he can see the very answers written on my soul. Finally he leans down and presses a soft kiss to my lips. "Then let's begin."

CHAPTER 22

HOOK

I consider Gaeton and Tink. As much as I want to get right down to business, there are other matters I can't shuck off tonight. "Strip. Shower." I level a look at Gaeton. "You can tease her, but no coming." I turn the same look on Tink. "The same goes for you."

She gives me a saucy smile. "I'll try to remember that order. Don't be gone too long." No questioning that I have to leave for a moment. She knows that Colin is sweeping the building, just like she knows I'll need that report before I can finally devote my full attention to the pair of them. It's been barely thirty minutes, but we have enough men that they should be damn near done. If things have gone terribly wrong and there *is* someone dangerous in here, Gaeton will keep Tink safe. He's brutally efficient when it comes to taking down threats, and he'll protect her.

She jumps when Gaeton slaps her ass, and he booms out a laugh. "Come on, Tink. I can practically hear your pussy calling my name."

"You are so full of shit." She waits for him to walk into the bathroom to lean up and kiss me. "I'll keep him occupied for as long as you need."

Does she realize that she's stepping into the role we spoke about, shifting to act as a partner instead of someone fighting me every step of the way? I'm not sure, but I appreciate it all the same. I take her hips and pull her against me, savoring the contact. "Your sacrifice is duly noted. Try not to come all over his face before I get back."

She laughs, low and wicked. "What happens if I do?"

I turn her around and bring her back flush against my chest. The feel of her in my arms drives me fucking wild, but I muscle down the physical reaction. I can't be walking around with a cockstand while I'm dealing with this bullshit. I nibble on the curve of her ear. "If you disobey me, then I won't let Gaeton come all over you and then fuck you against his chest."

She whimpers and arches back against me, rolling her hips and instinctively seeking my cock. "So rude."

"You love it."

A shaky laugh. "Maybe I do."

I want to look into her words, to demand an explanation about whether they go beneath the surface level. I don't. I just press a kiss to her temple and give her ass a swat. "Don't give him time to think." Distracting Gaeton has the added bonus of distracting Tink. Tonight won't fix the damage Peter did by destroying her things, but it will still be a good thing.

"Yes, Sir!" She puts a little extra sway in her walk as she saunters to the bathroom, and I let her catch me enjoying the view when she glances over her shoulder. "Perv."

"You're putting on such a show. It'd be a shame if I didn't appreciate it."

Tink shakes her head. "Go deal with Colin. We'll be here

when you're done." Then she's gone, and I hear the low murmur of Gaeton's voice and the shower turning on.

I don't want to leave. But the sooner I'm gone, the sooner I can get back.

I find Nigel in his office down on the main floor. For the first time in a very long time, he's not perfectly put together. His hair is more mussed from running his fingers through it than by design, and his clothes are rumpled. He looks up as I cross the threshold. "We're clear."

"He's already done?"

"Yeah. It was all hands on deck. We've shut down the exits and closed the gate in the garage. Colin is sweeping that one last time, just in case." Nigel sinks heavily into the chair across from my desk. "How long do you think we have?"

"I'm drawing him out tomorrow. One way or another." I haven't talked about it with Tink, but we can't keep going like this. Peter has already proven he'll indulge in guerrilla warfare. The only people who will be hurt by a prolonged siege are the innocent ones.

"You sure about this?"

No. Not even a little bit. I know I can take Peter in a fair fight, but the man is incapable of fighting any way but dirty. He won't come at me from the front, no matter how pissed he is. I don't know if I can beat him, but I can't tell that to Nigel. I can't tell it to *anyone*. They need to believe in victory. In me. "Yes."

Nigel looks at me for a long moment. "I have your back. No matter how this plays out."

"I appreciate you, cousin."

He shakes his head. "Yeah, yeah. We have this covered. Go back to your woman and that asshole Gaeton."

"Actually—"

"Hook." He crosses his arms over his chest. "You don't

have to carry the world on your shoulders. We can handle this tonight. Fuck, cousin, *let* us handle it."

I finally nod. He's right. Maybe I micromanage shit too much. I don't know. It's hard not to wade in and do shit myself. They put so much faith in me to lead them. I want to be worthy of that. "Call if you need anything."

Nigel rolled his eyes. "We'll see you in the morning. Get out of here."

This time, I don't argue.

I don't allow my pace to increase as I head back up to my suite. Anticipation is just as important as allowing my people to see me. They've mostly retreated to their individual apartments, but I catch Colin on the way back down. He gives me a tight nod. "We have this covered."

"Thanks." I clasp him on the shoulder and keep moving.

The first thing I see when I walk into my suite is the outline of Gaeton and Tink against the glass of the shower. They're obviously putting my hot water to the test. I sit on the bed and pull off my boots and socks and then simply watch for a few moments.

Tink has her hands braced against the tile, each finger a clear outline in contrast of the hazy image of their bodies. Even so, I can see Gaeton bent over Tink, one hand cupping her breast and the other between her thighs. It's not exactly easy to forget how huge Gaeton is, but there's something about seeing him wrapped up in smaller people that does shit for me.

I grab a condom from my nightstand and stroll into the bathroom to lean against the wall, just outside the tile of the shower. "You've been busy."

Gaeton shifts easily, rotating so I can see exactly what he's doing to my woman. Her pale skin is flushed, both from the heat of the water and desire. Tink's never quite sweet, but she's almost past the point of mouthing off right now, her eyes half shut and her lips parted as her breath shudders out. "You were taking too long."

"Mmmm." I cross my arms over my chest and make a show of raking them with my gaze from their feet to the tops of their heads. I've watched Gaeton scene with Tink before, watched him make her come until she screamed herself hoarse. It made me so jealous, I couldn't see straight, knowing she allowed him a closeness she'd never allow me. The jealousy no longer applies. She's mine, by choice and by vow.

I always was a sharer.

"Gaeton." I put enough snap in my voice to draw his head up. "Sit on the shower bench."

It takes him a moment to disentangle himself from Tink, and I allow it. We both watch him stalk to the bench and sink onto it, sprawling on it with his big thighs spread, his massive cock at attention.

Tink gives herself a little shake and focuses on me. I like that she looks to me first even though he just had his fingers in her pussy. It's such a small thing, but it feels momentous. A clear indication of how things have shifted between us.

I hold up the condom. "Do you want Gaeton's giant cock, beautiful girl?"

She licks her lips. "Do *you* want me to want Gaeton's giant cock, Sir?"

Fuck, I love this woman. "Yes. I want to watch you ride his cock, knowing it's a gift I'm only too happy to give you." I grin and rip open the condom wrapper and then hold it out to her. "Give me a show and I might just let him make you orgasm."

"You're too kind." She's a little too breathy to make the sarcasm work. She carefully takes the condom from me, but doesn't immediately move to Gaeton. Tink tilts her head back, her eyes flaring in challenge. "Maybe it's not *me* you have to worry about coming without permission."

"I heard that," rumbles Gaeton. "Get that fine ass over here, Tink. I'm dying to fill you up."

She shivers, but her attention is entirely on me. I touch her chin with a single fingertip and she eagerly goes up on her toes as I guide her mouth to mine. All the bullshit waiting for us tomorrow falls away at the first brush of her lips, at the way she eagerly opens to me. I allow myself to sink into the kiss until Tink moans and reaches for me.

I catch her wrists and turn her around. "Gaeton is feeling left out."

"I can see that," she murmurs.

He creates quite the picture, and he's vain enough to know it. He looks like some kind of warrior that wandered into the wrong century, his body giving the impression of someone who *works* instead of spending a hell of a lot of time in the gym. Hair dusts his chest and descends to his solid stomach, its trail leading the eye right to his cock. Long and thick and more than ready.

As I eye-fuck him, he gives his cock a rough stroke. "Don't mind me." He gives a lopsided grin. "I'm just enjoying the view."

"Now," I murmur in her ear. "Give me a good show, beautiful girl."

"Yes, Sir." She walks slowly to Gaeton, and fuck, the shows starts before she ever touches him. Tink was made to be put on display, her curves inviting a look, a touch, a need to hold her and never let go.

She bends over Gaeton, and my breath catches in my throat at the glimpse of her pussy. My woman knows it, too, and takes her time rolling the condom over his cock before she slowly rises.

I have to work to keep my voice from going hoarse with need. "Gaeton. I want her on your lap, facing me."

He loops an arm around her waist before I've finished speaking, dragging her onto his lap and spreading her legs to hook on the outside of his thighs. I will be able to see every inch of him sinking into her from this angle. Perfect.

Tink braces herself on his thighs and lifts her hips enough that he can notch his cock at her entrance. "Slowly," I grind out. "Take him slow."

My whole body goes tight at the sight of his cock sinking into her pussy. At the sound of Tink's little gasp. At the way Gaeton's big hands flex on her hips like he can't decide if he wants to slam into her or slow her down so it never stops. Inch by inch, he disappears into her until he's sheathed to the hilt.

I somehow drag my gaze to Tink's face to find her watching me, lust written across her features. I let her see my appreciation. "Ride him, beautiful girl."

She leans back against Gaeton's broad chest and lifts one hand to the back of his thick neck for leverage. And then she begins to ride him. Long, slow rolling strokes that have me fighting the desire to stride into the shower and join in. Gaeton's getting off on the show just as much as Tink is, his dark eyes watching me just as closely.

Waiting for my next command.

"Her breasts, Gaeton. Pinch her nipples the way she likes."

He obeys immediately, her breasts filling his hands. Tink moans and slams down on him. She seems to fight to keep her eyes open, to keep her gaze on me. I'm all too willing to reward her for that. "Now her clit. Gentle, Gaeton. Tease her."

"I don't want gentle," she gasps out.

"I know."

Gaeton rumbles a laugh and obeys. He presses two

fingers to her clit. Not circling, not stroking; just applying something for her to grind against as she fucks him. But every time Tink tries to chase that pleasure, he shifts a little away. Denying her as I ordered.

Her eyes go a little wild, and she grabs his wrist with her free hand, trying to force him closer. She knows it's not a fight she can win, but that doesn't stop her from straining to get him the last millimeter closer to where she needs his touch. *"Please."* She fucks him harder, lifting nearly completely off his cock before slamming back down. It's not enough, not without that last bit of stimulation. "Fuck. *Fuck.* Please, Jameson. Please let me come."

I will never get enough of this woman begging. For how sweet the jolt of power is, yes, but also for the clear indication of her trust. Tink doesn't beg for anyone, but she does for me.

My cock is so hard, I'm distantly worried that it will split the seams of my jeans. We're almost there. Just a little longer. "Gaeton."

He's watching me with just as much lust, just as much anticipation as she is. We all know this is only the warm up. The main event is still to come. Just like Tink is. "Make her orgasm. Don't follow her over the edge."

"Yes, Sir," he grinds out.

Tink's gasp is filled with elation. She moans and grinds down hard on Gaeton's cock as he finally strokes her clit like she needs. "Thank you, thank you, *thank you.*" She's wound tightly already, and it doesn't take long before her back bows hard enough that Gaeton has to band an arm across her chest to keep her in place as she comes. It's *my* name on her lips as her orgasm takes her. I've never heard anything sweeter. She might only let down her barriers enough to call me Jameson when she's on the edge of oblivion, but she still does it.

I turn off the water and walk into the shower. The tiles

are warm against my bare feet, but I barely notice. My entire attention is wrapped up in these two. Gaeton guides Tink to her feet and holds her as she wobbles. I don't hesitate to scoop her into my arms and turn for the door. "Come."

"Just did." She laughs, sounding punch-drunk. "Fuck, that was good."

"We're not done yet, beautiful girl." I head straight to the bed and carefully set her on it. "Back against the headboard. Use some pillows and get comfortable."

She hesitates. "Do I get your cock tonight?"

I lace my fingers through her hair and pull her in until I'm speaking against her lips. "You get my cock whenever you want, however you want. But first I'm going to give it to Gaeton. I think he deserves a reward, don't you?"

She shivers. "I suppose I could get on board with watching that."

"Tink." I put a little censure into my tone. "It's a reward. Do you know what Gaeton loves just as much as getting his ass pounded?"

The man himself answers. "Oral sex."

"He's going to eat my pussy as long as you fuck him. Just like you promised that first night." Tink smiles slowly, her eyes lighting up. Greedy girl.

I don't look back him. "Yes." I lick her bottom lip. "Consider this permission to come as many times as you're capable."

"Is that a reward or a punishment?"

I laugh darkly. "You'll find out soon enough."

CHAPTER 23

TINK

This whole thing feels like a fever dream. Gaeton crawling across the bed to settle between my thighs. Hook kneeling at his back with a bottle of lube and a heated look in his eyes. He smooths a hand down Gaeton's back and then squeezes and parts his ass cheeks. My angle isn't quite right to see everything, but I can't find the breath to say much as Gaeton drags his tongue over my pussy. The way he growls against my skin, there's absolutely no doubt that he's enjoying it just as much as I am. I've never met a person who loves oral sex on quite the same level as Gaeton. It's damn near a fetish.

Hook urges Gaeton's hips up a little, and he is all too happy to comply. It bends his back in a way that has my body clenching. I watch Hook's expression, the concentration as he spreads lube over Gaeton's ass and then rolls a condom over his cock. They've done this before, but he's too methodical to take anything for granted.

Or that's what I think until Hook slams into Gaeton hard enough to drive his face against my pussy. Gaeton curses, and then there's no more time for talking. Hook gives several rough strokes and smacks Gaeton's ass. "Don't you dare come. Not until I'm finished with you."

Gaeton murmurs his assent against my clit. He goes after me with a ferocity that leaves me breathless. I can do nothing but cling to him and enjoy the ride. I've been in threesomes—and moreseomes—before, but this feels different. It's more than Hook dominating both Gaeton and me. As I meet his gaze over Gaeton's back, it feels like …

Almost like we're a team. Like we're taking our pleasure, yes, but also acknowledging that this is as much about Gaeton's comfort as it is about some kinky good times. I've never felt that before. It's always been me against the world, frantically scrambling to patch up the holes in my worn walls, a never-ending effort to keep the dangerous sea of emotions and caring for other people out. It never quite worked, but this is different. Maybe it's always been different with Hook.

He sinks fully into Gaeton and drags his hand down the other man's back. Gentling him. Tormenting him. "She tastes good, doesn't she? Like a little bit of paradise, right there on your tongue." The tiniest of pumps. "Suck on her clit. You know the way she likes it."

Gaeton obeys without hesitation, completely lost in Hook's commands. He *does* know the way I like it, and pleasure has me shaking. The look on Hook's face has me shaking even harder. He's watching my expression, and there is a world of possession and lust and something like joy in his dark eyes. "Come for me, beautiful girl."

Come for me.

Because Gaeton's tongue is simply an extension of Hook's will. I don't know why that's so sexy, but the knowledge crashes over me, and then I'm doing exactly as he commands. I dig my heels into the mattress and arch up. Gaeton meets me there, letting me fuck his face as I orgasm.

"That's right. Just like that." Gaeton is too big for Hook to be able to touch me in our current position, but his voice does the work for him, licking along my exposed skin, a pleasure so acute I can barely handle it. He slaps Gaeton's ass. "Slow. Tease her back to the edge." His grin is downright wicked. "Try not to get too distracted by my cock in your ass."

Gaeton's laugh rumbles through my lower half, and he rests his forehead against my lower stomach. "Do your worst, Hook." He sounds a little hazy, as if he's drunk. I've seen Gaeton down half a fifth and be no worse for wear, so it's not the single shot that's put him in this headspace. It's Hook. The dance of dominance and submission, the cascading relief of handing the decisions to another person for a little while. And pleasure. So much pleasure.

Hook gives a laugh of his own. "Don't worry. I will." And then he starts to move. To fuck Gaeton in a relentless pounding rhythm that has the other man's hands spasming on my hips, his breath harsh against my pussy.

They're so beautiful, I can't stand it. Gaeton is like some massive canvas that's been laid out for our pleasure, and even as he keeps my hips caged, he's not really in charge. Behind him, Hook moves in rough strokes that put every muscle beneath his medium brown skin in stark relief. He's not holding back. He's not afraid he's going to break Gaeton. He knows the other man can take everything he has to give, and he's fully intending to push him right to the edge.

"Fuuuuuuck."

Hook's laugh is pure evil. "Sounds like you're distracted, my friend."

Gaeton shakes his head, the move dragging his mouth across my sensitive flesh. "Not even a little."

"Mmm." Hook barely pauses in his rhythm. "If you can't multitask, I'll have to slow down."

Gaeton moves so fast, I let loose a squeak of surprise. He wedges his hands under my ass and lifts me to his face. There is no finesse in this tongue fucking. Desperation drives him, and it's a heady thing to be on the receiving end of.

"Do you want to fuck her again?" Hook drops the words like a well-timed bomb. Gaeton lifts his head and blinks at me with pleasure-drugged eyes. Hook doesn't miss a single beat. "Do you want to sink into that tight pussy while I'm balls deep in your ass?"

"Yeah," Gaeton grinds out.

Hook lets the silence spin out between us, anticipation building with each second that ticks past. His arrogant smile hits me a beat before his answer. "No." He grips the bigger man's shoulder and thrusts deep. He can't quite reach Gaeton's ear from his position, but that doesn't stop him. "But I'll let her stroke your cock, my friend. I'll let her tell you where she wants you to come."

Gaeton is staring at me like he's seen the sun, as if he's not seeing me at all, but something far beyond the confines of this room. "She loves that shit."

"Yes. She does." Hook looks up and holds my gaze. "Tell us, beautiful girl. Where do you want Gaeton's come?"

Sheer lust weighs down my tongue, and it takes me several tries to speak. "My breasts."

Calculation flickers through Hook's dark gaze, and I know without a shadow of a doubt that he's going to make a mess of me tonight. Of all three of us.

I can't fucking wait.

Hook smacks Gaeton's hip. "Back."

It takes a little maneuvering, but we end up with them standing next to the bed, Gaeton bent over and bracing his hands on the mattress, me on my knees before him. He's tall enough to make it work, and I give myself a moment to just enjoy the sight of his big cock. I give him a stroke, but it's not right. "Hook."

I can't see him, but I don't have to in order to hear the satisfaction in his voice. "You want to suck him."

No lies between us. Not tonight. It doesn't even occur to me to try. "Yes, Sir."

"Do it."

I take Gaeton into my mouth and he shudders. Whether it's from my tongue against the underside of his cock or the fact that Hook's resumed brutally fucking him, I have no idea. It doesn't matter. As Hook said, this is comfort.

I lose myself in sucking Gaeton's cock. I've had some practice, but it's still a hell of a job, and my jaw begins to ache. His rough curse brings me up short. "Tink, now."

I barely get my mouth off him in time. He comes across my chest in great spurts and, holy shit, it feels dirty and decadent and oh so wrong. I shiver a little and give him one last stroke before I slump back against the mattress.

The position gives me an idea, though. I run one hand over Gaeton's thick thigh and reach between their spread legs with my other to cup Hook's balls. His strangled curse makes me smile.

At least until his voice lashes me. "Gaeton, on the bed. Tink, on your feet."

I scramble to obey. I'm sticky and a little sore, but we're not through yet. Hook tumbles Gaeton onto the mattress on his back and grips me by the back of my neck. Not hard enough to hurt, but a steadying rock-solid contact. He moves closer behind me, not quite enough to touch, but I swear I can feel the heat rolling off his body. "Are you sated, beautiful girl?"

Again, it doesn't even register that I should lie. "No." I lick my lips. "I don't know if I ever will be." Not when it comes to everything Hook seems determined to give me. I want to soak up his attention, his touch, his *love* until it fills me to the brim and chases away the last of the shadows lingering in my soul.

He gives my neck a light squeeze and lifts his voice. "And you, Gaeton?"

The big man stretches and gives a lazy grin that always means he's up to no good. "Dawn's a long way off yet."

Hook taps my jaw. "You can play for a minute. Make it count."

No mistaking his meaning. I crawl onto the bed and kneel between Gaeton's thighs. A quick glance over my shoulder shows Hook walking into the bathroom, likely to clean up. Anticipation zings through me, the feeling only getting stronger as I lean down and take Gaeton into my mouth. He's easier to manage now that he's not hard, and I take my time exploring him with my tongue. Enjoying myself.

It doesn't take long before his cock hardens. Gaeton always did have the stamina of a bull. I look up to find him lacing his hands behind his head and watching me with hooded eyes. "You look happy, Tink."

I don't bother to reply. He might just be running his mouth. It's also possible that he's testing for information. I don't *think* Gaeton would pull some shit like that, but we live in strange times.

Unsurprisingly, he doesn't seem to need a response. His gaze follows my lips as I suck him deep. "He's good for you. You're good for him, too."

That's about enough of that. I rise off his cock enough to frown at him. "Do you want a blow job or do you want to wax poetic about my potential relationship status?"

"Nothing potential about it." He jerks his chin to my hand fisted around his cock, the diamond twinkling obscenely in the lamp light. "You're married now, Tink. Call me sentimental, but I'd like to think you're happily married."

"Is there any such thing in our world?" I don't know why I'm entertaining this. Hook will be back any second, and this is *not* part of the scene.

Or maybe it is and I'm just skittish enough to want to avoid it.

Gaeton chuckles. "Don't ask me. I'm shit at relationships. Only one I ever wanted went down in flames because she couldn't choose." He shakes his head. "That's some fucked up shit."

I have my own thoughts about the Gaeton-Isabelle-Beast love triangle, but ultimately it's none of my business. I can see the attraction of both men, but the way Isabelle handled the situation was shitty. Then again, I'm biased as hell. I have absolutely no business offering love life advice but ... "World hasn't ended yet, Gaeton. You obviously still love her. Do something about it."

He raises his brows. On the surface, he still looks like the good old boy he mostly pretends to be, but now something dangerous lurks in his dark eyes. "Leave it alone, Tink. I'm not in the mood tonight."

"You're never in the mood." I give his cock a squeeze. "But I'll make you a deal: you stop trying to divine what the fuck is going on with me and Hook, and I'll stop giving you relationship advice."

He finally nods. "Point taken." Gaeton jerks his chin. "Now get back to sucking my cock like a good little cum slut."

I don't need to be told twice.

I'm so busy following that order, I don't hear Hook come back into the room until he gently touches my hip. He trails his fingers over my ass and down to my thighs. A slight pressure that is a silent command I'm only too happy to obey. I spread for him.

And then his cock is there, sliding into my pussy in a way

that feels like coming home. I can't explain it. I'm not sure I want to. Hook fucks me in a lazy rhythm, as if he has all the time in the world, as if he isn't aware how close I am to coming. I can't normally orgasm from penetration alone, but after a few times, that rule no longer applies.

He braces his hand against the small of my back, pressing me down a little and then, holy shit, he's hitting my G-spot with each stroke. I don't want it to end, but I can't hold out any longer. I cry out around Gaeton's cock as I come. Several rough strokes, then Hook pulls out and comes across my back.

He winds my hair around his fist and guides me off Gaeton's cock. My body has gone boneless, pleasure making me drunk, and I'm only too happy to slump next to Gaeton's hip while Hook takes Gaeton's cock into his mouth. I lazily reach between them to cup Gaeton's balls, playing them against my palm and drawing my finger along the sensitive flesh behind them.

It's enough.

He orgasms with a muted roar and Hook drinks him down. It's so hot, I can barely stand it. I impulsively kiss him as he comes up, and then I'm in his arms between them, his mouth on mine. And it's perfect.

We stumble to the shower for the second time tonight, though there's little sexual about this. It's pure comfort. Glancing touches. All of us soaping each other up. Hook washing my hair again.

It hasn't *fixed* anything. Not really. Tomorrow, real life will intrude. Gaeton will still be swimming in grief. I'll still be terrified. Hook will still have a crisis on his hands. Somehow, none of that matters in this moment. We've carved out a little space to breathe. If it's temporary, it's no less valuable for it.

"Stay, Gaeton."

Gaeton nods, his eyes already half-shut with sleep. "Yeah, I guess I will."

Hook takes my hand and leads us back into the bedroom. There may only be a few hours left in this night, but we can rest here safely.

That's what he's offered us.

What he's offered me.

Safety.

CHAPTER 24

HOOK

*I*t's late by the time we change the sheets and collapse onto my bed. I'm not surprised Gaeton took me up on the offer to stay overnight, just like I'm not surprised that he wanted to be fucked until he couldn't think straight instead of talking about it. My friend has some shit to work out, but ultimately it's going to be up to him how he handles things. He hits the mattress on the other side of Tink and, within two minutes, his breathing evens out, and he's snoring lightly.

She rolls to face me, though I can't read her expression in the starlight from the windows overhead. "Thank you."

"Don't thank me. I got just as much out of it as you did." I hesitate, but I'm tired and in danger of thinking too hard about tomorrow. In the end, it's the simplest thing in the world to pull Tink to me and arrange her head on my chest. She doesn't tense up like I half expect her to.

"Jameson ..."

Here in the dark, it feels like we've finally turned a corner. I don't know if it's too late. I can't afford to believe that, to let myself be fatalistic. Failure is not an option. Not with so much on the line. I gather her closer and rest my chin on her head, giving her time to get out whatever she's been chewing on for the last few hours.

She shudders out a sigh. "You really don't make this easy."

"Nothing in life is easy, Tink. Least of all people. If it seems like it is, someone's lying."

Strangely enough, that makes her relax. "I don't understand how you always know what to say."

"I don't." Fuck, I definitely don't. I've been in a tailspin for months, my people looking to me for answers that I don't have. I'm doing the best I can, but I'm muddling through like everyone else. I smooth my hand over her hair. "We have a similar way of viewing things once you cut through the bullshit. That's all."

She runs her hand up my chest. A touch not meant to seduce; one simply done for the sake of doing it. "This might sound a little cliché, but I feel like I'm running out of time to say it."

"Tink—"

She touches two fingers to my lips and lifts her head. I still can't see her expression clearly. "I love you, Jameson. It makes me kind of cranky because I didn't plan on this, but it's the damned inconvenient truth."

I don't smile, but it's a near thing. "Loving me is an inconvenient truth."

"Stop being amused."

"Only you would fall kicking and screaming into love and then pout about it." I move her hand from my mouth and press it back to my chest. "We're not running out of time."

I don't have to see her expression clearly to know her mouth has twisted into a frown. "Save your comforting lies for the people who believe it. I know what Peter is capable of better than anyone. Unless you've been hiding things from me, we don't know where he'll strike, only that he's revving up for some kind of attack." She takes a shuddering breath. "Actually, that's a lie. We know exactly where he'll strike. Me."

I frame her face with my hands. Tink never feels fragile, not really. She's too strong, fills a room with her energy too effectively just by walking into it. But at the end of the day, she's only human and she's about to come face-to-face with someone who's done her immeasurable amounts of harm. "I won't let him touch you. I promise."

"Don't make promises you have no way of keeping."

I start to argue, but she kisses me before I can get another word out. It would be the easiest thing in the world to break that kiss, to keep talking in circles until we're both blue in the face. That's not what we need right now. Tomorrow is coming, for better or worse, and neither of us is that good at masking our worry. It's there, a lurking presence that drags its nails along the edges of my mind, a taunting whisper of all the things that can and will go wrong.

Touching her is the only thing that silences it.

I kiss her back with everything I have, taking the comfort she offers and giving it in return. I reach between our bodies, and she lifts herself just enough to give me access without breaking the kiss. Part of me wants to rush this, to lose myself in the feeling of fucking her again and again, until we have no energy left for fear. That can be comfort in its own way, but that's not what I want right now. That's not what she needs. Instead, I tease her, palming her pussy and exploring her with my fingers. Denying us both.

Or at least that's the plan. Tink has other ideas. She grabs my hand and moves it away from her. "I need you."

"Tink."

"I don't want to wait." She presses my hands to either side of my head. Not so much holding me down as giving herself leverage. I could free myself without effort, but I can't quite catch my breath. This isn't domination and submission. This is something else. Something that goes even deeper.

She laces her fingers with mine as she grinds against me, each slide of her pussy against my cock teasing at the possibility of penetration. "You make me lose my mind." Her voice weaves a spell as thoroughly as her slow, rolling movements. "This shouldn't work. *We* shouldn't work."

It takes everything I have not to grab her hips and slide her onto my cock. To maintain stillness and let her guide us. "Who gives a fuck about 'should,' beautiful girl? We work. It's enough."

"It's enough." She does another of those hip rolls that has my cock notching at her entrance. I hold my breath, my body a single line of tension as she keeps us hovering on the precipice. Tink's laugh is breathy and a little amazed. "I really do love you, Jameson. I really, really do." She slams down onto me, taking my cock in a single stroke even as she takes my mouth in a kiss that leaves me dizzy.

This woman might kill me, but what a fucking way to go.

She moves her hands to tangle in my hair, and that's all the encouragement I need to stroke up her thighs to her hips and ass, squeezing and urging her to move. Then there is no more need for words. We've said all there is to say; we're both content to let our bodies continue the conversation.

She rides me slowly and kisses me like she'll never get enough. That makes two of us. I can't touch her enough, can't keep my hands still. I want everything. Fucking *everything*.

When Tink comes, she does it with my name on her lips, a soft moan that I drink down like the best kind of whiskey. I want to hang on, to make this last, but she feels too good, and this is too important. Pleasure shoots down my spine, and then it's too late to worry about anything but the orgasm turning me wild, pounding into her from below with a single-mindedness I can't shake. I don't bother to try.

We lay tangled together as our heartbeats return to a normal pace. "Stay with me. Stay married to me."

She gives a little laugh. "Most people would hear 'I love you' and start making assumptions."

Most people don't know Tink as well as I do. "Stay with me," I repeat. I cuddle her closer and play my last card. "Marry me again. Big church wedding and all that shit. Spend a couple years solidifying our power structure in this place, getting us as far out of the criminal shit as we can manage." I pause, all too aware that she hasn't taken a breath since I started talking. I should leave it at that. It's a lot to dump on her all at once, but hope is a treacherous and slippery slope. "Have a family with me. Make a *home* with me."

She exhales slowly. Carefully. "It's really shitty of you to start dangling that kind of thing in front of me. We don't even know if we're going to survive the next week."

"Yes, we do. We're going to remove that bastard, and we're going to win." If I say it enough times, it will be true. We will win tomorrow without any losses. We will embark on a future together that I want more than I've wanted anything in my life.

"Jameson."

Every time she says my name, it's like she's reaching right into my chest and giving my heart a squeeze. "I wouldn't say it if I didn't mean it."

"I know." She lifts her head enough to give me a ghost of a smile. The fact I can see her expression more clearly now means the moon has once again fled the sun. Dawn isn't quite here, but it's close.

She reaches up and runs her fingers through my hair. "Wanting a family is what got me into this mess to begin with."

"No, *Peter* is what got you into this mess." I make a face.

"Well, Peter, then Hades, and now me. He used your hope against you."

"And you aren't?"

The comment stings, but it's a fair question. I shift her closer, enjoying the way she fits against me. "You know who my father was."

She blinks, obviously thrown by what appears to be a change in subject. "Only in passing. He was one of Peter's generals. Peter kept me away from most everyone."

"He was about what you'd expect." Not as bad as some. If there's a ranking of shitty parents, Hugh Hook lands somewhere in the middle. He only roughed me up a handful of times and was usually just a sloppy drunk, not a mean one. But he ran my mother out of town at some point when I was young enough to only have flashes of memories, and he ensured that the apartment we lived in, no matter how nice, was littered in figurative eggshells I had to navigate whenever he was home and conscious.

Tink frowns. "You mean he wasn't winning any father of the year awards."

"No. Not by any stretch of the imagination." I don't bother to try for a smile. I'm not trying to charm her. I'm dead fucking serious about this. "I want a home, Tink. You know what I mean when I say that. A real home, not just a nice fucking place to sleep. I have my cousins and the people who have become family over the last few years, but I want a *family*."

Her lip quivers the tiniest bit. "You know there's no guarantee I can pop out a few kids. That's not always how the world works."

The fact she's arguing this means she wants it just as much as I do. She's just afraid to grab it with both hands, and with good reason. She's been slapped down so many times over the years. Tink deserves a win. That's not always how

217

the world works, but it's how *our* world is going to work. "I want you, beautiful girl. I *love* you. The rest will fall into place as it's supposed to, regardless of what form that takes. Maybe we work on getting you pregnant and, as you said, popping out a few kids. Maybe we adopt. Maybe we change our minds about kids and get a small pack of dogs instead. The only rules are the ones we make."

"Just like that."

"Just like that."

She frowns harder and finally sighs. "Can we talk about this after we get through the next hurdle? I don't think I'm superstitious, but I'm about to find some salt to throw over my shoulder or something because I don't want to jinx us." She shifts against me and rests her head on my chest. "I'm afraid to want what you're offering."

"I know." I press a kiss to the top of her head. "But you're right. We'll talk about it when the future is cleared of this last barricade." Of Peter. His death won't magically fix all the issues in this territory, but it will remove the leader the dissenting voices are trying to rally behind. Without Peter pushing things forward, I'll have time to actually fix things here. Our operations will never go completely clean. Even with all the money in the world, if we go completely legit, someone else will try to move in. Finding the right balance is a challenge I can't think too hard about because there's still so much to be done to get us to that point.

"Jameson?"

"Yeah?"

"Thank you for tonight. It doesn't magically make the pain go away, but it was exactly the distraction I needed."

"Anything for you."

I hold her as her breathing evens out, nearly matching Gaeton's on the other side of her. In the morning, the big man will be off to fight his own battles, but he sleeps in the safety of my bed now because it *is* safe. If we ever go to war with—Well, it's not the Man in Black's territory anymore. I suspect it will pass to his eldest daughter, Cordelia.

She and her wife will hold the center, though I shudder to think about going up against them. I've only met Cordelia a handful of times, and she's easily as ruthless and ambitious as her father was. Her wife, Muriel? People who cross Cordelia have a way of disappearing, and I am nearly certain it's her wife behind it. One wouldn't know that they're a pair of the most dangerous people in Carver City when standing next to them, watching them make eyes at each other.

Cordelia is the eldest, the most ambitious, the leader, but she's arguably not the most dangerous of the Belmonte daughters. The middle, Sienna, is a certifiable genius and one of the coldest people I've ever met. The only exception to her icy attitude is her sisters, and her husband who's a startlingly normal guy. And the youngest? I look at Gaeton, relaxed in sleep. Isabelle Belmonte might seem like a nice girl, but she's playing a dangerous game with Beast and Gaeton and doesn't seem to care.

No, it's in everyone's best interest if the inheritance of power happens seamlessly. There have been too many changes lately in the city. All it takes is someone rocking the boat, and we'll all end up underwater.

I cuddle Tink closer and close my eyes. Dawn is nearly here, and we have more than enough problems without borrowing from the future. We'll figure it the fuck out.

We don't have another choice.

CHAPTER 25

TINK

*I*f not for the delicious ache in my body when I wake up alone in Hook's bed, I could almost convince myself I imagined everything that happened last night. Not the sex. No, the scariest thing that happened last night was admitting my feelings to Hook. They aren't going away, and that terrifies me. I don't know if we're going to live past the confrontation with Peter that's barreling down on us.

The possibility of a future? A *family?*

If I reach for it, grasp it with too much enthusiasm, will the universe respond favorably? Or will it kick me in the teeth for having the audacity to believe I deserve a happily ever after?

The only way to know for sure is to jump and hope I learn to fly on the way down.

Hook walks out of the bathroom. He's got on slacks and nothing else and seeing his bare feet peeking out from beneath the black fabric feels strangely intimate. Silly considering everything we've shared in less than a week, but the strangest things become kicks to the chest with this man.

He studies me in that way of his, as if he knows I'm sitting in his giant bed and having a silent freak-out. "You want to talk about it?"

"I don't believe in happily ever after." As soon as I blurt out the words, I feel foolish. I don't know what I want him to say. I'm precariously perched on a cliff edge, and one word will send me back to safe ground, and a different one will push me right over the edge. I don't know what I want. I don't know what I *need*.

Hook turns, freeing me from his gaze, and pulls open one of the wardrobes. All his clothing was cleaned in record time and put away the day after I sent it to be dry cleaned, though I have no confidence it will stay that way. This man is a hurricane in motion. He shrugs into a cream button-down and does it up with deft fingers. "There's no such thing."

My heart sinks, even as I tell myself that to be grateful he's being honest with me. "Oh."

Hook crosses to the bed and holds out a hand. "All the stories end with the villain vanquished and the happy couple riding off into the sunset. That's what happily ever after is. They never have to work on their relationship, never have to get their hands dirty when facing the challenges living a full life creates. They're caught in stasis, without conflict, without problems, without *life*. That's no way to live."

I blink. Of all the things I expected him to say, this isn't one of them. "You read a lot of fairy tales, Hook?"

"Don't do that." He gives me a tug, and I climb gracelessly to my feet. "When I say I love you, and I want a life with you as my wife, I mean a *life*, Tink. The problems and the victories and the day-to-day mundane bullshit. I want everything." Another tug closes the distance between us, and then I'm pressed against his chest. He skates a hand down my spine and gives my ass a squeeze. "That's better than any fictional happily ever after, don't you think?"

"How can you be so damn confident all the time?" I whisper. Compared to him, I'm wobbling on my feet like some unsteady newborn creature.

He shakes his head. "It's not confidence, beautiful girl. It's the truth, and I try to always be honest with you." He grimaces a little. "At least since we've been married."

The caveat gives me pause. I lean back and narrow my eyes. "You would have saved me anyways, even without the ring."

For the first time in a long time, he actually looks a little uncomfortable and won't quite meet my gaze. "Maybe."

"Jameson," I say his name slowly, enjoying watching him fidget. "Are you sure you're really the monster you claim? Because I think you might have a tarnished suit of armor stuffed in that wardrobe somewhere."

He kisses me, a deep, rough kiss that has me weaving on my feet. Hook lifts his head before I'm ready for it to end. "Get ready, beautiful girl. Wear comfortable shoes."

Because I might be running for my life before the day is through.

The thought weighs down the lightness in my chest brought on by his words. I grab his hand and give it a squeeze. "I want to live not-happily-ever-after with you, Jameson."

His grin is blinding. "I love you."

"I love you, too." The words feel strange on my tongue but not entirely unpleasant.

I rush through getting ready, moving quickly to avoid thinking too intensely about what comes next. I opt for comfort, slicking my hair back into a ponytail and pulling on a pair of jeans and one of my graphic T-shirts. Boots round out the outfit. I stare down at them, wishing that they were steel-toed instead. The thought brings a hysterical giggle to my lips. What would I do with steel-toed boots? I might be a fighter in the survival sense, but when it comes to actual combat, I'm a flail-violently-and-hope-for-the-best kind of woman.

Why the hell didn't I pick up some kind of training in the last five years? Or at least take Hades up on his offer to get me shooting lessons? I know enough gun safety not to shoot myself in the foot, but the thought of spending that kind of time with a weapon that still reminds me too much of Peter ... I couldn't stomach it. Even the taser, I purchased and stuffed in my bug out suitcase and promptly forgot about it.

There's no use worrying about it now. There's no other way forward. We were too far to go back the second I met Peter, and I can't afford to think too hard about that, about paths not taken.

I ended up here. I don't know if I believe in fate any more than I believe in happily ever after, but I want this future Hook paints for us. I want it desperately enough to fight for it.

We meet up with Nigel and Colin in Hook's office. If I wasn't already on edge, the serious expressions on all three of the men's faces would put me there. Nigel shuts the door behind me, and I move to perch on the corner of the desk. "What's the plan?" The sooner we get moving, the better.

"He's watching you." Hook speaks low, as if he really doesn't want to admit it. "He's had a couple people on this building since you showed up, and one of them followed you from Hades's place."

I shoot him a sharp look. This is new information. "Were you just not going to tell me?" I should have suspected Peter had me followed. How else would he know the exact moment I left the safety of Hades's place?

"You were stressed enough without that added to the mix."

His logic is flawed, but I'm not willing to get into it in

front of his cousins. The end result is all that matters, and the end result is that Hook kept his promise and kept me safe. Now it's time for me to do my part. "So the second I leave—"

"He'll know." Nigel has himself locked down. "Yes."

Hook shifts, drawing my attention to him. "You won't be alone with him. We just need to draw him out. We'll go together."

There's one huge flaw in his plan, loathe though I am to point it out. "He won't do it if you're there."

Hook's mouth goes flat. "Absolutely not."

"You know I'm right." I turn to his cousins. "*You* know I'm right."

Nigel is silent, but Colin looks at the ceiling as if it's the most interesting thing he's ever encountered. "She's not wrong."

"Stay out of this."

"Listen to me, cousin." Colin finally meets his gaze. "We'll only have one shot at this. We have to make it count."

"Fuck that. Then we make some calls to one of Nigel's shadow contacts and have a sniper take out Peter." He still isn't looking at me.

Nigel finally makes a sound suspiciously like a sigh. "If that were an option, we would have done it years ago. You have to do it yourself or it paves the way for assholes to undermine you in the future."

"He doesn't get his hands on her. I'll deal with future assholes as they arrive. That's tomorrow's problem."

Oh, Hook. I want to kiss him and strangle him at the same time. I glance at his cousins. "Could we have a second?"

Nigel and Colin don't hesitate, which tells me they've been having this conversation with him for longer than I realized. As soon as the door closes, I turn to Hook. He's already shaking his head. "Don't even think about it."

"We don't have a choice."

"That's bullshit, and you know it. You're reacting emotionally."

I might laugh if I could breathe past my racing heart. "I'm not the one reacting emotionally." Or at least not the only one. I move closer until he can't look anywhere but down at me. "If we only have one chance to get him, then we have to do this right. Peter's too smart to fall for the same ploy twice." He might be too smart to fall for *this* one the first time, but I don't say that aloud. It's something Hook will have already considered. We have to try.

His mask flickers, and I get a wave of torment from his dark eyes. "I promised he won't get his hands on you again. I meant that promise."

I desperately don't want to be anywhere near Peter. Even now, part of me is searching for another option, another way to go about this. But Colin is right—there are rules of engagement, so to speak. Hook is only the top dog because he's instilled enough fear and loyalty to ensure no one will challenge him. But all the loyalty in the world won't hold people back from doing exactly that if they get a whiff of weakness. Our world only respects strength. Sending someone else to do his dirty work reads like he's afraid of Peter, which paves the way for people to doubt him.

The next challenger might learn from Hook's mistakes and kill him when they take over so there isn't an enemy at their back.

The thought sends ice cascading down my spine. I press my hands to his chest. "Jameson." I wait for him to meet my gaze. "He's already laid a hand on me. He's already done his worst."

"Not his worst," he says darkly. He doesn't need to finish the thought for it to beam right into my head. *Because I'm still alive.*

Peter will kill me if given half a chance. That thought

should terrify me—and it does—but there is a steely determination rising up within me. "I was always going to play bait. Let me do what you intended."

"That was before." Hook rakes a hand through his long hair. "And even then I had my doubts."

Fuck, but I love this man.

"I was always going to play bait," I repeat softly. "Walk me through how it should have gone."

He doesn't want to. That truth couldn't be clearer. But he finally jerks his chin in a rough nod. "Cell phone tracking. We follow you in. Take him and his people out from there, burn their shit down."

There are a thousand things that can go wrong with that plan, which I'm sure is why he's balking now. I cup his face in my hands, his beard rough against my palms. "Then that's what we do."

He covers my hands with his. "I'm not risking you."

"If Peter stays in the shadows and keeps undermining you, then you *are* risking me." I have to work to keep the shake from my voice, to sound as strong as he needs me to be in order to agree to this. "I can't stay in this building for the rest of my life, Jameson. I can't. At some point I'll have to leave, and then he'll strike. We either choose the time now, or we live with the threat of him hanging over our heads."

Still, he hesitates.

So I go in for the kill. "Did you mean it when you said you wanted a partner in full?"

Hook tenses, already knowing where I'm going with this. "Don't start that shit."

I steamroll right over him. "Either I'm your partner, or I'm not. Either you want a true future with us, or you still see me as some damsel to be saved and locked up for my own good. There's no gray area here. It's one or the other."

"You can't just logic your way out of this, Tink."

"Watch me." I drop my hands, but he laces his fingers through mine, maintaining contact. "Answer the question."

He curses long and hard, and I stand still, waiting him out. It's not fun to be painted into a corner, and he's entitled to feeling pissed. There was a time in my life when this wave of anger would make me flinch, would send me back several steps to ensure I'm out of reach. Maybe it still would with a different person, but though Hook may be loud as hell with every single one of his emotions, he'd cut off his hands before he touched me in anger.

I didn't flinch when we fought in the kitchen, either.

Acknowledging that feels like sliding home the final piece of a puzzle I didn't realize I was building.

Finally his shoulders drop the barest amount. "I'm not letting you out of my sight."

"Okay."

"There will be three teams on your location, all from different directions."

"Sure."

"The second we have him off the streets, I move in and handle it. You don't play the hero, and you stay the hell out of my way and as far from him as you can manage."

I squeeze his hands and give him a confident smile that I don't feel. "I promise."

Another of those world-weary sighs. "Then let's get this shit rolling and over with. The sooner, the better."

I only hope this won't end up being the worst mistake of my life.

CHAPTER 26

HOOK

I never should have agreed to this. Watching Tink walk away from me, her ponytail swinging in the bleak morning light, I can't shake the feeling that I'm never going to see her again. That we flew too close to the sun when we dared strive for happiness.

"She'll be fine."

I don't look at my cousin. Nigel has been saying some variation of the same thing since I begrudgingly agreed to this shitty plan. The fact that it was *my* plan originally makes no difference. It's shitty. End of story.

Tink turns the corner and moves out of sight. "Let's go."

"Not yet." He steps half in front of me, forcing me to a stop. "We have three teams on her. She's won't be out of sight at any point during this. But *you* need to be out of sight. Peter won't strike if he thinks you'll be there to counter."

He's right. I hate that he's right.

I force several deep breaths into my lungs. It does nothing to dispel the feeling of impending doom. "We'll take a parallel route."

Nigel hesitates, but he must realize that this is the only option that will keep my head on straight. "Let's go."

Tink's route isn't exactly random. She's heading to a little fabric boutique that's been owned by the same family since before either of us were born. They paid their dues to stay out of Peter's mess, and they've done the same with me, though I lowered the rates. My goal isn't to drive my people's businesses into the ground. It never was.

We move at a decent pace, and Nigel keeps his phone in his hand as a stream of texted updates come in. Nothing yet. No sign of Peter.

The farther we get from my core territory, the worse the feeling of something about to go terribly wrong. We're well outside the main patrols I have scheduled, though my men do regular checks through the entire territory. Not regular enough to keep Peter out, though, which is why we're in this mess to begin with.

We keep walking, and half my attention is on Nigel. Every half block or so, he shakes his head. *No Peter.*

Where the hell is the bastard?

We turn a corner, mirroring Tink's path. The buildings this far out haven't gotten the face-lifts of the ones closer to the center of the territory. It's a never-ending project, trying to keep everyone above water, and the money flows in fits and starts. In another five years, there won't be buildings falling down, and the only shady shit happening in alleys will be sanctioned by me. We're not there yet, and this street only drives that fact home. Bars on windows. Everything feeling a little grungy, as if covered in a layer of dirt.

We're close to where the line between my influence and Peter's is blurred. My steps slow without my intending them to. "Nigel."

"She's fine." Nigel shakes his head, his attention on his phone. "She's almost to the boutique."

"It's not that. It's—" I see the blow coming out of the corner of my eye and lunge forward, shoving my cousin out of the way. The baton takes me in the shoulder instead of him in the head. Pain flares, intense enough to leave me woozy. "Get Tink."

Nigel curses. "Are you fucking with me?"

There's only one attacker, and their mask tells me this is a diversion. "Tink. Now, Nigel. I got this." If he thinks I'm distracted, Peter will move on Tink. He'll *hurt* her. "Go!"

"Goddamn it, Hook. I'm sending Colin's team this way."

The baton comes whistling at my head again, and I have no breath to argue. He's obeying, and that's enough. I barely dodge the blow this time and kick out, aiming for the masked man's knees. A crunch as my boot makes contact, and he goes down. I step forward and kick the baton from his hands and then lean down to yank off the mask.

I don't recognize him, but the guy is more kid than man. If he's eighteen, I'll be surprised as hell. Peter always liked to surround himself with teenagers. They look at him like he's a god, and it feeds his ego something fierce. "Who the hell are you?"

"John." He grins suddenly. "Gotcha."

"What the hell?"

This blow, I don't see coming. It knocks me off my feet, and I land hard on the ground, asphalt grinding against my face. I'm still trying to relearn how to breathe when a boot catches me on my injured shoulder, the force of the kick knocking me onto my back.

I already know who I'll see before the bastard leans over me, a satisfied smirk on his face. Brown hair, blue eyes. A face that might be trustworthy if a person didn't know better. I know better.

"Fancy seeing you here, Hook."

"Fuck off, Peter."

"Hook and I are long overdue for a conversation." He motions to the men who appear at the mouth of a nearby alley. "Get him up. Let's go."

CHAPTER 27

TINK

I know something's wrong the second Nigel appears at my side. I don't get a single word out before he's hauling me down a side street, his grip firm but not hurting my arm. He barely checks his stride so I can keep up with his longer legs. "There was an attack."

"*What?*" I look around, but the handful of people on the street are very pointedly not paying attention to us. "What are you talking about?" Understanding dawns, and I almost trip over my feet. "Is he okay?"

"Hook can handle some asshole with a baton." Nigel doesn't look convinced, though. He glances at me. "He sent me to make sure it wasn't a diversion so they could go after you."

I look around. Peter doesn't burst out of anywhere. "It wasn't a trap for me. It was a trap for *him.*"

"That's what I'm afraid of." He types on his phone while barely looking at it. "We have backup closing in. Both teams shadowing you will be here."

"And the third?"

"I sent them to Hook as soon as he sent me to you." Nigel's jaw goes tight. "They aren't checking in."

I thought I was afraid before. It's nothing to the feeling that washes over me when we arrive at the spot where Nigel says he left Hook, only to find a spatter of blood and nothing else. I speak through numb lips. "Where is he, Nigel?"

"Fuck." He drops his hand and stares at the blood as if he can divine Hook's direction if he just concentrates hard enough. "*Fuck.*"

The truth crashes over me hard enough to make me stagger.

This wasn't about me. It may have started that way, but Peter is too savvy to blow his chance to take out the true threat—Hook. "Where is he, Nigel?" I repeat, louder this time. "Where the hell is he? Where is the team?"

"If I knew where Peter was, we wouldn't be in this fucking mess to start with." He turns away from me, typing furiously on his phone. No doubt trying to find the missing team. My gaze lands on the blood again. Peter took Hook. If he got the drop on him, he could have killed Hook, but he *took* him.

He'll have gone back to his secret base, back to the spot where he feels safest. My breath stills in my lungs. "I know where he is."

Nigel stops typing and gives me his full attention. "How the hell do you know where he is?"

"I … I don't know if I know where he is. But I know where his new woman is." I found her once before, after all. She didn't want to be saved, and I got a black eye for my efforts, but it was more than worth it if I can keep Hook alive. "Peter won't be far from her. He won't want to let her out of his sight longer than necessary." *That* I know for truth. For four years, my survival depended on anticipating his every whim and need and desire, on watching him closely to judge his mood and course-correct as needed to ensure I stayed ahead of it. I never once thought I'd be grateful for that knowledge.

I draw myself up. "We can't go in with force. He'll kill Hook."

Nigel shakes his head. "You're not wrong, but we need more backup than just me."

"More than just *us*." I start walking before he can argue. The lack of time will work on my side for this debate. Nigel can't force me back to the safety of Hook's building, and he can't spare anyone to haul me there. "It's on this block." I rattle off the address where I found the woman before. It's possible they've moved, but the set up seemed pretty permanent when I snuck in.

I still can't believe I had the courage to do that. Or that I'm about to do it again.

Nigel falls into step beside me. His phone buzzes nearly constantly, and his expression is a mask of concentration. "You are not going into that building. I've rerouted the two remaining teams to set up a perimeter. Colin and I will go in after him."

I don't bother arguing. I'll agree to anything that ups Hook's chances of survival, including being sidelined—as long as I'm in the vicinity. Inside that building, I'm a liability. I won't get anyone killed for my pride.

It takes us a mere ten minutes to reach the location I found before. Nigel glances at his phone one last time and hauls me down an alley and through a back door into what appears to be an abandoned laundromat. He moves to the taped-over window and carefully peels back a section of it. The glass is grimy, but I can clearly see the apartments where I found the woman. "Yes, that's it."

"Good."

Fewer than five minutes later, seven people pile into this

building. I don't know what I expected when Hook said he'd have three teams on me. Maybe pseudo soldiers? The five men and two women are all dressed in street clothes and are completely indistinguishable from the normal foot traffic in this territory. They must have been spread out around me the entire time, and I had no idea.

"Tell them what you know, Tink."

My heart beats too fast I as clear my throat. "The third-floor apartment overlooking the street." I jerk my thumb to indicate the one behind us. "My information is a couple months old. I didn't see any of Peter's people in the building when I was there last, but we have to assume they're inside now, and—"

My phone rings, cutting me off.

I almost ignore it, but something has me pulling it out of my purse. *Unknown number.* I go cold and swipe my thumb over the screen. "Hello?"

"Hey, baby."

I swing around to look at Nigel. He motions for me to put it on speaker. Part of me doesn't want to obey, doesn't want to give Peter that power, but it'll be easier for everyone if they can hear both sides of the conversation. I carefully hold my phone away from my face and put it on speaker. "Give him back."

"Come and get him." He sounds happy. Too happy. He's riding high now, but anything going wrong will send him crashing down in an instant. I've seen how that pseudo-joy can flip on a switch. "Don't take too long, though. You know how I get bored."

"Peter." His name tastes like the ash of broken promises. "This won't end the way you want it to."

"Yes, baby, it will. I have Hook. You're too soft to let him hang for you, so you'll be arriving shortly. You know the place; you tried to take something of mine a few months back. Don't make me wait." He hangs up before I can form a response.

Nigel's already shaking his head. "Absolutely not."

"We don't have a choice."

"Yes, we do. And the choice is to not walk into Peter's blatantly stated trap."

I shove my phone into my pocket and glare. "If we don't go, Hook will die." Hook will *die*. I just found him, just allowed myself to hope we might have future and a life together. A family, whatever that looks like for us.

Now Peter wants to take it from me. From us.

Just like he's taken everything I've ever valued. My pride. My strength. My self-confidence. My *freedom*. I fought and clawed and reclaimed those things for myself, day after day, year after year.

I'll take back Hook, too.

"You have ten minutes to come up with a plan. After that, I'm walking in there." I hold Nigel's gaze, letting him know that this is no bluff. We need to move, and we need to move now. Every minute Hook spends with him is a minute Peter might lose his temper and snap.

Nigel curses and turns to the men standing around. I step back, letting them handle this part. I've never infiltrated a building, have never orchestrated a coordinated attack on an enemy. This isn't my wheelhouse.

I might not survive what's coming.

The realization has me pulling out my phone again and firing out a quick group text to Meg, Allecto, and Aurora. My fingers shake as I type.

Me: You guys are the best friends I never realized I had. Thanks for that. Kind of wish I'd been less of an asshole so we could have hung out more.

I send it before I can talk myself out of it. It takes all of three seconds before a flurry of responses appear.

Aurora: We've been friends for years. It's okay that you never noticed!

Meg: Tink ... Why the hell does that text sound like a last letter to your loved ones before you make your last stand?

Allecto: Who do I need to kill? Peter or Hook?

Meg: There's no way it's Hook, so it must be Peter.

Allecto: I'll get the car ready.

I blink. That escalated quickly.

Me: This is territory business, ladies.

Allecto: That's bullshit. Meg, tell her it's bullshit.

Meg: Unfortunately, we can't interfere without a formal invitation.

Aurora: Screw that. Tink, where are you?

Meg: Aurora, no.

Aurora: I can help, so I'm going to help. Tell me where you are, Tink. I can be out of here in five.

Apparently I misjudged the depth of our relationship on a fundamental level. I've barely come to terms with the idea that these women are friends with me, and now they're willing to ride into battle without explanation or hesitation. My throat goes a bit tight, and I have to blink rapidly a few times.

Me: Stand down, ladies. I'll text you tomorrow, when everything's over.

Me: Thank you, though. I really appreciate it.

There's no point in saying that I might not survive the night. That will just panic them. Hell, I've probably *already* panicked them without intending to. I pocket my phone again, this time ignoring the series of vibrations that signal incoming texts.

Nigel motions me back over. "You're with me. You walk where I walk and obey my every order."

I don't have the wherewithal to make a joke, so I just nod. "Okay."

"Let's go."

We file out the back door and half the men split off. I don't ask where they're going. Nigel has a plan, and my only role is to not get anyone killed while we save Hook. I wish I were more confident that we'll come out of this conflict victorious.

Our group circles the building, and all the men except Nigel melt into the deep shadows caused by broken streetlights. Nigel moves to the main door, and I shadow his steps.

Impossible to push through this rickety door without remembering the last time I did it. I still can't believe I had the balls to come here alone, to bet my life on Peter being gone. I found the woman in the apartment on the second floor, an old one-bedroom filled with secondhand furniture. Compared to where Peter kept me five years ago, it was a palace.

I'd only been there five minutes before the woman realized what I was trying to do and punched me in the face. My cheekbone gives a phantom throb in remembrance. I don't blame her for the attack or for kicking me out. Didn't I do nearly the same thing to Hook when he offered me a way out? It was something I should have considered before I even tried, but being confronted with a past version of yourself has a way of messing with a person's mind.

The door leads into a narrow hall with an out of service elevator and a stairwell leading up. Nigel keeps his gun down by his side. "Stay close."

I nod. "Okay."

We inch past the second door and the third. Every muscle is so tight, I'm surprised I can take a step. Something bad is coming. I just know it.

When it does, it happens fast.

The door behind Nigel eases open, and then two men appear. One knocks his gun away. The other punches him in the back of the head, sending him to his knees. They look at me. "You go up alone."

I haven't even had a chance to move. I clutch my purse close and try not to look as terrified as I feel. "Let him go, and I won't fight."

They exchange a look. The guy on the left finally shrugs. "Whatever you say, lady." They haul Nigel to the front door and toss him unceremoniously out. I wince at the sound of impact, but at least he's alive. I hope.

They follow me up the stairs, a weight at my back that prevents me from running. As if that's an option. It feels like the last five years have been leading me to this place, to this moment. I never wanted this confrontation. I only wanted to live without the threat of Peter dragging me down.

I should have known he'd never let me go unless I forced him to.

I cling to my purse and walk to the same door I knocked on two short months ago. The doorknob turns easily in my hand, and then I'm inside. I'm not sure what I expect. A bloodbath. Hook, broken and bleeding on the floor, maybe even dead. To be shot the second I step over the threshold.

Instead, the scene I enter might be mundane if I didn't know the history of the players. Hook sits on the couch. He's got a trickle of blood still flowing from a cut on his temple, and his hands are cuffed in front of him, but he doesn't seem too much the worse for wear.

Peter is … cooking.

I stop short and look around. Where's the woman? Maybe the bedroom. It stands to reason that Peter would keep her out of it. Unless … "Where is she?"

"You always did have a hell of a time minding your own damn business."

The scent of bacon slaps me in the face, making everything that much more surreal. "What the hell, Peter?"

"I got tired of waiting for you." He doesn't look at me, seeming to concentrate on the pan on the stove. "Get over here, baby. I want to show you something."

"Tink?" Hook shakes his head slowly like he's not sure I'm really here or some phantom in his imagination. "No." There's something off in his tone. I'm no doctor, but he's definitely concussed, which means he won't be able to help. It also means that one more nasty hit to his head could kill him.

I thought I was afraid before. I didn't realize that the bottom of my terror could drop out and leave me in a freefall that feels strangely like rage. "He hit you."

"I'm fine." Hook frowns at me. "What are you doing here? Get the fuck out."

That's the one thing I can't do. I don't know if I can get Hook out alive, but if I leave now, I definitely won't. "I'm sorry." I turn my attention to Peter as I take the handful of steps required to get me into the little kitchen. Not quite close enough to grab, but close enough to be obedient. To pacify. It takes more effort than I could have dreamed to shift my tone to obedience instead of screaming in his face. "I'm here. Let him go."

"Did you think I'd really let you go, Tatiana?"

He's said something similar before, but it's only now that I finally have the strength to answer. "You don't own me."

"Wrong." He turns and leans against the counter, so casual that I might relax if I haven't seen this song and dance before. Peter likes to lull his prey into relaxing before he strikes. He gives me a slow smile. "You've been mine from the second I pulled you out of that shit hole foster home. I didn't ask for much, and you turn around and betray me the first chance you have."

Hardly the first chance, but I know better than to say as much. It took a very long time to gather up what little strength I had left and flee. "You shouldn't have attacked Father Elijah." As if that's the sum of his sins. The thought is almost laughable.

"He shouldn't have meddled with what's mine."

"I am a person, not a toy. You don't get to throw a fit that I escaped before you broke me and threw me away."

Peter holds out a hand. "Come here, baby."

My heart is simultaneously trying to beat its way out of my ribcage and also cower somewhere around my spine. I don't want to do this. I don't, I don't, I don't. I know the shape of this trap intimately. I've been here before. I can move through the next steps by memory, even after all this time.

I *will not* go back to this.

I hug my purse tighter to my chest, an inadequate shield if ever there was one. "You're going to regret this." My hoarse voice might read like fear but anger rises with each ragged breath. He thinks he can simply pick me up and make me his again because he wants to. That he can kill the man I love and the future I'm desperate for out of spite.

No. I won't let it happen.

"Don't make me ask again." He motions me closer with a tense flick of his fingers.

I don't know where Nigel's people are, but they won't crash through this door in time to prevent what comes next. I'm on my own. If I falter, both Hook and I pay the price.

I've never done anything but falter where Peter is concerned.

Not this time. Never again.

It takes every bit of strength I have to move one step closer and then another. To willingly put myself back within his reach again. I don't make it a third step. Peter moves faster than he has a right to and grabs me, yanking me the last bit of distance and plastering my back to his chest. He's built shorter and slighter than Hook, but he's still strong enough to hold me easily in place.

"Do you know what a grease burn does to skin? Especially when it's good and hot?"

I look down at the pan. The bacon is burnt to a crisp, practically floating in viciously bubbling grease. That kind of thing won't kill me, but it will hurt like a bitch. It will scar. "You'll never make it out of this place alive, Peter." My voice sounds eerily calm, even to my ears. "Hook's people will kill you first."

"You and Hook won't live long enough to enjoy that. No one crosses me without consequences. You know that better than anyone. It's time to pay the piper, baby." He nudges us closer to the stove. To the grease-filled pan. "Give me your hand, Tatiana."

"Okay." I jerk my hand out of my purse and press my taser to the bare skin of his arm. The volt of energy makes him grip me tighter, but the second I let go of the trigger, he collapses to the floor. I go to my knees next to him and press the taser to his throat. This time, I hold the trigger for a five count, until his eyes roll back in his head. When I lift it away from his skin, he doesn't move.

I stare down at his unconscious form. It happened so fast. I did it. I fought the monster who's haunted my nightmares for years. "No one touches me without permission anymore, asshole." He can't hear me, but it feels good to say. So fucking good.

Even though I want to rush to Hook, I take a few seconds to pat Peter down. I find a gun tucked into the waistband of his pants and the keys to the cuffs. Only *then* do I climb to my feet. Hook meets me halfway. "I can't believe you came here." He's weaving on his feet in a way that alarms me, but at least he's moving.

"We don't have a lot of time. Hold this." I carefully press

the gun into his hand and focus on the cuffs. It takes me three tries to fit the key into the lock. I can't stop shaking. It's not over, and fear and determination and anger have me in a stranglehold. I toss the cuffs to the ground. "I have to get you out of here."

"Tink."

I ignore him and shove the taser back into my purse. "We have to go. Right now."

"*Tink.*"

I look up, but he's not focused on me. He's focused on something over my shoulder. I desperately don't want to turn around, don't want to see my nightmare rising to stand. I open my mouth, but Hook moves before I can say a word. He drags me to his chest, and lifts the gun. A bang. Another. A third. A thump as something large hits the ground.

Silence.

His big hand keeps my face pinned to his chest, but he relaxes the smallest amount. "He's gone."

"Hook." I try to push away, but he doesn't let me go. "Jameson. I need to see."

"No."

It's tempting, so tempting, to just give in, but I can't shake the feeling that if I don't look now, I'll always be glancing over my shoulder. "Please. I have to."

"It's proof that I'm a monster." He says it so softly, I can't tell if he's talking to me or himself. "It was always going to happen, but I thought I'd hesitate."

"No." I stop fighting him and pull him closer, as if I can hug him hard enough to chase away that emptiness in his voice. He's shaking, and it makes my heart ache for him. For both of us. "You are *not* a monster. You are not like him, Jameson. You're a good fucking person and a good person does what it takes to protect the protect the people they care about." I take a slow breath. "Let me see."

"Don't take this on, beautiful girl." He sounds hoarse and almost sorry. "It's not your burden to bear."

It's one he fully intends to take for himself so no one else has to. Even with the mess inside my chest right now, I don't think I've ever loved him more. I hold him tighter. "I need to see, Jameson. I need this to be over once and for all." When he still hesitates, I say the words I'm suddenly certain he needs to here. "I love you. There isn't a single thing that's happened today to make me love you less. Do you understand me, Jameson? I love you and he doesn't get to take that from either of us."

Finally, a small eternity later, he loosens his grip enough for me to twist in his arms. Peter lies on the floor of the kitchen, three gunshot wounds in his chest, his blue eyes staring sightlessly at the ceiling. I take it in with a single sweep, waiting for reality to sink in. He's gone. Really, truly gone. Then I see the pan beside him, the spilled grease. "He was going after me." The grease might not kill me, but a blow or two from that pan would.

"Yes," he sounds firmer, more centered.

I turn back and bury my face in Hook's chest. "I love you, Jameson Hook. Take me home. Please."

CHAPTER 28

HOOK

*I*t takes longer than I'd like to get things sorted out. Fighting a pounding headache and bone-deep exhaustion makes dealing with Peter's people surprisingly easy. Exile, rather than a full purge. I don't care where they go, but they are no longer welcome in my territory. I know all too well what a charismatic and compelling asshole Peter could be. They don't deserve death for following him, but they can't be trusted to follow *me*, either. They'll figure it out. Or they won't. Either way, they're no longer my problem.

I send Nigel back home to get checked out, which he only agrees to on the condition that I follow shortly. Colin handles the sweep of the surrounding area for any further problems.

Then, and only then, do I take Tink's hand and go home. She's been silent since we left the apartment, and I can't shake the feeling that I've damaged something beyond repair. She knows what I'm capable of now. It's not a new trait, but seeing it firsthand is something entirely different than knowing it in theory.

I killed Peter.

He might be an abusive asshole, a monster, but he was still a person. A person no longer drawing breath because of me. If she can't handle that, if she needs to leave … I won't stop her. I refuse to be a chain around her ankle, no matter how much I selfishly want her to stay.

I have every intention of going straight to our bedroom and washing off the blood coating my skin, but when we walk into the building it's to the sound of raised female voices. Tink curses under her breath and I give her a mild look. "Is that Aurora I hear?"

"Um."

"I don't think I've ever heard her yell before." She's normally such a sweet little submissive, but admittedly I've never interacted with her outside of the Underworld.

Tink actually blushes. "I, uh, we should take care of this."

"By all means." I motion for her to precede me and follow her to the front entryway.

The scene we find there has me simultaneously wanting to laugh and also find a shield to protect myself. Meg, Allecto, and Aurora are in my home. At the same time. Meg has her arms crossed over her chest and watches things play out as if deciding whether to step in or not. Allecto is caressing the gun in her holster the way children soothe themselves with blankies. And Aurora? She's in Edgar's face, which is a feat since she's barely an inch or two taller than Tink. I don't see a weapon on her, but appearances can be deceiving. Aurora shakes a fist in his face. "Tell us where she is *right fucking now*, or I'm going to burn this place to the ground."

Holy shit.

I give Tink a nudge. "Your friends means you deal with it."

"Coward," she snarls.

"Guilty."

She straightens, throws back her shoulders, and marches into the fray. "I'm here."

"Tink!" Aurora stops menacing Edgar and rushes her friend. I don't miss the way the big man slumps back against the wall, and I make a mental note to give him a raise and maybe a change of position. He's dealt with more than his fair share of confrontations in the last couple days.

Aurora nearly takes Tink off her feet with her hug. "Your text messages freaked us all out and then you didn't respond and I thought the worst."

Meg and Allecto follow, though they don't mob Tink the same way. Meg glances at me. "I trust we can keep this from being considered an infringement of territory."

I hold up my hands and wince a little when the move pulls at my shoulder. "I'm going to assume you came to ensure Aurora didn't literally burn my building to the ground."

She gives me a knife-sharp smile. "She was packing containers of gasoline into the trunk when I found her."

I really don't know how to process this new information. I turn to look to where Aurora is whispering fiercely to Tink. "I always thought she was such a nice girl."

"She *is* a nice girl." Meg starts to turn away. "There's also no lengths she won't go for the people she cares about. You'll do well to remember that in the future, Hook."

I sure as hell won't forget it. I carefully lean against the wall and watch as Tink assures the other women that she is, in fact, okay. I don't know if it's strictly the truth, but she *will* be okay. That's all that matters. We have time to figure shit out now, to actually chase the future we tentatively spoke about ... Was it only this morning? It feels like it was a thousand years ago.

It takes twenty minutes and promises they'll meet for coffee tomorrow for the three of them to finally allow themselves to be ushered to the front door. When Tink turns around, she's got a soft smile on her face. "I have friends."

"Yes, you do. Very scary friends."

We head up to my suite, and once the doctor has checked me out and declared I have a concussion and need to take it easy for a while, we shower and clean up. The whole time, she doesn't say a word. I can't tell if she's still marveling over the fact she has friends, which seems to be a sort of revelation, or if the events of the last few hours are finally sinking in. Maybe a combination of both. Either way, I don't press her. She deserves that much and more.

Tink shuts off the water and turns to me. "I want a fall wedding."

I blink. "This concussion is worse than I thought, because I could swear that you just said you want a fall wedding."

"That's because I did." She hands me a towel and wraps a second one around herself. "We're married in every way that matters, but I want a real wedding. One where we invite your family and our friends. I want to design my own dress. I want the whole ridiculous spectacle of it." She crosses to me and cups my face in her hands. "I want the world to know that I choose you and that this is real."

I'm still having a hard time catching up. She wants to stay married to me. She really *does* want the future we painted together this morning. Still, I promised I'd be honest and so I have to tell her the truth of my plans. "I was going to offer you a divorce in the morning. You were going to be free."

Tink's smile is sweet and the tiniest bit salty. "I think that's the most romantic thing you've ever said to me." She stops short and frowns. Tink drops her hands. "Unless you really want a divorce, in which case ignore everything I just said."

Oh no. Fuck that. If she's choosing me, there's no way in hell I'm letting her get away. I grab her hand and sink unsteadily to my knee. "Tink Petrov, would you do me the honor of marrying me? Again." I clear my throat. "You're the strongest woman I've ever known, and I love the shit out of you. Marry me, and we'll spend the rest of our lives bickering and fucking and raising a family of little hellions while we run this territory the way it should be run."

The shadows flee her expression, and she beams down at me. "Yes, Jameson Hook, I very much would like to do all of that with you and more." She tugs me to my feet. "I love you. I want to live not-happily-ever-after with you. Yes, of course I'll marry you. Again."

* * *

THANK you so much for reading Hook and Tink's story! They're very special to me, and I hope you enjoyed reading them as much as I enjoyed writing them. If you did, please consider leaving a review!

Need more Hook and Tink in your life? Sign up for my newsletter and get a BONUS short giving a glimpse of what happens after the events of A WORTHY OPPONENT...and what happens when Tink finally calls Hook's bluff about challenging him in public.

The Wicked Villains series continues in THE BEAST, which takes a look at what happens when Isabelle Belmont is forced to do whatever it takes to bring Gaeton and Beast back to her territory...even agree to a sex pact. Things are destined to get explosive!

Looking for your next sexy read? You can pick up my MMF ménage THEIRS FOR THE NIGHT, my FREE novella that features an exiled prince, his bodyguard, and the bartender they can't quite manage to leave alone.

* * *

KEEPING READING for an exclusive first look at THE BEAST...

Gaeton kicks one of the chairs in front of the desk so that it is angled to see the entire room and drops into it. The man doesn't know how to sit without sprawling, and even with fury darkening his expression, this is no exception.

Beast shuts the door and moves to lean against the desk, unconsciously mirroring the same position Megaera took when I spoke to her. He crosses his arms over his chest and watches me. Waiting.

Gaeton has no such patience. "What the hell are you doing here, Isabelle?"

Now's the time to lay out my argument, but the words dry up in their presence. I lick my lips again, and give him the same answer I gave Beast. "I'm here for you. For both of you."

Gaeton doesn't look impressed. "Yeah, I don't think so. We tried that and it blew up in our faces. I'm not doing it again."

If I don't talk fast, they'll pack me up and send me on my way and this will all be for nothing. Failure is not an option. It can't be. "Come back to the territory. Resume your positions. We need you."

Beast raises an eyebrow, but it's Gaeton's cruel laughter that echoes through the room. "I should have known this is all power and games. It always was with you." He leans forward and braces his elbows on his big thighs. "I don't pretend to speak for this asshole, but there's nothing in that territory for me now."

Nothing. Including me.

It shouldn't hurt so much to be rejected by a man who already dumped me, but it does. Sweet gods, it does. I turn to Beast, but I might as well seek solace from a glacier for all the warmth he gives me. Hopelessness rising in my chest, threatening to send me to my knees. I can't fail. I *can't*. My bottom lip quivers the tiniest bit before I shut my reaction down. "Please."

Beast looks at me a long moment. His lips slowly curve, the barest hint of a cruel smile. I've seen that expression on his face before, always preceding his delivering one of my father's punishments to someone who's crossed him. "Get on your knees, Isabelle. If you're going to beg, do it properly."

Gaeton flinches like the other man struck him. "What the fuck, Beast?"

Beast doesn't look away from me. It feels like the intensity of his gaze is a weight across my shoulders and chest, driving me slowly, inexorably, to my knees. "You heard me. How bad do you want us back?"

"You don't speak for me," Gaeton rumbles.

I already left my pride at the door. I can't afford the luxury when I'm bargaining for the lives of so many. In the end, it's far simpler than I could have dreamed to give into the Beast's gravity and sink to my knees. The carpet is surprisingly soft against my bare skin and I shiver. "Are you happy now? *Please* come back."

Beast rises and moves slowly around me. It's a struggle not to twist to keep him in sight. Instead, I focus on Gaeton, on the way he watches us so closely, his gaze jumping from me to Beast. "What are you up to, you bastard?"

Beast digs his hand into my hair and tugs sharply, bowing my back and drawing a gasp from my lips. In all our time together, he was always devastatingly gentle, until I thought I'd go out of my mind and scream in his face to *touch* me. Pain flickers to pleasure and back again, and I have to bite back a moan. I stare up into his beautiful face, but he's not looking at me. He's looking at Gaeton. "I propose a bargain."

"You're out of your fucking mind."

"Gaeton." Beast says it almost gently. "*Look* at her." He

gives my hair another sharp tug. This time, I can't stop the moan. My body doesn't feel like my own. My skin is too tight, my nipples pebbling and my pussy clenching with an ache only one thing can assuage. What is he *doing* to me?

"Get your fucking hand off her." Gaeton's voice is low and strangled. "Now."

Beast releases me in an instant and I slump forward, barely catching myself before I crumble into a ball on the floor. Dazed, I touch the smarting spot on my scalp. I should be furious that he dared touch me like that, but all I can focus on is how much I *need*. I straighten back to kneel with some effort. "What's your bargain?"

"No."

Beast ignored Gaeton and resumes his position leaning on the desk. "The three of us for a limited duration. At the end, you make a choice once and for all. Him or me. Regardless of your decision, we will both stay in the territory and resume our roles." There it is again, his cruel little smile. "And you will pay penance, little Isabelle."

I shiver. "What does that mean?"

"It means that you played us to your heart's content for months on end. Now it's our turn." He turns to Gaeton. "You're furious about how things fell out."

"Yeah," the word feels almost forced out of him.

"We played by her rules and cut off pieces of ourselves to be worthy of her." Beast turns those eerie blue eyes back to me. "Now we drag her down into the dirt with us."

Gaeton folds his hands together and seems to be actually considering it. "Explain what the fuck you mean when you say 'us.'"

"We top her together."

My gaze jumps back and forth between them. Surely they're not saying… "*Together.*"

Gaeton doesn't look at me. "Careful there, Beast. Might

start to think you're sweet on me."

Beast doesn't blink. "It's an efficient use of time and effort." He's on the move again, but this time he circles Gaeton, coming to stop behind the big man's chair. He leans down, not touching Gaeton, but close enough that I catch my breath at the sight of him so close to the bigger man. His rough voice is pure sin. "Think of every depraved thing you've wanted to do to that sexy little body. All the times you held back. All the fantasies you kept locked down."

They're both looking at me like a pair of wolves who happened across a lamb in the forest. I can't stop another shiver. I came here with the intention of walking out with both of them. I didn't bargain on *this*. Any of it.

Beggars can't be choosers, though. I clear my throat. "State your terms in explicit detail."

Beast still hasn't moved back from Gaeton. "Gaeton and I dominate you. We fuck you. We are your gods and masters for the duration of two weeks. You will have a safe word and will use it when necessary, but otherwise will obey our every whim. At the end of the timeline, when we've balanced the scales, you will make a decision and stand by it."

The loss of power is staggering. They want me trapped and helpless. A safe word, yes, but we all know I have no choice in this. If I say no and walk out of here without them, there's a very large chance that my territory will fall. Cordelia is ruthless and a good leader, but the loss of our father and his two top generals at the same time is too high a cost. Already our enemies nip at our borders, testing us. We need Gaeton and Beast back, and we need them back now. "What will you do to me?"

"Anything we want."

Pre-order THE BEAST now!

ACKNOWLEDGMENTS

A huge, huge thank you to my readers. This series has been a wild ride so far, and that's in no small part due to your enthusiasm. I am so happy you're loving these villains as much as I am!

Big thanks to Andie J Christopher and Jenny Nordbak for being my first readers and telling me to stop worrying about this book. I adore you.

Endless thank yous to Manu from Tessera Editorial and Lynda M. Ryba for helping me get this book into the best version of itself. Special thanks to Christa Desir, too!

As always, thank you to my family for your endless patience while I work for "just a little bit longer" and for dragging me away from my computer on a regular basis. Last, but never least, thank you to Tim. Love you like a long song!

ABOUT THE AUTHOR

Katee Robert is a *New York Times* and USA Today bestselling author of contemporary romance and romantic suspense. *Entertainment Weekly* calls her writing "unspeakably hot." Her books have sold over a million copies. She lives in the Pacific Northwest with her husband, children, a cat who thinks he's a dog, and two Great Danes who think they're lap dogs.

Website: www.kateerobert.com

Printed in the USA
CPSIA information can be obtained
at www.ICGtesting.com
LVHW040302070923
757355LV00022BA/81